SCOURGE

An American Horror Tale by Dalton James

Illustrations by Braden Maxwell

Scourge: An American Horror Tale

ISBN: 978-1-7334719-0-9

For those who supported my dream:
Your encouragement means more than I could ever say.

Chapter 1
Of a Simple Life Disturbed

The dawning of that Thursday morning gave no indication to John or Eli that anything strange or mysterious was afoot, save for the slight chill that brought them both from their deep slumbers. John was first to rise from bed, and as was his custom, he stretched all the while listening to the sounds of the outside world. It was quiet that morning, and that always brought a smile to John's face. The quiet.

He went to Eli's bed on the other side of the room and placed a gentle hand on his brother's shoulder. His brother's eyes snapped open, and he stared wide-eyed at his older brother, a brief glimmer of sheer terror in his expression, before exhaling and recognizing John.

"Just me, Brother," John said calmly.

Eli nodded.

"Bad dream?"

Nod.

"Well, let us get to work then," John said. "That always settles the mind."

John had tilled the soil and planted the crops himself. He was stronger of the two brothers and always had a knack for the more laborious upkeep of their farm. He was taller than Eli as well as fifteen years his elder. He enjoyed the hard work. The feeling of exhausting his muscles made him feel satisfied of a hard day's work. He was proud of what he had built here and appreciated Eli for joining him here. He never forgot to thank his little brother for all of his contributions on the farm, no matter how small the deed.

Eli was more inclined to the "simpler" tasks of the farm's day-to-day activities. Rather than join his brother out in the fields, he preferred to collect the eggs from the few chickens they owned, milk their sole cow (Beth, they called her), and keep their cottage clean and tidy. He enjoyed being around their two horses they had inherited as well. Often, John would find Eli brushing them and talking to them soothingly.

Eli was the lovelier of the brothers. His skin was flawless, and women, young and old, had often stopped to stare at him when he left the house. Growing up, he had his fair share of young women who desperately, almost pitifully so, desired his courtship. He was quiet and shy, however, and was under the careful and constant watch of his mother.

"No one is good enough for my sweet Eli," she had said.

It was widely known that he was bullied by other boys for "being unable to stop suckling from his mother". His father wanted him to defend himself, but he had grown old, and the lessons in self-defense had been taught to John long before Eli had been born. And so, Eli remained mostly indoors growing up, save for those occasional trips to the market with his mother.

On this particular Thursday, the brothers had finished most of their chores early and sat outside their cottage, admiring their land. John sat in his wooden rocking chair he had crafted himself while Eli sat on the grass, stroking their old sheepdog, Tom. The farm was spacious but humble. One cottage where John and Eli shared living space, one barn that housed the chickens and the cow, and a well-sized plot of land devoted to the crops John tirelessly worked on. They never felt hunger and always had enough money from extra harvests to fulfill any needs the land could not provide them. A small forest lay in wait past their crops where John would occasionally hunt small game, and just before that was the well where their water came from.

"I am proud of us, Eli," John said, "proud of what we built here."

"You built most of it," Eli said quietly.

"Come now," John said, "your contributions here make this place what it is. I could not do it all by myself."

Eli allowed himself a smile.

"Now," John said, "I think we have enough day left to go into town. I have some things we need to go and get. Coming?"

Eli nodded. They tied up Tom to his post (he was an old dog and enjoyed laying in the grass, anyway), mounted the horses, and rode for town.

Town was a good distance away, but time passed quickly for the brothers. John hummed a tune, and Eli sang quietly for the two of them. When they arrived in town, they tied their horses to a hitching post and walked the street. John had gotten used to being ignored by all the pretty girls who only had eyes for Eli. Eli, not purposefully, would ignore them. The two of them knew they only needed one another, and that was what quelled the jealousy in John's heart and brought comfort to Eli's.

"Lots of pretty ones out today," John said.

Eli did not reply, instead reading the weekly paper.

"Must be some new fashion from England," John said, eyeing a blonde woman walking with some pompous aristocrat.

"Hm," Eli acknowledged.

"Something more fascinating there?" John asked.

"Politics," Eli muttered.

"More taxes?" John asked.

"The colonies are demanding more rights," Eli said.

John sighed, "We are heading into a war, Eli. I promise you."

"A war with England?" Eli almost laughed. "The most powerful country on earth? Not likely."

The two entered the general store, and John produced a list for the clerk. The clerk gave a curt smile, a nod, then scurried to find the items indicated. John leaned against the counter and watched his brother read the paper. Eli was more educated than John, but that did not bother him. It was useful for times when someone would try to take advantage of John, and Eli would be swift to point out what was taking place.

John also came in handy when someone attempted to challenge Eli. Eli had once caught the eye of a married woman, and she spent close to five minutes attempting to exchange pleasantries that obviously made Eli uncomfortable. When her husband saw his wife with Eli, he had ridiculed him mercilessly until John stepped in. A few insults here and the threat of a good row set the husband in place. Aside from John, Eli had become *more* timid around others than when he was younger. John did not know the reasons for this and never pried. He assumed Eli would tell him when the time was right.

"Everything is in order, sir," the clerk said, breaking John's thoughts. "Hatchet, small parcel of gunpowder, tinderbox, and candles. Everything is here, sir."

The brothers returned to the farm just before nightfall to find Tom barking frantically. The brothers dismounted their horses and tied them to the post before checking on the dog.

"What is wrong?" John asked, kneeling beside the sheepdog and staring in the direction of his aimed barks.

The last rays of sunlight lent little aid to assist the search of what had upset Tom. John stared in the direction of the forest.

"I do not see anything, Tom," John said. "You are getting old and paranoid—"

Something darted into the cover of the trees. John did not see what exactly, but he definitely saw movement.

"Eli." John called his brother over.

"Hm?"

"Go grab the musket," John said.

"What is going on?"

"Just bring it to me, please," John said. "Quickly."

Eli obeyed. John stared, never blinking, at the tree line. He had dealt with his fair share of predators that lurked from the forest. The occasional wolf or even a fox trying to get into the chicken's coop. But whatever he had registered in his mind at the tree line was a lot larger than either of those possibilities. In fact, he was not fully convinced it was an animal he had seen. Of course, he had chased off rambunctious children before who wanted to cause trouble.

John even had a standoff or two with a drunk or a traveler too far from town.

Eli returned with the musket before long, and John gripped it with familiarity. It had been a little while since he had last used it.

"Loaded?" John asked.

"Yes," Eli said, "already prepared it for you. And here."

Eli handed John the hatchet they had purchased from the store earlier. John tucked it into his belt.

"Stay here," John ordered, "I am going to see what was bothering Tom. Call out if I am needed. I will be back."

Eli nodded as John marched out to the forest line. John felt the annoyance build internally. He was ready for bed after the ride home, but now he had to deal with this nuisance. He walked past the fenced plot and then past the well, nearing the trees.

"Best to clear out!" John announced. "You are trespassing, and I will protect my land!"

He stood and listened a few moments just outside the forest line. The trees in the waning light seemed sinister, like the branches were arms that reached out for him, inviting him into their clutches. A chill he had not experienced since he was a boy ran through him. He became very aware of a cold sweat at the base of his neck that slithered down his spine. John was unfamiliar with the sudden unease that began to clutch at his heart, but staring into the darkness of the woods, he felt like a small boy again, yearning to be in bed and pulling the blanket over his head to shield him from the terrors that crept in the night. The trees seemed to inch closer to him, and he thought the forest may swallow him in that moment.

He frowned and shook off the boyish fear that had settled inside his stomach. He called out several more times. No response.

Was it an animal? No. No, it could not be. Wolves do not run on two legs...

If it was an animal, it must have been scared off by now. John's brow furrowed as he scanned what was visible within the forest. Nothing.

Then why do I feel as if I am being watched?

John forced that thought away. He called out once more then let himself chuckle. He was being foolish. He uncocked the musket and allowed himself to relax. When he turned his back on the forest and began walking back to the cottage, John's uneasiness smashed into him with a sudden and tremendous impact like a horse bucking him in the chest. He felt eyes digging into his back with intensity. He whirled around.

"Hey!" he shouted.

Nothing.

"This is ridiculous," John muttered to himself.

But even as he acknowledged his own foolishness, he walked backwards, facing the forest, for a good distance until he reached the well. Only then did he turn around and walk to the cottage, albeit with a slightly quicker stride.

Eli and John sat at the small wooden table eating their supper. Eli had prepared a stew, and they both ate in relative silence. Tom was laid down beneath the table, praying for some fallen morsel to escape either of the brothers' spoons. He had calmed down when John returned and had not made a sound since.

"Find anything out there?" Eli asked.

John shook his head. "Nothing. Old Tom must have gotten spooked by his own shadow."

Eli smiled.

"You did well on the stew," John said.

"I am glad to hear it," Eli replied.

The rest of their evening was peaceful. Eli read the newspaper to his brother, who listened intently. John did not read so well, so he was thankful his brother was there to keep him updated on the times. Soon enough, the both of them readied for bed. They wished each other (and Tom) a goodnight before blowing out the candle and curling up in their beds. John had since forgotten about the experience near the forest and had just finished counting to ten for the third time before falling into a deep sleep.

Eli, on the other hand, had trouble falling asleep. This was normal. He had problems sleeping ever since he was a boy. His mind was loud most nights, and tonight, the nausea had already settled into his belly. He tried to calm the anxiety he felt by breathing deeply and reminding himself that he was safe with his brother. John was just a few feet away in the other bed. He was *safe*. John would always protect him. John had promised to keep him safe, after all. And that promise always made him feel at ease when he thought back on it. Eli's eyes grew heavy, and he felt sleep begin to take him.

DO YOU REALLY WISH TO DISAPPOINT ME, ELI?!

Eli shot up in bed with a gasp. The dream, the nightmare of a life before, had come again. He looked around frantically at the darkened cottage and forced himself to breathe. He was *safe*. His brother was in the bed a few feet over. His brother would always protect him. Tom licked Eli's hand, and Eli gave him a gentle pat.

"Good boy," Eli whispered.

He felt his bladder expanding and set to burst. Eli cursed in the darkness and swung out from the bed. He wrapped his blanket around himself and searched around for the candle. Upon finding it, he lit it, and the light from the flame made the remnants of his nightmare fade away.

"I am going to relieve myself," Eli said quietly to John.

John grunted in his sleep. Eli opened the door to the cottage and walked out behind the barn with Tom following closely behind. The cow and chickens were asleep, so he crept a little further past the barn to a small bush. Eli lifted and tucked his bed shirt under his chin. He held the candle steady and relieved himself in the shrub. He sighed happily, and, when finished, he rewrapped himself in his blanket and began to walk back to the cottage.

"Come on, Tom," he whispered.

The dog followed. Eli thought about how cozy his bed would feel at this time of night as he went. He looked up then. The sky was clear, and the stars shone brilliantly against the dark backdrop. The moon's light dazzled, and Eli almost stopped for a moment just to take in the artistry of the night sky. He smiled. He loved his life here. He passed the barn and examined the sky once more. Then he turned to the threshold of the cottage, and his smile faded. A cry became lodged in his throat and turned to an icy grip of fear at what he saw.

Upon and around the door were symbols scrawled in what looked like blood. The symbols were crude in the moonlight and seemed hastily drawn. Eli did not know if it was a language, but they were indeed menacing. A bloody handprint was at the window as well, as if whoever had done this had leaned against the wall to peer inside. Eli felt his heart pounding. His ears rang. Panic began to boil within.

"John," he whispered so quietly, he was not certain he had even spoken.

Eli was frozen in place. Not since he was a boy had he felt this kind of fear. He tried to convince himself that it was just children playing a joke. But those symbols. The blood. What child would be morbid enough to do something like this? Especially so far from town.

Eli tried to call for John again, but his voice managed only a small whimper. Eli would remain frozen in place until dawn came. Until John awakened to begin the day would he stare at the symbols on the threshold. Until John would come outside and ask what he was doing, then look and see what Eli's unblinking gaze beheld.

Chapter 2
Of the First Signs and the First Visitation

"Eli," John said softly but firmly, "you must eat something."

Eli shook his head and wrapped the blanket around him tighter. His brows were furrowed, and his eyes were wide.

"I am telling you," John said, pushing the plate of bread toward his brother, "it was only children. Children play jokes."

"I heard nothing outside the house," Eli said, "nothing. What child would do something as sick as drawing bloody runes on someone's home?"

"Then explain what you believe happened," John said, continuing to eat his breakfast.

Eli only shook his head and remained silent. John had found Eli outside that morning and found the bloody scrawls upon their home. He had led Eli back into the cottage and had asked him what had happened, but Eli was too fearful to speak. John had examined the symbols, and, seeing how it was blood, he had checked on the chickens, the cow, the horses, and old Tom. They were all unperturbed and unharmed.

"Kids," John grumbled.

John finished the rest of his breakfast and then stood from the table.

"Well," he said, "children or no, we still have work to do today. So let us get everything done. See if you can scrub away the blood while you are at it today, alright?"

Eli did not respond.

"Alright?" John said a little louder, firmer.

"Alright," Eli said softly.

Eli had milked Beth and stored it in the cellar. He pet her soothingly and made sure the chickens were well. He had brushed the horses and then took a bucket to the well and drew from it. He then fetched a rag and did his best to scrub away the bloody scrawls from the cottage.

John had tended to the crops and, when satisfied, had taken the axe from the cottage to chop some more firewood. He had once asked Eli to help him in this task for when winters came, but upon seeing Eli's ability (or lack thereof) to cut wood, he had thought it best to handle this duty himself. They always had enough wood for winter. Even managed to sell their extra logs every year.

John had found the art of chopping wood to be soothing. Another form of mental peace. The work was simple and built his strength. The callouses on his hands were rock-hard. He laughed to himself when he remembered Eli first cutting a log. His whimper at a splinter and how John had teased him for his "womanly" hands. Eli had told him to make his own supper that evening, and when John had gone to bed with a failed soup (if you could call it "soup") in his stomach that night, he had never teased Eli about his hands or had him chop wood again.

John added the newly-cut logs to the growing pile outside their cottage and then went to Eli, who he found vigorously scrubbing at the blood. Eli had put in a great deal of effort as most of the scrawls were faded, though not entirely gone. Eli threw the rag down in frustration.

"They are still there," he groaned.

"You have done well," John said. "Most of it is gone."

"It is not all gone though," Eli said, massaging his aching hands.

John went to him, took him gently by the wrists, and looked over his brother's hands. His fingertips were red, irritated, and appeared to have begun to swell. Eli had been putting in every ounce of effort he had to scrub away the defaced doorway.

"Womanly hands," John whispered to himself with a smile.

"What?"

"Time for a break," John said, walking past Eli on his way to the horses. "Come along."

"No, what was it you said a moment ago?" Eli said, following his brother.

"Nothing," John said, stifling a laugh.

He could never stomach his own cooking again. Never again.

They rode to town and hitched the horses. John had mentioned something about visiting the church, which Eli had almost laughed at. They were not church-going men, and the idea of it made Eli scoff. Yet, his brother had insisted, so he followed him. John entered the church meetinghouse. A large crucifix was erected proudly on an altar in front of rows of simple, wooden pews. It was a humble place. John and Eli respected the solemn and silent few patrons that prayed in the pews. They two quietly walked past them and up to the priest, who had just finished praying with another man. He greeted the brothers warmly.

"Hello," John said, "I am John, and this is my brother, Eli."

"A pleasure," the priest said. "I am Father Benjamin. What can I do for you both?"

The priest's smile, while friendly, annoyed John, who had no desire to be here longer than needed.

"We, my brother and I, own a farm some distance outside of town," John explained. "And recently, last night that is, we experienced something odd."

"Odd?"

"We found bloody marks on our cottage," John said, "strange drawings or runes. We wondered if you might have heard of any pranks that local children may have taken part in? Or if anyone else has experienced that around here?"

"Now let me think," the priest said.

He was an older man, probably in his sixties, and his wrinkles seemed to chisel a life story of stress and toil into his face. He closed his eyes in thought and scratched at his chin.

"Well, I know that Mary and William recently punished their children for blasphemies, but aside from that, no one has come forth about anything you have encountered," Father Benjamin said. "Confessions have not been brought forth either."

"I see," John said.

"If you expect tomfoolery," the priest said, "I will certainly keep my ears open for you. A child drawing runes in blood would be a difficult thing to keep secret. Either they wounded or killed a small animal, or they had to wound themselves. I will inform you if I hear of anything. A 'joke' like that is no laughing matter and must be punished severely."

"We just want to make sure our farm is safe," John said, "you understand. Cannot go thinking our livestock is safe with blood on our walls."

"Of course, of course," the priest said. "Now is there anything else I may assist you with?"

"No, Father, thank you," John said, nodding his thanks.

"I hope we see you on the Sabbath day," Father Benjamin said with a smile. "We shall be seeing praises from the Psalms this upcoming Sabbath."

John gave a fake smile, and he and Eli saw themselves out.

"Singing all day?" Eli asked John quietly. "We... we are not going to that. Are we?"

"Not a chance," John said.

Two days passed without incident. Eli had managed to get the blood completely off the cottage by chipping the wood it clung to with a hatchet. John had not protested this as the markings were unsettling to him as well. On the third morning, John awoke with his usual routine. A light rain had woken him, and the dark clouds that covered the sky blotted out any trace of sun.

He stretched and was about to go rouse Eli when he looked out the window. Someone was standing at the edge of the wood. John could not tell man or woman from the distance but saw a raggedy cloak drawn about them. Their hood was pulled up, and darkness covered the face. Two, bone-thin bare legs held up the person. Whoever it was watched John through the window.

Old Tom began barking at them from his post. Eli awoke with a start. He stared at John.

"What is Tom barking at?" Eli asked.

John did not answer immediately, instead watching the person intently. Something was wrong with them. The way the person stood there, or perhaps just their very presence, unnerved him. He found the sensation odd since no one frightened him. Not anyone living, that was.

"John?" Eli asked again. "What is he barking at?"

John turned his head to look at his brother. "Someone is out there."

"What?"

John turned to look at the figure again. It was still there.

"Do they need help?" Eli asked.

John did not respond, so Eli got up and joined his brother at the window. He saw them as well, and a chill ran down his spine like the one from his childhood.

"What is the matter with them?" Eli asked quietly.

"I do not know," John said. "Maybe they are lost?"

They both stood there watching the figure. Neither wanted to go outside to confront whomever it was. Finally, John mustered his courage and thought it ridiculous to be afraid of a stranger. Especially one so skinny. He opened the door.

"You are going out there?" Eli asked.

"Well, they are not leaving," John said. "I will see what they need. I will be back. Try and calm down Tom, will you?"

John strode out of the cottage and into the rain. He kept his eyes fixed on the cloaked figure. With every step, dread built in his heart. For whatever reason, he did not want to confront this person but knew it had to be done. He walked past his fenced plot, and when he made it to the well, the details of the cloaked figure became ever clearer.

The cloak was made of poorly sewn rags, muddy and travel-worn. The flesh upon the legs was grayish and clammy from the rain. John saw every detail of bone within the legs. Knobby knees and almost bowlike shins stood unwavering in the cold. The hood was drawn over the face, but John noticed the neck was also grayish. Blue and green-colored veins seemed to bulge from it, and long, greasy, raven-colored hair seemed to accentuate them. John could distinguish just enough to tell that this was a woman. She was barefoot, and the flesh there repulsed him. He stopped a good distance from her before the dread could overwhelm him.

"Hello," John said, voice cracking subtly.

No answer.

"I am John," he said, forcing his voice to feign courage. "This is my farm."

No response. No movement. Just the rain and the light wind responded.

"I live here," John said. "My brother and I, we both do."

John turned his head to locate his brother. He saw him with Tom near the cottage. He pointed at him.

"There he is," John said, turning to face the woman again.

That was when John noticed something new about the woman before him. Blood was seeping from her legs from small wounds.

"Are you--" he began, but then he noticed.

The wounds were in the exact shapes of the scrawls that had been on the cottage. John took a step back, watching the rain merge with the pool of blood around her deformed feet.

"You are unwell," John said. "You need a doctor. Who did this to you?"

A quiet croaking sound came from her. John felt like fleeing, but his fear cemented his feet to the earth. He thought he could see two glowing eyes from within the hood but for only a moment, and he was not sure if he had imagined it or not.

"John!" he heard Eli cry out.

Tom's barking had increased in ferocity and seemed to be closer. He turned his head and saw that old Tom had broken free of the rope that tied him to his post. He was now bolting at the woman like a feral wolf. John saw the woman then turn and dart into the woods with great speed. Tom took off after her. Eli ran to John.

"Tom is going to attack them!" Eli said, panting.

John was quiet. He stared at the blood-soaked ground where the woman once stood. Eli did not notice it.

"John, we have to go get Tom!"

John did not answer. He did not blink. He just stared. Eli then shook him from the trancelike state.

"John!"

"I do not know who she is," John said, "but something is wrong with her."

"What?"

"There is no time," John said. "I will go retrieve Tom."

"Are you sure?"

John did not respond, uncertain of his choice even as he ran into the forest. He cursed his false sense of bravery and ran after the sounds of Tom's barking.

"Tom!" he called.

That woman could not have outrun Tom, he thought.

He followed the barks further in. Rain was falling harder, and the wind was stronger now.

"Tom!"

John ran further along. He did not notice the branch that stuck out of the ground, which grasped at his foot and tripped him. He fell, and his head struck something hard. The world spun, and his vision grew dark.

"Tom," John groaned.

Only the wind greeted his ears before he fell unconscious.

When John stirred awake it was quiet. The silence defied nature. Wind did not blow, and birds did not make themselves known. His breathing and his own heartbeat were all he could hear. John's head was spinning, and a dull pounding aided in stewing the nausea in his stomach. He placed a hand to his forehead and felt the wet stickiness of blood. He groaned a curse and stood up slowly. Pain shot through his head like a metal ball from a musket, and it made him dizzy. He leaned upon his knees and groaned again.

The woman and the dog were gone. He knew that much, at least. He took several deep breaths and tried to gain a sense of where he was. The woods were like an abyss, and if you did not pay attention, they would swallow you. John looked for a landmark. Of course there was none. How far did he chase Tom into the forest? He cursed himself for not being more careful.

"Eli!" he called out.

Nothing.

John's heart thudded in his ears, and with every beat, his head spiked with pain. He called for his brother several more times to no avail. He cursed again and began to walk slowly in the direction (or so he thought) of the farm. Leaves crunched beneath his feet, so loudly they may as well have been cannon fire. He stopped. The noise made him feel as if he was drawing attention to himself. The feeling of being watched made the hair stand up on his neck.

That woman. Her very presence was in his mind, unnerving him, and now, with her at the forefront of his brain, he felt like a scared young boy.

MAN UP!

The familiar voice rang in his head. A voice he had not heard in years. John frowned.

"Impossible," John said to himself.

He took another step. The leaves crunched, loud as thunder. John felt like every terror, every evil, that lurked in the forest would bear down on him any second. For a moment, John even closed his eyes, not wanting to see what may pounce.

Silence.

He opened his eyes. He was being foolish. He was being a child. He took another step, and the sound of the leaves made him turn into that scared little boy again.

YOU ARE AN EMBARASSMENT!

"You are wrong!" John yelled instinctively, whirling around to face the speaker.

Nothing was there. Nothing but the trees and the branches that seemed to inch closer, as if they were reaching for him. John took a deep breath. This was nonsense. All a figment of imagination. The hit to his head was making him hear things, making him feel unnatural. Everything would be fine when he got home. John's legs did not respond to his logic. Fear still gripped at him.

YOU HAVE ALWAYS BEEN WEAK!

The voice became deafening.

WEAK!

COWARD!

PATHETIC!

DISAPPOINTMENT!

John felt tears begin to build in his eyes.

"No..." his voice cracked.

STUPID BOY!

YOU ARE WORTHLESS!

"No..." John whispered, bringing his hands over his ears.

IF ONLY YOU HAD NEVER BEEN BORN!

The insults and taunts overcame him. The tears were released from their brown-eyed prison. The voice felt as if it was ripping his mind into fragments, and it brought John to his knees.

"I hate you," he said softly in between soft sobs. "God damn you."

The voice did not cease.

Eli waited patiently for his brother at the cottage. It had been a long time since John had bolted after Tom and the woman, and Eli had grown worried and restless.

"John," he had muttered while pacing the cottage, "where are you?"

Finally, the restlessness became too much, and Eli marched outside. He strode past the barn, the crop, and the well. Then, he hesitated at the tree line. The forest loomed before him. Uncertainty seemed to drown him.

"John!" he yelled.

There was no answer.

"JOHN!"

Nothing. He made up his mind. He would go in after his brother.

"You know nothing!" John screamed.

The voice bellowed its curses in his head.

"I AM MORE THAN YOU EVER WERE!"

A firm grasp dug into his shoulder, and John roared and swung his fist blindly. A squeal came from the target, and John, in a blind rage, leapt upon the individual.

"I am stronger than you remember!" John yelled.

"John! John! John!"

John's fist was cocked back ready to strike. Then, Eli's face broke through the fog of his hatred. He was horrified. The younger brother's face shined with frightened tears. His lip was split, and a small amount of blood ran down his chin. John felt immense shame.

"Eli..." he whispered, hand relaxing. "Eli... I... I am so sorry."

"John?" Eli whimpered.

John had sworn to protect Eli. He had promised himself he would always keep his little brother safe. The guilt he felt of being the source of his brother's fear and sadness in this moment racked him. He grabbed his little brother by the shoulders and yanked him into his embrace. He apologized profusely, bitter tears streaming down his cheeks.

"John, it is okay," Eli said. "Your head is bleeding."

"It is not okay," John said. "I struck you. Forgive me. I did not know it was you."

"I know, John," Eli said, trying to wriggle away from his brother's embrace. "I know."

"No," John said softly. "You do not."

"What happened?" Eli asked. "I found you because you were screaming at someone. Was someone here?"

John did not respond. He squeezed his brother once more then wiped his face.

"John, who were you screaming at?" Eli asked.

"We must leave this place," John said, helping his brother to his feet, "Lead us home."

Eli obeyed.

The brothers did not speak as Eli led them out of the forest. Occasionally, Eli would look back to check on John, and he would catch John looking around frantically for a few moments before settling down and focusing on the ground. He knew something had happened out there with John, but he knew John would not say. His screaming and cursing seemed to be directed at someone he was familiar with. Eli had thought it best to ask him about it later. Much later.

Once they had returned to the farm, John sighed in relief and became visibly more at ease. Inside the cottage, Eli began preparing supper. John sat at the table, resting his head in his hands.

"John, did you find Tom out there?" Eli asked.

"No," John said, "I lost him. I tripped and hit my head. When I woke up, he was gone."

Eli sighed.

"He knows the way home," John said, trying to lighten the obvious sadness that sat with Eli.

"Right..." Eli said.

Eli loved old Tom. They were best friends since he was a boy.

"I am sorry I lost him," John said.

Eli did not respond.

They ate and then decided to turn in early. John had nursed his head injury and was feeling better. He had cleaned the gash and wrapped it as best he could before turning in. Eli did not go straight to bed though. He waited outside, hoping, praying, that Tom would show. When night took away all light, he gave up. He wiped his eyes and made peace that his friend was probably not returning.

"Goodbye, Tom," he said sadly.

Sleep, as usual, did not come easily for Eli. Nighttime always plagued him. He had reserved himself to the fate of a near-sleepless existence. He relaxed in bed and forced himself to remain still. He simply counted, having to start over a few times, before feeling drowsy. The dreams would come soon, and he would do his best to combat them.

Coming to bed, darling?

Eli's eyes snapped open, dissolving the beginnings of a nightmare. He was lying on his side facing the wall. He pulled the blanket over his shoulders and up to his chin. He forced his eyes closed. The quiet within the cottage normally disturbed him, but tonight, he was too tired to care. The bed was hugging him perfectly. He felt at peace. Then, he heard it.

A noise from behind him filled the room. The sound was like wet feet stepping across the wooden floor. Someone was inside the cottage. Eli did not move. Fear baptized him as he stared at the wall.

Slap.

Slap.

The wet footsteps indicated that they were searching for something. Eli begged for them to leave. Begged for John to awaken and confront the intruder. The footsteps crossed behind him and past the supper table. He thought he heard heavy breathing. He was too frightened to recognize it as his own. His heart beat like a drum, his ears thudding with the beat.

"Please, leave," he mouthed. "God, please."

He remained still. He tightened his grip on the blanket as if it were a shield that would protect him from harm. The wet slapping had gone, and Eli began to wonder if he had just imagined the noise.

Are they gone? he thought to himself. *It is safe now. If they wanted to hurt you, they would have already. Just relax. Go to sleep. John will keep you safe. John will keep you safe. John will keep you safe.*

Then, a faint dripping sound could be heard from the corner of the cottage. A leak? The wind did get pretty strong earlier that day. He would help John patch the roof tomorrow. Eli yawned. Exhaustion made his lids grow heavy.

Drip.

Drip.

Drip.

Eli's eyes opened again. That was going to get bothersome and quickly. He adjusted in bed and sat up. The darkness of the cottage made it difficult to see, but in the corner, he saw something unfamiliar.

"What?"

Drip.

Drip.

Drip.

Eli lit the candle on the bedside table. The flame caught the wick, and slowly, the room filled with a soothing light. The darkness would be at bay, and Eli's mind was lulled into safety as the flame warmed his face. His eyes adjusted to the light. He shined it at the corner, and he screamed.

Tom was pinned upside down to the wall. The dog's blood dripped to the floor rhythmically from a massive slash in his stomach. His entrails spilled out onto the floor like snakes. Tom's eyes were wide and unblinking. His discolored tongue hung to the side of his broken jaw. His teeth were gone. And all along the walls of the cottage were runic drawings and scrawls in Tom's blood.

John had shot out of bed when Eli screamed and witnessed the scene before him. He felt sick at the sight and nearly released the contents of his stomach. He cursed.

"John...." Eli whimpered.

John saw his younger brother pointing at the floor by John's feet. A piece of cloth, like a muddy rag, lie there by his bedside. A rag that would have belonged to a dirty, travel-worn cloak.

Chapter 3
Of the Burial of Old Tom

The brothers had remained in a state of shock for a prolonged time. The drip of old Tom's blood was almost hypnotic. When they were finally released from the trance, Eli felt like weeping for his old friend but bit his lip and remained strong.

"Still think it is a child's prank?" Eli asked bitterly.

John shook his head. As they went to take Tom off the wall, they realized that pieces of his own skeleton were pinning him in place. It required a hammer to remove the makeshift nails. Tom's body hit the ground with a sickening splash of blood and entrails. Eli left the cottage in a hurry. He did not wish to remember his oldest friend this way.

He stood outside, leaning over his knees, and tried to keep from being sick. He retched dryly, his stomach tightening into a painful knot. He heard John come outside.

"Eli," John said sadly, "get me the shovel. I will deal with it, Brother."

Eli nodded his thanks and went to retrieve the shovel from the barn. He entered slowly; in his depressed state, he moved sluggishly. He patted Beth on the head gently, and she mooed her approval before going back to chewing on her cud. Eli grabbed the shovel and left the barn. He handed it to John then sat in the grass with his back to the cottage.

"I will let you know when he is buried," John said.

Eli nodded. He heard John's retreating footsteps, then the cottage door swinging open and closed. He stared off into the wood past their well. The sun's first rays would begin to illuminate the sky soon. He thought he saw something in the forest, but he did not care. He began to toy with the blades of grass before him, rolling them between his fingers absent-mindedly. Then, his ears picked up the sounds of John's toil. Eli winced with every crunch of the shovel as the hole was dug for Tom's final resting place. He shut his eyes and clamored for reprieve. He searched through his memories for something, *anything*, that would bring just an ounce of joy.

"What does he want?" Katherine barked at her husband.

"I do not know," James replied, still staring from the upstairs window, "but he will not go away."

Eli stood in the corner of his parents' room, watching them argue about someone who had come knocking. A small, fragile, beautiful boy of twelve, Eli flinched whenever they raised their voices. James, his father, looked wearier and definitely older than normal on this day. He had recently celebrated his fifty-sixth birthday by getting drunk and sleeping on the porch, leaving his wife, Katherine, and Eli alone. Katherine was of a similar age as her husband, and yet, she did not look a day over thirty-five. She had a beauty about her that deceived young men and intrigued the older.

"Tell him to go away," Katherine ordered.

James was not one to argue with his wife when she used that famous tone. He looked out the window once more, frowned, then left the room to go tend to the visitor. Katherine peered out the window again then closed the curtains. She walked to her son and smiled.

"Do not be worried," she said, sweetly cupping a hand to Eli's soft chin. "He will be gone soon."

"Who is out there?" Eli asked staring at his mother.

"Do not worry about that," she said. "Your father will deal with him, and we can get back to your lessons."

Eli shuddered when she left. He did not attend traditional school, not anymore. His mother had insisted on instructing him herself from home. He loathed it. Loathed her. But those feelings were secret. He hid them for he sensed that any disrespect toward her would be construed as an act of hostility toward his father.

Eli left the room and crossed the hallway toward the stairs. Outside, the raised voices returned, and soon, they grew into roars. His father was shouting his voice hoarse. He had heard that shouting directed at him only once before. He did not want to revisit it. The shouting fell to a more hushed urgency until another voice thundered over them. One he had not heard in a long time.

"Eli! Eli!"

The front door opened quickly, and John, now a grown man, stood there in the doorway. John looked up the staircase, and their eyes met. Eli grinned. John smiled warmly through his untrimmed beard.

"Eli!"

"Eli," John's voice broke through the memory. "Eli?"

"Hm?"

His older brother's hand rested on his shoulder.

"Come."

John led Eli to a small clearing. A dirt mound with the shovel resting atop it sat beside a small hole.

"I shall fill it," John said, "then if you want to say a few words, you can."

Eli nodded and watched his brother fill the grave where his oldest friend was being buried.

Buried.

Such a fitting state for the only friend Eli knew. One more commonality shared between them.

"Eli!"

The younger brother raced downstairs to greet John. They embraced for a brief moment. John then took him by the shoulder and led him outside. James looked at the both of them with a disapproving stare, but John ignored this and guided Eli to a small horse-drawn wagon on the dirt path in front of the house. The house was a stone's throw from the city of Boston, where Eli suspected John was working.

"John, you are back," *Eli said happily.*

"I am," *John replied,* "but not for long, unfortunately."

"Are you going to leave again?"

"I am. More work needs to be done. I am saving most everything I earn. I have plans, you understand?"

"I do," *said Eli,* "but you will stay for supper, right?"

John weighed this question, looking at their father on the porch then at Eli. Eli swore he saw a violent hatred in John's eyes when he had looked at their father.

"I am afraid not," *John said,* "I am expected back at the port soon."

Eli's face fell with disappointment. John bent on one knee to face his brother eye to eye.

"Listen to me, Eli," *John said,* "one day and one day soon, I will come back for you. And I want you to come with me."

"Go with you?" *Eli asked happily.* "Where?"

"Away," *John said firmly.* "Away from here. Away from... them."

Eli understood who "them" *referred to. The brothers were silent for a moment. Eli looked into John's tired eyes. It was obvious, even to a youth like Eli, that revisiting his old family home was troubling for him.*

"You look old," Eli said.

"Well, I should," John chuckled, "I am fifteen years your elder, boy."

"Is work going well?"

"Very."

"That is good."

John nodded. He looked around the estate. His eyes looked sullen as he gazed around the place he spent his childhood. John then gripped Eli's shoulders with firm, almost vise-like, hands.

"Ow!"

"Eli, listen to me," John said very seriously now, "are you listening?"

"Yes, John," Eli said, wincing from the grip.

"How are they treating you?"

"Who?" Eli asked, even though the answer was obvious.

"Your parents," John said.

"John, you are hurting me," Eli said.

John's grip relaxed somewhat, but the urgency remained.

"Answer me," John said.

"Father gets drunk some nights," Eli said with a trained response, "but he does not lay a hand on me or Mother."

"And she does not harm you?" John asked.

Eli bit his lip. His eyes began to shine.

"Eli? She does not harm you, does she?"

"No," Eli said finally. "No, she does not."

It was not a lie, but he could not find the words to explain.

"Are you certain?" John asked.

"Alright, that is enough time," James said, striding up to them. "You can be on your way now."

"Give me a moment with my brother, old man," John ordered his father.

"You already demanded a moment," James said with a rising temper, "threatened me for a moment. I granted it, and you have had it. Time is up. Eli, back in the house."

Eli retreated slowly back to the house and meekly watched his brother from afar. John stood and faced their father. James looked up at his eldest son, who was now a head taller than he. John looked him in the eye with a vengeful gaze that burned through the old man, and for a moment, just a moment, Eli saw a trace of fear pass through his father's cold, gray eyes.

"Mark this," John said quietly, "I will be back for him."

Eli trudged back to the house, no longer able to hear the exchange between his brother and father. He slowly walked up the porch steps, and at the doorway, he turned to look at the two men. They were still speaking.

"Eli!" John called loudly. "A parting gift for you!"

Eli turned and saw a young, Welsh sheepdog pup bounding at him. Its tail wagged furiously as he pounced on Eli, drenching his face in licks. Eli laughed and petted the young dog.

"His name is Tom!" John called from the wagon. "Take care of him! I will return!"

James scowled all the way back to the house. He entered and slammed the front door behind him. Eli remained on the porch with his new friend, watching his older brother wave from the slowly disappearing wagon, back to Boston.

"Would you like to say a few words for him?" John asked.

Eli swallowed hard. A knot in his throat had formed. He looked to his brother for strength.

"Tom was a good companion," John said. "A finer dog, I do not believe there is one."

John wiped a single tear from his eye before it could fall down his cheek. Eli stood there a moment. He calculated what he would say, even rehearsed a couple lines in his head to honor the dog, but nothing came forth. He was overwhelmed. John draped an arm across his little brother and squeezed him gently.

"Whoever is responsible will get theirs," John said.

Eli did not respond as tears coursed down his cheeks. He quietly sobbed as John mourned alongside him. Eli then looked at John.

"I miss him..." he cried softly. "I miss him."

Chapter 4
Of the Priest and the Wolf Beside the Stream

When the brothers had finally said their goodbyes to old Tom, they still had their chores to do. John tended to the crops while Eli checked on the livestock. When John returned to the cottage, his eyes were immediately drawn to the bloody symbols on the walls. Eli was not there. Disturbed and unsettled, he left and went to the barn that held the animals.

"Eli?"

John found his younger brother in the pen with Beth. Her head was nestled in his lap, and he gently stroked her muzzle.

"I did not want to go back inside with those... markings upon the walls," Eli said, not looking up from Beth.

"I understand," John said. "They do have a disturbing essence."

"It is evil, John," Eli said.

John agreed with his brother inwardly but did not voice this.

"Whatever it is," John said, "it cannot continue."

Eli nodded then said something that took his brother aback.

"Perhaps we should see the priest. Father Benjamin."

"What?" John almost scoffed. "What would he do?"

"I do not know," Eli shrugged, "but I would feel a lot safer if he blessed the house. If he blessed the farm. *Anything.* Because whatever occurred is not... holy."

John, in any other circumstance, would have openly mocked the idea. He would have laughed in his brother's face, but after what they had seen and with those markings and the voice in his head--

"Fine," John agreed.

They walked up the stairs of the church and took a deep breath at the doors. The sun was beginning to set now, and neither of them had any idea how to proceed with the priest. John stared at Eli before finally speaking.

"I can try to explain the situation," John said.

"Thank you," Eli said quietly. "I still... do not quite know how to explain it to myself."

They entered and found Father Benjamin praying before the cross at the altar. The church was empty, and in its emptiness, a certain beauty was impressed upon the brothers. They had entered too quietly for the priest to hear as he still murmured through his prayers. They sat in the pew a few rows behind Father Benjamin and patiently waited for him to finish. It was several long minutes before they heard him utter the "amen". The priest turned and gasped at the unexpected visitors.

"Oh!" he exclaimed.

John and Eli stood at the same time with apologies written on their faces. John spoke.

"Forgive us, Father," he said, "we did not mean to startle you. Truly. We did not want to disturb your prayers."

"Oh, it is fine, gentlemen," he responded, a warm smile spreading across his features, "your scare did not send me to face our Heavenly Father early, so you are forgiven."

John chuckled, and Eli smiled.

"I remember you both," Father Benjamin said, "the farm lads being toyed with. I am afraid I have not heard of anything yet, but--"

"No, sir," John said. "At this point, I do not think we are dealing with the jests of children."

"Oh?"

"My brother believes we are dealing with... an evil," John said, searching for the right words.

"An evil?"

"I still hold hope that there is a logical explanation for what is occurring at our farm, but after last night," John said, "I fear my brother may be right."

"I see," Father Benjamin said. "And what is it you require of me?"

"Well..." John hesitated.

"Will you come bless our home?" Eli blurted.

"I am not sure what good it would do," John said, "but I know it would help Eli."

Father Benjamin raised his eyebrows and pondered their words.

"So, as I understand," the priest said, "you want me to come and say a prayer over your home?"

"Sure," John said.

"And how far is your farm?" the priest asked.

"Some miles away," John explained. "About a half day's ride from here. Maybe less."

"I see," Father Benjamin said hesitantly.

"We will pay you," Eli said.

"Eli," John said sternly.

"It is fine, John," Eli said. "I have some money tucked away of my own. Please, sir. I will make sure it is worth the travel. Just a simple prayer, that is all."

Father Benjamin thought about this, knowing he (and the church, of course) could really use the money.

"Just a prayer or two?" the priest asked.

"Yes," the brothers said in unison.

"Very well," the priest said. "But since this is... short notice, I trust you can wait a day or two? I assume you will both be there when I arrive?"

"We do not leave often," Eli said. "Just as soon as you possibly can come. Please. I will have the reward waiting for you."

"Very well," Father Benjamin said, "I will make preparations. I must take care of my flock's needs first and foremost. Their needs come before... well... absent attendees. I am sure you understand. I will be out there tomorrow morning, if that is agreeable?"

"Yes, yes!" Eli said. "Absolutely!"

John then explained where the farm was in great detail, and when he was certain the priest understood, the two brothers dismissed themselves and left the church.

"Do you think it is God's will that drives him or a need for money?" John asked his brother.

"At this point, I do not care," Eli said.

The brothers returned to the farm after dark, using the moonlight as a guide. There was nothing out of the ordinary at the farm (save for the bloody markings that remained on the walls of the cottage) when they returned. They hitched the horses, checked on Beth and the chickens, and when all seemed peaceful, they went inside.

Eli and John sat upon their beds pondering things. They said goodnight to one another. Eli remained awake. Given the circumstances, it would have been surprising if he slept on this night. John also remained awake. He sat in his bed, keeping watch over the cottage. He thought the idea of having a priest here was foolish. Something logical was taking place here. That woman from before must have killed old Tom. But how would a woman of such a fragile-looking state be able to lift the dog and use his own bones to pin him to the wall?

Given more thought, John concluded that having a priest pray over their home was not the worst idea. Maybe it could do some good.

John soon settled into a dreamless rest. He was not asleep, nor was he awake. He was something in between. Aware and unaware. Still, the day came, and in the early hours, he got up, rubbed his eyes, and decided to go for a hunt. Just something to keep his mind occupied. He grabbed the musket and his pack, which would carry more ammunition and gunpowder, then he tucked the hunting knife and hatchet into his belt. John went over to Eli's bed and, as was customary, saw his brother's wide, bloodshot eyes staring in terror at him.

"Just me," John said.

He was used to announcing himself to Eli every morning like this. His brother *never* slept properly, and at times, it concerned John, but his brother had never wished to discuss what plagued his ability to rest, despite John asking more than a few times. Eli had never faltered on his duties around the farm, so John, in their previous discussion of it, merrily told Eli that he was there for his brother and that he was free to come to him with anything. He had hoped Eli understood that, but Eli's lack of transparency in certain matters made John feel more like a stranger than brother. Still, he knew Eli cared for him, and the brothers shared a bond (unspoken, yet still present) that ran deeper than even they understood.

"I am going on a hunt. Do you want to come?" John asked.

Eli shook his head, then he turned his back on John and faced the wall, begging for just a little bit of rest before the day.

"Alright," John said, "I shall return."

He hesitated before entering the forest. It was brief, but it was there: that ominous feeling that something was watching him. Ever since purchasing the land and building the farmstead all those years ago, he never had experienced a sensation like this one. Still, he proceeded into the forest and shouldered the musket in search of game.

Hunting had become another one of those pastimes that John always fell back on whenever his mind was in turmoil. Since his mind *was* in turmoil these days (and understandably so), he was crouched in the forest, studying and observing the tracks that were on display before him. A small rabbit had lingered here then had bounded off. He also noticed why: a paw print nearby that belonged to a wolf. The heavy male (an alpha, most likely) had surely scared it off.

John studied the wolf's tracks and took a deep breath. At times, he felt that this was a flaw within his character. The desire to seek out danger during a hunt thrilled him. The adrenaline would build in him like a snowball rolling downhill. It would gain speed and become an uncontrollable force of destruction. John would think on that sometimes. *Destruction.* Did he seek out his own on these hunts? Would the wolf be a worthy adversary? He felt the desire to discover that answer rise like smoke from a fire in his stomach, and its suffocating fumes clouded his mind and judgment. He smiled to himself. He would find out.

The tracks were inconsistent as he went along. Occasionally, the alpha had taken pause and would (or so John thought) sniff the air, listening for its prey. When it had left, it treaded lightly upon its padded feet, and it made John's job of tracking difficult. Upon the trail, he found a tree that the creature must have stopped to scent rub. Its fur clung to the bark, and it left behind a myriad of claw marks. It had taken time to sharpen its nails to an acceptable point in order to kill.

John imagined finding the thing. A glorious battle played out in his mind. A duel for the ages between man and beast. John would hurl himself at the wolf and pound it with his fists. It would claw at him and make impressive wounds that created a fountain of blood. But John would roar, and it would cower at his battle cry. John would continue to attack. Man would become the beast, and the beast would become prey. He would snap its neck with his bare hands, and he would skin it to wear the fur like a prized cloak from war. Victorious.

The illusion broke when a twig snapped beneath John's weight. He looked down and shook his head. How long had he been daydreaming? He heard the sound of the nearby creek. Its water lapped against the land in perfect symbiosis as it was guided downstream. John knew where he was. This landmark had often saved him from losing his way. He was only a couple miles from home, but he had lost track of the wolf. His imagination had gotten the better of him. That is when he heard it.

Small smacks of a tongue pulling water into its mouth alerted John to the far bank. John did not move and turned his gaze to the thirsty alpha that had not taken notice of him behind the cover of several trees. He took in the sight of the creature. The muscles in its neck and arms bulged impressively as it leaned down to drink from the stream. Its fur was like untainted snow with winter's pure, white sheen, save for what looked like some blood upon the crown of its head. He must have found that rabbit and eaten sloppily. If it had been winter, it would have been impossible to spot, but John *had* seen it, and the element of surprise was in his grasp. He shouldered the musket and lay the barrel upon the branch of the nearest tree. It helped steady his aim as he cocked it slowly, trying to make as little noise as possible.

Click.

The sound of the lock may as well have been thunder in the silence of the moment. The wolf's ears perked up, and its head looked side to side, trying to find the source. John's heart pounded like a drum, and he forced himself to calm down. After a short time, the wolf was lulled back into a sense of safety and began to drink again. At first hesitantly, but then greedily. John eased the lock of the musket down once more until it was in readied position to fire.

Click.

Now, the alpha had the sense of where the sound came from, and its eyes leveled in John's direction. It did not move, though. It began to snarl, its lips curled around knife-like teeth as it glared at John. The beast was ready for battle. John rested a shaky finger upon the trigger. He knew if he missed, he would have to go for the hatchet quickly or risk destruction. Still, thrill fired through him, and he wondered if he would miss the shot intentionally. If only to find out if he had the strength to duel the wolf on equal footing. John leveled the barrel of the musket in line with the wolf's head. Its responding snarl was louder, cautioning John.

A thousand thoughts ran through his head. A thousand voices of doubt and fear and anxiety screamed at him. He would not disappoint this time. Not again.

If you miss, you are no son of mine!

John hesitated. The shot was clear, but his father's voice rang like a church bell in his ears. He blinked several times. The wolf barked its warning now and dug its paws into the ground, ready to pounce. Then, as John prepared to finally fire, the blood upon the alpha's head demanded John's attention when he realized what it was. A symbol. One not unlike those that had appeared at the cottage. John's eyes widened. The wolf had stopped snarling. It had begun to whimper softly as its head twitched once then twice.

John's finger fell from the trigger, and he watched as the whimpers intensified as if it was in a great deal of pain. It suddenly ceased making noise of any kind, then its head snapped to John. Its eyes were now a pale, milky white color, as if blind. The fur on its back began to raise, and a low guttural sound formed in its stomach then traveled into its throat. A hacking cough came from it, and John stood in shock and fear as it spoke.

The words were quiet but just loud enough for him to hear. John was suddenly overwhelmed with the thought that he was not facing a Godly creature as God never intended animals to speak human language. So when the two words came from the throat of the wolf, John was horrified and sickened. The possessed thing uttered them in a perverse and unnatural way, but John heard. And worse, he understood. Fear gripped his heart in an icy and unbreakable grasp as he began to question his own sanity.

"**Hell cometh...**"

John felt a cold sweat trickle down his spine as the wolf tried to fight the control of whatever power held it. It cried and twitched with pain. The bloody symbol on the crown of its head pulsed, and John gripped the musket harder, finding the trigger.

"Shoot the thing," John whispered to himself as it cowered away.

His courage was failing. His mind was attacking itself.

"SHOOT, JOHN!" He shouted at himself.

The control upon the beast was relinquished, and the wolf vomited the half-digested remnants of a rabbit carcass. It gagged again and then eyed John. It seemed weary and broken. They held eye contact for a few brief moments, then the wolf walked into the forest, leaving John alone to make sense of what had occurred. He remained there for what felt like an eternity, his hand clutched the musket with a grip that pained him. That pain broke him out of the trance.

All the way home, he could not piece together the previous events. He could not make sense of any of it and began to wonder if his mind was lost.

"Animals. Do. Not. Speak. John."

He repeated this to himself again and again and again in the hopes that when he got home, he would begin to believe it. But he knew that he would never forget what had transpired. If Hell was indeed real, then he had seen one of its guardians. John felt overwhelmed with paranoia and sickness when he arrived at the cottage. He found Eli doing his share of work and, when Eli asked him how the hunt went, John had chosen not to respond with honesty.

"Nothing happened," he said, "I did not see anything."

"You alright, John?" Eli asked. "You look ghostly."

John did not answer.

Chapter 5
Of the Visitation of Father Benjamin

John did not sleep that night. His mind was at war. One side of his brain was debating the other over the reality of the events from the previous day's hunt. In the real world, wolves did not speak, and yet, he had not been dreaming. But still, the words the wolf had spoken kept sleep at bay. And when the sun's first rays of light began to creep across the sky, John blinked and revealed the pain of exhaustion in his eyes. John made up his mind as he got up from bed that he would put the wolf out of his mind and focus on his duties of running the farm. Nothing else was important now.

As John tended to the crops and as Eli was beginning to awaken, Father Benjamin came riding up on a small horse. John left the gardening tools upon the ground and extended a raised hand in greeting. The priest waved back with a small smile as he tied his horse at the hitching post along with the others.

"I hope the journey was not too difficult," John said evenly, pushing his thoughts of the wolf from his mind. He had already failed to keep his mind focused on work.

"Not at all," Father Benjamin replied. "It is certainly a ways from town. I trust privacy is not hard to come by."

John chuckled more than he normally would have at the quip and shook his head. There was a pleasantness about the remark, despite its actual quality, that made him feel a wave of ease. Jokes, no matter how small, were an invited distraction from yesterday's events (as he still found himself questioning his own sanity).

"Did you build this place yourself?" Father Benjamin asked.

"I did," John said proudly. "I was able to build a life here for my brother and myself."

"That is excellent," Father Benjamin replied. "I hope for a life like yours one day. But for now, I am, well, the Lord's instrument. I go where I am called."

John nodded.

"Where is your brother?" Benjamin asked. "Eli, was it?"

"Yes," John said, "he is inside. He does most of the minor work around here so I can tend to the crops and build and repair things."

John beckoned the priest to follow and opened the door to the cottage. John entered and saw Eli sitting at the supper table in quiet thoughtfulness. The priest did not immediately enter the home. He stood at the threshold, frowning. The priest's eyes were closed in a quiet meditation.

"Father Benjamin?" John asked.

The priest's eyes slowly opened, and he stared at the two brothers with an expression of concern.

"I feel something," he said quietly.

"What is it?" Eli asked.

The priest did not respond and instead entered the home. He looked around and saw the fading, bloody runes on the walls opposite where the brothers slept. He walked to the wall slowly, eyes transfixed upon the shapes and odd scrawls that decorated the room.

"And you do not know who did this?" the priest asked without breaking his gaze upon the blood.

"No," John said.

The priest studied the runes and occasionally uttered short prayers that the brothers could not distinguish. He placed a hand on the wall itself and prayed quietly, then he beckoned the brothers over to him.

"I do not know what has been occurring here, but evil has certainly been present," Father Benjamin said. "Come. Take hands. We will pray."

They stood in a circle holding hands. The men closed their eyes (the brothers more out of respect than actual belief in the power of prayer), and Father Benjamin began to pray.

"Dear Lord, our Heavenly Father," the priest said reverently, "we come before You now in need of You. There is an evil here, oh God. A presence unwelcome and unholy in Your sight. We plead, oh Lord our God, remove that which plagues this land and ease the minds of Your two sons here. Father, we pray these things in Your Son's holy, precious, and beautiful name. Amen."

The brothers echoed the "amen" quietly. They quickly released hands.

"Is that all that is needed?" John asked.

"If I may," Father Benjamin said, "I would like to walk the grounds and pray blessings. With your permission, of course."

Eli nodded as John agreed.

"I will not disturb you or your duties," Father Benjamin said. "You will hardly notice my presence. I will alert you when I have finished."

The brothers nodded once more, and Father Benjamin nodded back with a small, encouraging smile. He saw himself out of the cottage.

"Do you think this will work?" Eli asked.

"I am not sure," John said as his mind returned to the wolf in the forest. "But the priest is right. Whatever visited us was indeed... unholy."

The brothers returned to their duties around the farm. John tended the crops and occasionally watched the priest wander the farm. He was blessing every inch of the place, it seemed like. When Eli had gone to tend to Beth and the chickens, the priest had asked if he could pray over the animals. Eli, seeing no harm in it, allowed him to do so. The brothers finished most of the work by the time the priest had concluded his final prayers.

"I believe I have done all that I can," Father Benjamin told them.

"Will you stay for dinner?" John said. "We insist after everything you have done."

"Well, I suppose some supper would not hurt." Father Benjamin smiled. "I accept."

Eli prepared a stew with some bread. He set the table and placed the food before John and the priest. John and Eli were about to dig in, but Father Benjamin opened up in a prayer that lasted much longer than the brothers' aching stomachs desired. When he concluded, all three ate greedily.

"This is quite delicious," Father Benjamin said.

"Thank you," Eli said quietly.

The satisfied sounds of slurps and belches filled the room. Deafening laughter followed from everyone after a rather lengthy burp from the priest, who flushed with embarrassment.

"Forgive me," he chuckled, "it just had to be set free."

The brothers laughed at this. When they finally finished the meal, Father Benjamin thanked them profusely for sharing their food and home with him.

"I hope to see you both at Sunday mass," Father Benjamin said, standing at the threshold of the door once again. "And thank you again for the wonderful meal."

"We appreciate you taking the time to come out here," John said.

"Of course," the priest said, turning slowly to head to his horse, "I always wish to help when I can."

"I trust you can find your way back to town?" Eli said.

"I believe so," Father Benjamin said. "Do not worry about me. I--"

He stopped speaking. His eyes fixed on the outskirts of the farm. The brothers exchanged glances with each other as the priest stared, unblinking, at something in the distance. The brothers squinted in the direction he looked, and in the dying light of the sun's final rays of the day, only the forest and the well and the crop were present.

"Father Benjamin?" John asked. "Are you alright?"

The priest whispered something so quietly, the brothers could not hear. Eli thought he heard him say a name but was unsure. Eli reached a hand out and touched the priest's shoulder. The priest whirled around in a fit of sudden rage.

"What evil is this?" he asked wildly.

"What--" John began.

"What evil have you brought me to?" Father Benjamin asked. "What is this devil magic?"

The brothers stood perplexed at this sudden change in the priest. Father Benjamin took a few steps from the cottage and placed his hands on his head in confusion. Quiet whimpers escaped his lips.

"How is this possible?" he said to himself. "How is this possible? Lord, what is this?"

"Father Benjamin?" John said, attempting to gain some clarity on the situation.

The priest now extended a hand in the direction of the forest and cried out.

"Samuel!"

The priest began to take more steps toward the forest. He cried out the name again. The brothers watched the scene play out. The priest looked from the direction of the forest then at the brothers. Tears flooded his eyes. He looked back at the wood and took a deep breath.

"Samuel!" he cried. "By God's goodness… Samuel."

The priest then ran as fast as he could to the forest, crying out the name like a madman in the night.

"Priest!" John shouted. "Do not go in there!"

"Father Benjamin!" Eli called.

John made up his mind and tore after the priest. He gained on him, but as the priest entered the woods screaming the name, Samuel, John stopped dead at the tree line. A paralyzing dread seized his limbs, and he watched Father Benjamin take off into the darkness. Flashes of the wolf filled his head. Those milky eyes. The tortured sounds that came from it. That voice. That horrible voice thundered through his head, driving him into madness.

Hell cometh.

Hell cometh.

HELL COMETH!

The repeated phrase in that guttural, disturbing voice brought John's mind to the brink, and he collapsed to the ground. His head was splitting, and pain shot through him. He screamed.

"John!"

Eli was by his side now, pulling him off the ground. He dragged him away from the forest as John continued to scream.

"HELL COMETH!" John wailed.

"What?" Eli cried out. "John?"

But John did not reply, and unconsciousness overtook him. Eli dragged his brother back to the cottage with tears filling his eyes. Fear gripped his heart as he got his brother into bed. And Eli watched his brother stir violently in his sleep from his own bed, the blankets pulled up to his eyes as if he were that young boy again.

Chapter 6
Of the Search for the Priest and of the First Plague

Sometime in the night, John shot up in bed with a loud shout. His body was drenched in a cold sweat, and his eyes darted around in a state of near deliriousness. Finally, his eyes rested on his brother, who was staring at him from behind his blankets, body petrified and eyes wide in horror.

"Eli?" John asked.

"You passed out," Eli whispered a voice just barely louder than a mouse's squeak. "I put you in bed, and you were thrashing around and screaming."

"I was?"

Eli nodded timidly.

"What happened?" John asked, more to himself. "I remember running to the edge of the forest to get Father Benjamin and then... darkness."

"You were screaming when you passed out, John," Eli said, still cowering behind the blanket.

"What was I screaming about?"

"You kept saying..." Eli hesitated now, the fear he felt like a thick fog that would cover him and strangle him in its density.

"What?"

"Hell cometh..." Eli whispered so that the devils of the Earth could not hear.

John looked away from Eli and frowned. His brows furrowed. The wolf's presence came to the forefront of John's mind to the point where he thought he saw it pass through the shadows out of the corner his eye. Those blind eyes. That horrible voice. It was cursed company, and yet, despite his best efforts, it would not go away.

Hell cometh.

John shook himself free from the cold chill that traced its icy finger down his spine.

"I am sorry, Eli," John said. "I do not know what happened or why. Thank you for looking out for me."

"We are brothers," Eli whispered. "I know you would never let anything bad happen to me. I am here for you too, Brother."

John allowed himself to smile. He inhaled deeply and expelled the thoughts of talking wolves from his mind. He smiled at his brother once more, which brought a calmness to Eli.

"I do not rightly understand what is happening," John said, "but you are right. We are brothers. And we look out for one another."

Eli finally let the blanket fall from his face as he felt more relaxed. John looked around the cottage then. His expression went from smiling to confused.

"What happened to Father Benjamin?" John asked.

"I do not know," Eli said.

"What?"

"I do not know," Eli repeated. "He ran into the woods, calling to someone, and you went after him. You collapsed and started screaming. I had to look after you first."

"He has not returned since?" John asked.

Eli shook his head.

"It is still dark out!" John said, "He is out in the woods by himself at night, Eli!"

"Well, I was not going in there after him after you were screaming about Hell, John!" Eli responded defensively, feeling as if John was blaming him for leaving the priest in the forest.

"How long was I out?" John asked, getting out of bed and looking out the cottage window.

"Hours," Eli said simply. "I do not know for certain, but since Father Benjamin's disappearance... it must be more than a few hours."

"Oh, God," John said to himself, rubbing at his temples at a sudden developing headache.

"It is too late to search for him now," Eli said.

"Well, if we do not go out and find him, we are the ones responsible," John said. "Who knows what the town will think if their priest disappears without a trace after visiting our farm?"

Eli cursed inwardly as he got out of bed. They could not afford to be shunned by the closest town in a hundred miles, it was true, but Eli was taken aback by the fact that *that* was what convinced John to go after Father Benjamin. The only thing that kept Eli from going after him was his own fear for himself and his brother, he knew that. The idea of entering the wood that possessed John, his untouchable, indestructible elder brother, with fear made Eli sick to his stomach. But deep down, he knew they should go looking because if the same evil force that plagued their farm now plagued the priest, he needed help, even when that semblance of courage was nearly eclipsed by Eli's fear for his own wellbeing.

To think that John was more concerned about being ostracized than the priest's wellbeing...

Both brothers put on their shoes and readied two lanterns. John brought the musket and slipped the hatchet into his belt. Eli wrapped his blanket around his shoulders and kept it secured tightly with one hand while he guided his steps with the lantern in the other. The two walked to the edge of the forest, where they both stopped short simultaneously. That is when they noticed it.

The soundlessness of the forest was deafening. The usual sounds of the night were not present. The air lacked any breeze. The trees did not make a sound, nor did their leaves. The crickets were nonexistent. John was the first to take a step inside, and Eli followed after a moment of hesitation.

"Father Benjamin!" John called out into the night.

Eli winced at the sudden noise from John. He almost wanted to silence his brother, but not wanting to give himself fully to the paranoia that held sway over him, he called for the priest as well, although much quieter than John. Further into the wood they went, and the two of them almost seemed to agree silently (as if they had read the other's mind) not to stray far from each other. One was never more than a few feet from the other, and they always held the lanterns high.

The light from the lanterns brought little comfort to John's terrorized mind. Several times, he thought he saw the wolf's milky white eyes penetrate the darkness, peering into his soul. Several times, he had unnecessarily readied the musket to fire, but he always regained his senses before pulling the trigger.

"John, are you alright?" Eli asked.

"I worry for the priest," John said, lying to his brother about the terror he felt in his heart.

They pressed further into the darkness. The silence ate away at John, and the paranoia grew. Every crunch of dead leaves and gnarled twigs beneath their feet made John question whether some unknown terror was hiding just behind them, waiting to spring and destroy them. He felt like a young boy again, his imagination filling with visions of demons and monsters he feared lay under his bed.

Not until he began to age did he realize what true monsters really looked like.

"Father Benjamin!" Eli called, summoning his courage.

Eli's sudden outburst shattered through the last of John's resolve. He felt the trees closing in around him with twisted features, laughing at his immature lack of bravery. He could not continue.

"It is useless," John barked into the darkness, his tone tormented, "*useless*. He is not here. He is gone. Let us go home."

Eli sighed. "Poor man. I do not know why he ran off like he did."

"Neither do I," John said, "but we should get back. Now. Who knows what is out here."

Eli agreed, and they turned around and headed in the general direction (or so they guessed) of their farm. They went along as silent as the grave, the lanterns guiding their way. The idea of home brought John peace of mind. The thought of his bed pushed aside any vision of monsters or demons or evils of the night.

But as they walked, Eli felt a strange sensation course through him. It was brief, but it was there. It began slowly, like a breeze against the back of his neck. Then, a feather-light touch, as if someone gently stroked his arm. He felt his skin clam up. He shook his head in an attempt to ward off the feeling.

"Eli."

A voice, a whisper on the wind, drifted through the air out of the darkness of the woods and past Eli's ears. He turned around and squinted into the blackness.

"Are you alright?" John asked.

"I thought I heard something," Eli said.

"You are not playing a joke, are you?" John asked.

"No."

John stared in the same direction as Eli and saw nothing.

"Well, what did you hear?" John asked.

"I am not sure," Eli replied.

They stood there a moment, and when nothing occurred, they continued on their way. Eli felt that creeping feeling again. The trace of a finger across his arm. It began at his arm then ran up his shoulder and drew circles at the base of his neck. He shivered.

"Eli."

The voice was louder now but still faint. Eli ignored it, hoping it was just his imagination. The feeling of that caress was now tracing along the curvature of his spine.

"Oh..." Eli shuddered. The touch felt carnal, but it made a knot form in the pit of Eli's stomach

"What?" John asked.

"Nothing," Eli said, flushing, irritated. "Let us get home quickly, yes?"

"Eli."

The voice was louder still. Tender as before, but there was no ignoring it now. Someone called to him from the darkness. Eli spun around.

"Who is there?!" he cried out.

The sudden cry made John jump. He dropped his lantern, and the fire went out. John gripped the musket and looked where his brother was squinting.

"What is it, Eli?" John asked.

"Did you not hear it?" Eli asked.

"Hear what?" John replied.

"Someone is out there, calling me," Eli said.

"What?"

"You really do not hear them?" Eli asked. "They have called me three times now!"

"Eli, I have not heard a thing since we entered the wood," John said.

"Well, I am not making it up!" Eli said. "Someone is calling me."

John got in front his brother and forced him to make eye contact.

"Listen, Brother," John said, "it is late. We are both exhausted. Losing the priest, you having to drag me back to the cottage as I thrash about in an unconscious state, and the woods at night have left you delirious. You are *tired*. Your mind needs rest. There is nothing out there."

"Eli."

"There it was again," Eli said.

"I heard nothing," John said, starting toward the farm.

"But--"

"No!" John said. "No more. I have had my fill of this night. Come!"

John grabbed his brother, spun him around, and forced him onward by the shoulder. At first, Eli protested but soon came to understand his brother's words. He *was* tired. He had not slept properly in a long while, and he knew he needed to rest. His bed did sound wonderful. But the voice continued to call out to him, and while he did not confront it, he did occasionally turn his head to try and catch a peak at the source.

Soon, the farm came back into view, and the brothers both increased the speed in which they walked. The fear quickened their steps, but not wanting to seem cowardly to the other, the brothers kept a brisk walk and not an outright sprint.

The moment they cleared the tree line, the sounds of night seemed to come alive again. Neither brother made mention of it, but both noticed its oddness. Crickets made their presence known. As did a light wind. The leaves brushed against the branches, and an owl called out a farewell. They quickly entered the cottage, and John shut the door behind them.

"You left a lantern back there," Eli said.

"Well, you frightened me," John said. "We will get another one. I just want some rest now. Goodnight."

"Goodnight, John," Eli said, laying down and forcing himself to sleep.

"You know your brother is not welcome here," Katherine said.

"I do," Eli replied to his mother.

"Then why do you disobey our wishes and still pretend like he is a member of this family?" she asked him.

"He is my brother," Eli said, "I love him."

Katherine scoffed at this. She looked at her husband for support in this matter, but James said nothing and instead took a gulp from his bottle.

"What did he do to you, Mother?" Eli asked.

"It is not what he did to me," Katherine said, looking at James.

"Father, then?" Eli asked.

"It is not your concern," James said, his words beginning to slur. "He is an ungrateful cur."

Eli did not speak. The last time he defended his brother from his father's harsh words, he went to bed with an empty stomach for two straight nights. He kept his mouth firmly shut. He pet Tom beneath the table as his parents continued to lay insults upon John.

Eli had often wondered why his parents hated their own child so much. He had meant to get a straight answer from John about the situation, but he never had the courage. Neither would he ask his father about it again. That was just foolish.

Eli and his parents ate supper relatively quietly this night after the seemingly-ceaseless episode of insulting and cursing John. They placed the dishes on the floor so Tom could clean them up (and eat what was left since he had not eaten that day) and then went to the study. James did not stay long after he finished reading a few letters and announced he was going into town.

"Again?" Katherine asked.

"Again," James said. "The lads want to meet up."

"Go on, then," his wife said almost sourly.

Eli remained silent. A sickness began to bubble in his stomach as a familiar anxiety brewed. He watched his father put on his coat. He silently begged the man not to leave. James closed *the front door behind him, and Eli heard his footsteps down the gravel path begin to fade.*

Eli looked at his mother from behind the book he was reading. She was occupied with her own readings and paid him no mind. Eli almost sighed with relief. He continued reading. A small cough came from his mother. Eli looked over the book and into Katherine's piercing gaze.

"Eli?" she said.

"Yes?" Eli asked in a voice that wavered momentarily.

"I need your assistance for a few moments," she replied. "Can you come with me?"

"Well, I actually--"

"It is not a request, Eli," Katherine ordered.

Eli swallowed hard. He closed the book gently as if closing a door of safety. He slowly and reluctantly followed his mother out of the room.

Eli awoke in a cold sweat. The vivid dreams of his life as a boy never gave him the peace he prayed for. The anxiety and sickness sat in his belly like an anchor, and he felt like he would retch upon the floor. He managed to calm down, and the sickness he felt slowly died. Not long after, John sat up in bed, stretched, and looked at his younger brother.

"Get any sleep?" John asked.

"Some," Eli replied. "More than usual, so I am grateful for that, at least."

"Good," John said. "Today, see if you can remove the rest of the blood off the walls."

John pointed at the faded, but still present, bloody runes on the opposite wall of the cottage. Eli nodded as the sick feeling returned, the runic markings staring back at him.

Though faded, their presence was still a strong source of uneasiness.

"Do you want a bucket of water for a rinse?" John asked. "A bath may be good for both of us today."

Eli nodded as a feeling of uncleanliness materialized within him that ran much deeper than just his hygiene. He got up from bed to prepare a quick breakfast for John and himself.

The two brothers stripped off their clothing after finishing breakfast and, once outside, dumped their buckets of water on themselves that provided a small morale boost. A bath (no matter how simple or inelegant) always made them feel rejuvenated, lighter.

"Cold out?" John asked his brother, laughing.

"You should talk!" Eli chuckled. "You seem to have shrunk a bit, as if it were winter!"

John tossed the remainder of his water at Eli, who almost slipped trying to avoid it. They both laughed harder. Their troubles seemed to cascade off them, like the water off their bodies. In that moment, there was not a thought of nightmares, bloody runes, talking animals, the circumstances surrounding old Tom's death, or anything sad or frightening. For now, the brothers enjoyed each other's company. Laughter and lightheartedness made the two brothers' quiet dread dissipate. At least, for a short time.

Eli attempted to scrub away the remainder of the bloody runes within the cottage to no avail. They were fainter but never fully gone. He knew he would have to discuss that with John. He may want to board up the tainted walls or rebuild that end of the cottage entirely. John would not be happy about it.

Eli also could not ignore the bloodstain on the floor that old Tom had left behind. He felt waves of sadness hit him as he failed to scrub it clean. His friend was gone. Eli took a deep breath and tossed the bloody rag into the bucket. He walked outside and went to the horses' water trough to rinse his hands. He felt small stings on his fingertips from the amount of force he had put in to clean the dried blood.

He stared at his hands. They were indeed very feminine and unblemished in comparison to someone like his brother's hands: calloused and hardened from working the land. Perhaps if he scrubbed the wall harder, they would become tougher. He felt embarrassed by his hands; as foolish as it seemed, he longed to be more—well—manly in the eyes of his brother. He knew John would not trust him in the field, which made him feel like more of a younger brother than a trusted partner on the farm. While that hurt slightly, the system they had here worked. John was a farmer. A hunter. Eli was more a gatherer.

He dried his hands on his pants and watched his brother work from afar. He felt jealous sometimes of his brother's physique. John was impressively strong and capable, and Eli was--

"I am just Eli." He shrugged.

He walked into the barn and grabbed the milk bucket and stool. He settled beside Beth and patted her on the shoulder. She responded positively, and Eli looked at her from over her shoulder.

"May I?" he asked her.

Beth mooed and chewed her cud in response. It made Eli chuckle when she mooed almost every time he asked her permission to take her milk. He began the process and talked quietly to Beth as he milked her. He would talk sometimes about his day or how he was feeling. He even discussed his fears and dreams with her.

"Thank you for listening, Beth," Eli said once the bucket was full.

After Eli transported the milk to the root cellar that housed the farm's sellable products, he returned to the barn to gather the chickens' eggs. He snatched the basket near the door, which held soft hay that would cradle the eggs safely. Eli greeted the chickens and asked if it would be alright if he took their eggs. Eli pretended they answered with confirmation.

Normally, the chickens put up a bit of a fuss when he gathered eggs, but today, they were very docile. They did not react to Eli as he reached for them, which was strange to him. He grasped one of the eggs and was just about to place it in the basket when he noticed it.

The egg he held was a deep green color. It was revolting. The egg was rotting, and the smell made Eli retch dryly. He instinctively dropped it, and it cracked open, displaying a vile yolk that made the odor in the barn worsen. Its greyish, sickly color brought a frown to Eli's face. The chickens were perfectly healthy, and he had never seen them give rotten eggs before. He reached for the other chicken, which was as docile as the first.

The result was the same. An egg, vile and decayed, came forth. The smell made Eli drop the basket and flee from the barn. Once outside, he took deep breaths as the fresh air was a welcome reprieve for his nostrils. He gathered himself and went to John, who was still working the crop.

"John."

"Yes?" John replied, not looking up from his work.

"The chickens both laid rotten eggs," Eli said.

"Both of them?" John asked, now looking at his brother.

"Yes, both of them," Eli said.

"Did you not collect them in time?" John asked.

"I collect the eggs promptly," Eli said, almost annoyed, "you know that. I have never once seen a rotten egg."

"Maybe they are sick," John said.

"They seem perfectly fine," Eli said.

"Hmm," John replied. "Nothing to worry about then. We will see what they have in the next day or two. If it is more of the same, then we shall go back into town and replace the chickens. Sound good?"

"Alright," Eli said.

The next day was just like the previous. Eli went into the barn, and the eggs were putrid. The horrendous smell from yesterday was even worse than before. He ran to John.

"They must be sick," Eli said, "more rotten eggs."

John sighed. "Then, we will have to go into town and purchase healthy hens. Be patient. I am almost done here."

The brothers went to town and returned to the farm with healthy hens. They were more expensive than John had remembered, but that only increased their value in his mind. He had Eli hold the healthy chickens while John went into the barn and grabbed the two others. Eli brought the healthy hens inside and placed them in their respective nests.

John killed the two unhealthy birds. He discarded the heads in the woods and insisted they not put the meat to waste. He removed the feathers and began to clean them properly enough to eat. Eli did not like the idea of eating chickens that laid rotten eggs, but John insisted. That night, they went to bed with very full stomachs.

The next day, Eli went into the barn and took the basket in hand. He greeted the new, healthy hens, and they were unnaturally compliant. He reached and felt for the egg. The smell hit him like a hammer. He dropped the egg, and it burst upon the ground. Maggots and worms spewed around Eli's feet from the festering shell. They squirmed upon the ground, and that drew a disbelieving, disgusted cry from Eli's throat. He gagged at the sight and smell as the maggots feasted on the bile-like yolk.

"How?" Eli asked aloud.

The other chicken was just like the first. Another rotting, maggot-infested egg. It was not possible. They were healthy. Eli did not report his findings to John, fearful that his brother would become angry at the news of being cheated by the poultry trader. He instead decided to wait. Maybe they would produce tomorrow? Maybe it was just a horrible coincidence? However, the next day, as he went about his chores, Eli could smell the decay from the first hen's nest immediately.

"*Impossible,*" he muttered, "it cannot be!"

He reached into the other chicken's nest and fully expected to receive another rotting egg. His fingers instead felt something very different. It was not the shape or the consistency of an egg but of something else entirely. He pulled it to him, and his eyes widened in shock and disbelief. The smell was now the least of his worries as he witnessed what lay in the palm of his hand.

Resting in his cupped palm was a fetus. A small, putrefying chick covered in slime and blood. Its breast was torn open, and its heart, still connected, lay outside of the chest cavity, unmoving and unresponsive. Tiny maggots had burrowed within the fetus and were feasting upon its entrails. The shock of it all did not evoke a response from Eli, who simply stared in disbelief at this dead creature. What came next, however, would get the response.

The miniscule, underdeveloped heart of the chick *beat*. Slowly and without rhythm at first, but then, it beat faster. The chick opened its eyes suddenly and stared into Eli's. The sight horrified Eli. The fetus, the slime, the blood, the heart beating, and the maggots that were now eating this disturbing creature *alive* brought forth a cry that pierced even John's ears. Eli watched the oozing fetus fall between his shaking hands and ran from the place before it hit the ground. John rushed to Eli's side.

"Are you alright?" he asked worriedly. "What happened?"

Eli could not produce words.

"Eli!"

Eli babbled, unable to form a coherent thought. His mind raced. It was dead. Then alive. The maggots were eating it. The heart beat. How?

Dear God, how?

"They were healthy," Eli blurted out. "We saw them. We bought them. *They were healthy*. We saw their eggs at the market, John!"

"Eli, what are you talking about?" John asked.

"The eggs are rotten," Eli said. "The eggs are rotten, and the chicken... The other one... The other one..."

"What about the other chicken?"

"It was no egg, John," Eli said, disgusted. "Go look."

John went into the barn and soon returned. His fury was palpable, and it frightened Eli.

"That bastard merchant!" John yelled. "What did he sell me?"

They purchased new hens (from a different vendor this time). John had questioned the seller and demanded to see the eggs they produced. After being shown more than a dozen pristine eggs, John was satisfied with the purchase, as was Eli. As they left town, they heard people in the streets discussing the disappearance of Father Benjamin. The brothers had kept their heads down and prayed that they were not known to have been associated with him. The brothers quickly returned to the farm. When they placed the hens into their new homes, the brothers slept, both having itching suspicions that there would be rotten eggs in the morning.

Eli got up to begin his chores. He cleaned the cottage and milked Beth. John then accompanied Eli into the barn to observe the new hens. They did not receive rotting eggs.

The chickens they had newly purchased were dead.

Chapter 7
Of the Sounds Outside

John and Eli had taken the dead chickens and buried them deep into the ground. They decided against eating them, believing that they had been touched by some plague that affected the birds. John was upset at the loss of six chickens and wondered how this would affect the brothers' livelihood. The eggs fed not only them but also provided a fair amount of trade value. This worried John more than Eli, but the both of them, indeed affected by these occurrences, had decided to retire to bed sooner than normal to ponder what to do.

"What kind of illness could it be that it only affects the hens?" John asked, staring up at the ceiling, "Beth is just fine. We are just fine. We will just have to learn to live without poultry for a while. At least until I am confident that the plague has passed. Besides, we cannot afford to keep replacing them. We are not going to make much on this season's crop as it is. Those eggs always helped us. We might have to raise our asking price on the milk."

"Okay," Eli said softly.

He too stared up at the dark ceiling as his mind replayed the scene in the barn again and again. The premature baby chick, decomposing in his hands. Its heart coming to life and those lifeless eyes staring at him. An anchor sat in his stomach, and he knew sleep would be a difficult commodity to come by this night... Well, it always was.

"I may need your help hunting, too," John said, pushing aside the thoughts of the wolf in the woods. "We might be able to fetch a good price on pelts and meat. Especially the right pelts."

"Okay," Eli said in the same soft and melancholy tone.

"Are you alright, Eli?" John asked. "I know that what you saw was... unpleasant."

"I will be fine," Eli said almost automatically.

John was silent a moment and then wished his brother a goodnight. Eli responded the same and turned to face the wall. The brothers closed their eyes tightly and wished for sleep. The wish was not granted for either. Anxiety took root inside the mind of John, who wondered what they should do to overcome the damage done to the business end of the farm. Eli, on the other hand, envisioned the broken baby chick speaking to him. His imagination began to run away with those thoughts, then both brothers' thoughts were interrupted.

A sound from outside made each of their respective anxieties flow through their body like the blood in their veins. The door to the barn had creaked loudly open and slammed closed. John jolted up in bed and looked toward Eli, who was sitting up, terror filling his eyes.

"Was that the barn?" John asked his brother, hoping Eli would give him any excuse not to go and look.

Eli nodded slowly. His eyes were wide and brimming with fearful tears. Someone was in the barn. John felt his heart hammering in his chest. He supposed it could be Father Benjamin, but the notion was not convincing enough. Instead, he thought of the woman in rags and those bloody symbols in her flesh. He imagined her waiting in the barn to ambush them... Or worse.

"Beth," John said, "what if Beth is in trouble?"

Eli's eyes were unblinking, and he did not move or respond. He watched John grab the musket and prepare it. He watched him load it quickly, then John looked at him.

"Eli," he said, "I need you to be brave. Can you keep watch at the window and make sure nothing happens to me? I have to go check."

Eli felt himself slowly shake his head.

"Eli, please," John said, "if anything happens to that cow..."

Eli thought on it a moment. There was no chance of replacing Beth when they now had no eggs to sell and an unprofitable crop. He looked at John and nodded.

"Just keep watch from the window, alright?" John asked. "If anything happens, I will shout, but if you see anything, anything at all, I need you to warn me. Understand?"

Eli nodded again, slowly getting out of his bed.

"I need to hear you say you understand," John said.

"I understand," Eli replied, his voice cracking.

"Okay," John said.

The two brothers looked out of the window cautiously and surveyed the area. The moon allowed some light. They looked at the barn but saw and heard nothing. The farm was as still as ever. John was tempted to talk himself out of going to the barn, but he knew it had to be done. There was no wind blowing tonight, so that excuse would not do.

"Call out if you see *anything*, Brother," John said.

Eli nodded and watched as his brother went to the front door of their cottage. He placed his hand upon the handle. He held the musket firmly, enough to turn his knuckles white as snow, as he took a deep breath and then opened the door slowly. He quietly looked to his left and right, and when he saw nothing, he crept toward the barn. He looked behind him and saw Eli standing at the window, still keeping an eye on him. A fearful eye, but an eye nonetheless. He turned forward again and half expected to see some nightmarish horror spring in front of him, but it did not come to fruition. A blind, talking wolf also did not appear.

A wavering breath passed from John's lips as he pressed himself to the barn wall right next to the door. He tried to peer inside between the slats of wood but saw nothing. He yearned for his bed, to feel safe and cozy underneath the blankets. He wanted to cocoon himself within them and wish the night away. But these were the thoughts of a boy, and he knew he had a responsibility to himself, his brother, and their livelihoods. He looked back at the cottage. Eli was still there. John gave a small wave. Eli nodded.

John placed a hand on the barn door and took a deep breath. His heart beat so fast, it was deafening. He took several more calming breaths, and when his heart had settled to a more comfortable pace (though it still beat like a galloping horse), he opened the door slowly.

Creak.

John held the door open steadily and peered inside. He thought his legs would turn to jelly and he would collapse. The creak may as well have been thunder. He heard a shuffling within then, and John, in his panicked state, let the door go. It closed with a sudden slam, and although the door separated him from the inside, he knew he heard the shuffling noise again. He cursed his cowardice, but the presence of the ragged and thin and bloody woman came and burrowed inside of his mind. She was in there. He knew it.

The shuffling sound stopped. He stared at the door for what felt like an eternity. He found his grip on the musket had become slippery from the sweat of his palms, and he wiped his hands on his trousers. He cocked the gun and decided upon a forward approach. He would give a warning. If that woman was inside, she would have the chance to leave; if it was Father Benjamin, he could announce himself, and everything would be fine.

But John knew Father Benjamin was not inside. He knew this for a fact, and the sweat returned to his hands. The warning caught in his throat, and he almost choked. He took a deep breath, feeling as if he would suffocate under the paranoia. He exhaled and found his voice. He forced the words out in a strong and even tone he did not know he could be capable of in this moment.

"Whoever is in there," he called, "announce yourself immediately. Make yourself known this instant, or you will be shot."

The shuffling sound came again, and John pressed the musket to his shoulder and aimed at the door. His heart became like a pounding drum as it flooded his ears. He knew he had to open the door. He had to make the shot count or else he could find himself in a very terrible situation. His hand reached out to the door, and he gripped it tightly. The sound inside died the instant he touched the door.

John told himself he would fling it open on the count of three. But when he reached three, he found himself counting to ten. He restarted. The bloody woman awaited. He counted to three several more times. He cursed himself. He cursed the situation. He counted once more, and on two, his hand tricked him, and the door flung open.

BANG!

The musket fired into the darkness. The recoil caught John off guard and kicked into his shoulder. He was sent sprawling backwards. The massive amount of smoke from the shot blinded him further than the darkness alone. Beth's frantic mooing erupted, and John envisioned the crazed woman killing the cow.

"John!" Eli's desperate shout came from behind him.

There was no time. John found his courage and rushed into the barn, ready to use the musket as a club. He roared and swung the weapon. It hit something solid. The wall. John looked around wildly. Beth mooed, terrified, but John saw nothing. Just the cow. No one was here. He felt foolish as Eli came stumbling into the open doorway, lantern in hand.

"John!"

"It is alright, Eli," John replied, "it is nothing."

"You fired the musket," Eli said, "I thought the worst."

"It was my own nerves besting me," John muttered angrily. "There is nothing here. The cow is fine. Just shaken from my own stupidity."

"I can calm her," Eli said and moved to stand beside the frightened animal.

He set the lantern down and whispered to her. She slowly calmed. He stroked her gently, and she lay down in her bed of hay, which made a shuffling sound under her weight. John felt more foolish as he realized the source of the noise.

"Dumb beast," he whispered to himself just quietly enough so Eli, who he knew was fond of the bovine, did not hear.

John looked at the wall that he had shot at. He could barely make out the hole in it, so he reached for the lantern.

"She is alright, she is beginning to relax," Eli said.

"That is good," John said. "That is..."

He raised the lantern at the wall and found the hole the shot had created. He also saw something else. A single bloody rune hastily drawn onto the wood. His eyes widened.

"Impossible," John said. "It cannot be possible."

"Oh, God," Eli said, noticing what John was staring at.

John put the lantern down quickly, grabbed the musket, and raced outside. She was here. That woman with the rags and the bloody runes. She had been here! But how did she get out if John had not seen her? There was only one way in and one way out. They would have seen her leave.

"COME OUT HERE!" John shouted into the night air.

No reply came. Only the stillness of the farm responded. Eli came to John.

"Whoever made those runes in the cottage was in there, right?" Eli asked, terrified. "The one who hurt old Tom."

"It had to have been that woman," John said, "the one in those rags at the edge of the woods some days ago."

"She came back? It was *her*?" Eli asked.

"It must have been," John said, staring into the distance.

"What do we do?" Eli asked, a quiet dread building in his heart.

"Is Beth okay?" John asked.

"She seems fine."

"Get inside," John said. They went into the cottage.

He reloaded the musket, all the while keeping an eye on the window in search of anything or anyone. Eli watched his brother from beside the door.

"What do you want to do?" Eli asked quietly.

"Here is what we will have to do," John said. "If she was the one who killed old Tom, then she just warned us that that cow may be next. You remember what happened to Tom? She is sick. Demented. I will keep watch for a while. If she comes back..."

He used the ramrod to jam the pellet into the musket. He grabbed the chair beside the supper table and placed it in front of the window. He sat and watched outside.

"Is there anything I should do?" Eli asked.

"Get some rest," John said firmly. "I will keep watch as long as I can, and then, I will come get you to trade places. I need you to be brave again, Eli. Get some rest. You will need it. It may be a long night."

Eli nodded and settled into bed. His mind was racing as he peered at his brother from behind the covers. John had a death grip on the gun. Eli forced his eyes shut and did his best to obey his older brother. John settled into the chair and stared out at the farm. *His* farm. *His* life. He would protect it, no matter what the cost.

Chapter 8
Of John's First Watch

John had sat at that window for a long while. It had been perhaps two, maybe three, hours, and nothing happened. Not a sound, save for the soft and steady breathing of his brother ,who was asleep in the bed, and not a thing in sight. The adrenaline had worn off after the first hour, and after the second hour had come to pass, he found himself beginning to become weary. He shook off the feeling of exhaustion time and time again, but with each successful repel of sleep, it came back twice as hard. Soon, his eyelids became heavy, and they slowly, very slowly, began to close.

A horrid scratching sound reverberated against the stone of the well. John's eyes snapped open, and he aimed the musket. The moonlight revealed a young and curious squirrel that sniffed the air then darted from the well back to the woods. He calmed himself. A squirrel, only a squirrel. He rested the musket against the wall and leaned back in the chair. He stared out the window for a while longer and began to think about getting Eli to shift with him. But when he saw his younger brother finally sleeping soundly for the first time in a long while, he returned to the chair and resumed his watch.

He blinked the exhaustion away. His eyes felt dry, his vision blurring. They began to close involuntarily. Perhaps just a couple minutes' rest? He opened them again and slapped himself gently on the cheek.

"Come on, John," he told himself.

But soon, the weariness attacked him in full force, and the chair, though normally uncomfortable and stiff, felt like the most plush bed on God's earth. His eyes closed, and he leaned back. He promised himself just a few moments. Just a few, and then, he would have enough energy to continue the watch.

John knew he was in trouble. He knew that the punishment to come would be severe. The vase on the floor was shattered into a million pieces. He had been running too quickly to slow down in time, and now, he would pay for his incompetence. Tears stung at his young eyes. He could already feel what was to come. He thought of a million different ways of how to cover up the broken pieces, but they were all flung out the window when he heard a gasp from behind him. Katherine stood in shock at the scene.

"Mother," John said.

"John," she said sternly but with a trace of fear, "your father is going to be... furious."

John felt sick to his stomach, and tears began to flow.

"Please do not tell him, Mother," he cried, "please."

"And how do you propose we hide this from him?" she asked. "He will notice if the vase is missing. He will ask me, and then what? I lie to him?"

"I do not want him to be angry with me," John cried.

"I do not wish his anger upon myself either, Johnathan," Katherine said. "When he is not angry with you, his anger turns to me. And his wrath for your stupidity will not be on my head."

"Mother," John pleaded.

"No," she said, "you will be a man and take responsibility for your ineptitude."

Not a moment later, the front door to the house burst open and slammed shut. James was home. John could feel his legs shake, and he wondered if he would wet himself. The fear gripped him as James entered the study and saw what was before him.

"What. Happened. Here?" James said, emphasizing each word with measured malice.

"Your son decided to run around the house," Katherine said evenly. "This was the result."

"Is this true, Johnathan?" James asked, his temper rising.

John did not respond. Not immediately, which only fueled his father's anger.

"ANSWER!"

"It is true," John said, tears welling up again.

James snorted like a raging bull. His nostrils flared as he began to pace furiously. Katherine and John both stared at the floor like two guilty dogs that had relieved themselves upon the floor.

"You stupid boy," James whispered.

John embraced the flurry of insults that came, each one hitting heavier than the last. James's voice grew steadily until he was bellowing. Katherine winced at his every syllable, and John did his best to keep his tears from showing.

"What are you doing," James said then. "What are you... Are you crying?"

John whimpered, "No."

"You are!" James roared. "You are crying in my house. Did I raise a little girl?"

"No, sir," John whimpered, the tears spilling over like a broken dam.

"You look me in the eye when you address me," James yelled.

John obeyed.

"Stand up straight!"

John obeyed.

"You are a curse upon me, boy!" James screamed at his young son. "I knew it the moment I saw you."

John felt the hot, bitter tears falling to the floor. Shame built upon his chest.

"Stop crying," James said sternly.

"I am trying," John said.

"I am trying," James mocked.

Katherine remained silent.

"Get out of my sight," James said, "you are no son of mine. I thought we were raising a young man, Katherine. Not some common, sniveling, little shit. Go! GO NOW!"

John ran from the room, wiping his face as he did. He darted up the stairs as quick as his legs would carry him. He closed the door to his room behind him and felt a flood of emotions overwhelm his fragile mind. Rage and sadness and confusion ripped through him. He punched his bed repeatedly and swore that when he was older and stronger, he would stand up to his father. He would prove himself a man. He continued to pummel the bed until his small limbs grew tired and could no longer deliver a satisfying blow.

He slumped to the floor and wiped his eyes of their tears. He was just a child of eight, and he knew he was no match for his father. But one day, his father would fear him. He vowed it.

Then, he heard it. The heavy thuds of footsteps upon the stairs.

"Naughty children cannot go unpunished," James said in a low voice from the stairs.

John's eyes widened as he understood: the next phase. It never ended at insults. In his emotional state, he had forgotten that simple rule. The rage and the insults were just the first act of a play that John had not volunteered to be a part of. His father's steps became louder, more determined. He got up from the floor, raced to his dresser, and tried to pull it over to block the door. But it was too heavy, and his little arms were too weak. He felt himself begin to cry again.

"No," he told himself. "No. No more crying. No more. If he wants to hurt me, then he will get no response from me. Not now. Not ever again."

John wiped his eyes and stood in front of the door, attempting to hold it closed using his own body weight. James stood outside and tried to come inside. Not expecting the resistance, James was initially confused by the door not budging then laughed cruelly.

"Stupid boy," he said before throwing a shoulder into the door.

The door cracked at the blow, and the wood made a splintered sound. The sudden force threw John from the door, and he was sprawled on the floor as his father entered. John looked his father right in the eyes and saw the rage in them. John felt afraid, but as he had promised himself, he did not show it. He prepared himself for the second act of his father's production. A second act that John, only a child at the time, would become more accustomed to until he knew he had become strong enough some seven years later.

After his brother's birth.

John's eyes snapped open from the dream. Dried tears had melded to his cheeks. He realized after a few moments that he was at the farm. That he was a man. He calmed himself and looked to his brother, who still slept. He breathed a sigh of relief and rubbed at his eyes. He did not know what time it was, but it was still dark out. He surveyed the farm and saw that everything was still unchanged. He picked up the musket from the floor and leaned it against the wall again. He expelled a deep breath once more.

He blinked away the sleep and squinted. Something was out past the well. Near the woods. A man. He was stumbling slowly, as if he were drunk, from the tree line. John got up from the chair and went outside.

"Hello?" he called out.

He approached as the man gave no answer. As John edged closer, he saw he was not wearing a shirt, and his body was beaten and bloody.

"Sir!" John called again as he took another step closer.

As they neared one another, John recognized the features of Father Benjamin, but something was wrong with him. His eyes were empty and sunken. His face was expressionless and unresponsive.

"Priest!" John said, relief in his voice. "We searched for you! We could not find you!"

No reply. Instead, the priest took one shaky step after another and continued to look past John as if he did not exist.

"Father Benjamin?"

Step.

Step.

Step.

The priest trudged slowly past John, and John looked at him from behind. His eyes widened. His stomach became sour. And the fear returned with a cold malice. A rune, not unlike the one in the barn and the ones in the cottage, had been freshly carved into the flesh of the priest's back.

"Dear God," John uttered.

The priest took one final, wavering step and then collapsed into the dirt.

Chapter 9
Of the Priest's Return

John had rushed to the cottage and shaken Eli awake. As Eli slowly came round, he heard John yelling something incoherent in her ear, over and over, his tone desperate. Eli, in his confused state, looked at his brother through squinted eyes.

"Slow down, John," Eli said, "what?"

"The priest," John repeated loudly, "Father Benjamin. He is here. Help me!"

Eli jumped out of bed and followed his older brother outside to the crumpled heap of Father Benjamin. Eli noticed the blood flowing from the marking in his flesh. Fear seized his chest and stopped him from kneeling to help the broken priest.

"John..." Eli whispered.

"I know!" John said. "But we cannot leave him. He is hurt! Help me!"

Eli hesitated.

"HELP ME!" John roared impatiently. The sudden outburst took him aback: that was the tone of his father.

Eli scurried to assist then. He took the priest's left arm and threw it over his shoulder. Together, they hoisted Father Benjamin off the ground. They dragged him to the cottage, and John kicked open the door. The brothers carried the priest over to the table and lay him upon it on his belly.

"What happened to him?" Eli asked quietly.

"I do not know," John said, fetching a bucket and rags.

"That wound..."

"I know," John said, becoming more agitated as he collected supplies.

"It is just like in the barn and on the wall over there," Eli said.

"I know!" John said, almost yelling. He opened the door and left the cottage.

Eli watched his brother from the window and saw him fetch water from the well. John quickly returned and dipped a rag into the water, beginning to clean the priest's wounds.

"Is he going to be alright?" Eli asked.

"I do not know."

"What attacked him?" Eli asked.

"I do not know!"

"Where is his tunic?" Eli asked.

John abruptly stopped cleaning and threw the wet, bloody rag onto the floor. He grabbed his brother by the shoulders and pinned him to the wall.

"I do not have any answers to your questions, Eli," John barked. "I, too, want to know what happened, but he is hurt and needs our help now, not our questions. So either help me clean him and tend to his wounds, or stop talking."

Eli nodded, biting his lip, eyes watering. His brother *never* became cross with him like that. He grabbed a rag, soaked it into the water, and cleaned the priest. Various cuts and scrapes littered Father Benjamin's arms and legs. His bare feet were bloody, and Eli had to dig out some thorns that had buried themselves deep into the soles.

Eli thought it must have been a figment of his imagination, but when he tried to pull one of the thorns out, it seemed to dig further in, away from his fingers. Eli looked into the open cuts where the thorns made their home. They seemed to... move on their own. Eli reached again for one of the thorns. Then, *somehow,* it suddenly burrowed in Eli's thumb, buried deep in the flesh. Eli resisted crying out, not wanting to anger his brother by making noise, then removed it from his own finger before tossing it out the window. Several thorns found their way into his hands, and each time, he swallowed the urge to make sound. He wiped some blood from his own fingers then wiped the feet of the priest before tending to larger wounds on his legs.

John gently dabbed at the runic gash in Father Benjamin's back. The blood kept flowing with each dab. John then applied more pressure, leaning over the priest's limp body in an attempt to staunch the blood faster.

"What have you gotten yourself into, Priest?" John asked aloud.

Father Benjamin uttered a soft groan and stirred before becoming still again. John tossed his blood-soaked rag into the bucket and watched the blood begin to clot. John took up the bucket and went outside with Eli in tow. They rang out the rags into the bucket then tossed the bloody water out into the dirt, away from the barn, cottage, and crops. The brothers drew another bucket of water from the well before returning to tend to the priest.

When they came back inside, John saw that the wound had already, by some means, scabbed over. He paid this no mind as the priest stirred again. A louder groan escaped his lips.

"Father Benjamin?" John asked.

The priest moaned.

"Father, can you hear me?" John asked.

"I can," Father Benjamin murmured. "Where... Where am I?"

"You are back at the farm," John said. "You do not remember? You collapsed by the well."

"I... I do not remember how I got here," Father Benjamin said.

The priest struggled to get up from the table. John and Eli helped steady him, and they assisted him into one of their chairs. Eli brought the priest a blanket, and they watched him wrap himself in it with a shiver.

"Father Benjamin," John said, "you have been gone, in that forest, for a few days. Everyone in town is worried. I... I thought you were dead."

The priest sighed deeply and pulled the blanket tighter around himself.

"Do you remember what happened to you?" Eli asked. "You are really hurt."

"Give me a moment to think," the priest said softly, "I am tired."

They watched him calm himself. He groaned again as he leaned against the chair. He closed his eyes and frowned in thought. The brothers stood patiently, waiting for the priest to speak. After a quiet moment, the priest opened his eyes and stared at John and Eli.

"I do not know how to begin," Father Benjamin said, "and you will no doubt find what I have to say... unbelievable."

"Please," John said, "tell us what happened."

"Can I bother you for a drink of water first?" Benjamin asked.

Eli got him the drink, and the priest drank deeply until the cup was empty. He sighed and looked at his lap.

"Where to begin?" he muttered. "Where to begin?"

"What do you remember?" John asked.

"I remember... I remember my son," Father Benjamin said quietly, his eyes misting. "I remember seeing my Samuel."

Benjamin had torn into the woods without a moment of hesitation after seeing the boy. It could not be real. It was impossible. He knew this, and yet, he had chased after him. The boy was quick though, always a step ahead. Soon, Benjamin, who was in his elder years, had fallen behind and lost sight of the boy. Benjamin leaned over, hands on his knees, and gasped for air. His heart was pounding out of his chest, and he feared in that moment he might die alone in this forest. However, he eventually felt his heart slow its pace, and he was able to slow his breaths. Benjamin sighed.

"Samuel," he breathed, "how is it this is possible?"

He walked forward, and dead leaves beneath his feet crunched loudly. The air around him put him on the defense. The moon was bright this night and guided his steps, but with each step, he felt terror holding him back. He finally mustered enough courage in that moment to yell.

"Samuel!"

No answer. The silence was so heavy, he felt it suffocating him. He kept on, praying quietly to himself as he went. Several times, he begged for the Lord's protection, but as he kept pressing on, he felt the wood whispering to him. God had abandoned this place. Benjamin's ear twitched. He kept praying, feeling that if he stopped, something evil would break through the little protection provided to a holy man. His fear only grew. Soon, that fear became a lump in his throat, and his mind could only focus on its presence. The prayer was interrupted, and the words finally broke through into his mind, as if it had been waiting at the gates, waiting for the priest to conclude his connection to God.

The voice was quiet and cold. The effect upon his senses was immediate, and with each syllable, it was like a steel razor cutting into his brain. It stopped him in his tracks.

"A priest. Now that is interesting."

Benjamin whirled around, trying to find the voice's source.

"Then why is he all alone? I see nothing protecting him."

"The Lord is my protection!" Benjamin said, summoning his courage to combat the evil.

"We know what the protection of the Almighty looks like, and yet, I see... none."

The disembodied voice was laughing at him.

"You are a liar," Benjamin said. "You are a deceiver."

"Accusations. I have no reason to lie, Priest. I simply do not see the protection that should be hedged around a leader of the Church. You are alone."

"I command you, in the name of Christ, to leave me," Benjamin ordered.

"And here I believed we may have been friends."

"You are no friend," Benjamin said. "You are a demon sent from Hell to torment me. I command you, in Christ's name, to depart!"

"I do not take orders from those who do not have the Spirit within them. You, quite simply put, are a fraud."

"You lie!" Benjamin yelled.

"Again, I have no reason to lie, Benjamin. You may wear the frock of a priest and appear before your congregations clean. But inside, you are rotten. Rotten as a corpse."

"No..."

"Yes. But I do not wish to be a rude host. Please, Benjamin. Do not allow my words to hold you back. Come forward. Allow me to bestow a gift upon you."

"I do not want anything from a demon like you," Benjamin spat.

"Come now. There is no need for such vulgarity. I daresay you will very much like what I have to give to you. I promise."

Benjamin remained silent. The fear and air of unease seemed to lessen. He felt curiosity rise within him, and he silently debated his next decision. And soon, without any urging from the unknown speaker, Benjamin found himself walking forward, taking one step after another.

"I am so glad you can be reasonable. Continue forward, Benjamin. There is someone I think you will want to see."

Benjamin continued on until he came to a clearing in the forest. The moonlight seemed to become more intense and focused here; his eyes needed a moment to adjust. Standing in the clearing was the boy, Samuel, waiting for him. Benjamin did not hesitate to rush to him and embrace him. When the priest did so, he became aware of the fact that his son was soaked. His clothing was drenched, his hair dripping wet, but Benjamin did not care.

"My son," Benjamin wept. "My son. How? How is this possible?"

No answer. Benjamin wept and hardly noticed his silence.

"I love you," he continued. "My boy. I love you. I have missed you."

He placed his hands upon the boy's shoulders and extended his arms to see his son better. Benjamin's eyes were brimming with tears. Samuel, his son, his little boy, stared blankly back at his father. His body was bloated. His flesh was rotting and looked like fish has nibbled away at it. Water cascaded from Samuel's eyes and nostrils, and when Benjamin looked down, he saw the massive puddle it created.

"My son..."

Samuel blinked and narrowed his eyes then. He stared at Benjamin, and a brief recognition fell over their cloudy haze.

"Hello, Father," Samuel said, stinking and putrid water falling from his mouth.

"Oh, God," Benjamin whispered, "what happened to you?"

"But you already know the answer to that, do you not, Priest?"

The voice from before possessed his boy's lips. The diseased water spilling from his moving, rotted mouth. Benjamin let him go and began to take terrified steps backward.

"God, no..." he muttered. "God. No."

"But it is your boy. Your little Samuel. Are you not pleased?"

The voice was now behind him, and Benjamin did not want to see what had uttered the words this time. Still, a sick curiosity overcame him, and he slowly turned. When he finally made a half circle, he saw what had spoken, and he wished he had not. He desired nothing else than to flee this place. He no longer wondered what Hell was like after death for the unrighteous. For Hell was here.

"Are you not happy to see us, Benjamin?" his wife asked.

It was her. There was no doubt in the priest's mind, for she appeared to him exactly as he had remembered seeing her last. Her skin was pale, and those eyes were empty and soulless. Her gown was soaked a dark red with her blood. It ran down her arms from the long, deep vertical cuts in her arms. This state of being is the last he remembered of her, but he had not recognized her voice. It was warped, perverted, accursed. She extended her arms to Benjamin and gave a sad, disturbing smile as she took a step toward him.

Benjamin stifled a scream and stepped back. The smile turned into a scowl. Her arms fell to her sides. The blood dripped steadily from her fingertips, staining the ground. A bloody tear rolled down her cheek.

"Are you not pleased to see me, Benjamin? Are you not happy to see your wife?"

Benjamin felt his mind snap, and his legs collapsed underneath him. He let the scream loose from his throat. He heard the crunching of leaves under the feet of his wife and son as they approached.

"GOD! GOD!"

He fell unconscious and awoke periodically to the sound of tearing. His eyes would search frantically for the source of the noise, but then, he would pass out again. When he awoke the last time, it was facedown on the table of the brothers, John and Eli.

"That is all I remember," Father Benjamin said.

John and Eli stared at him. John's eyes were narrowed, and Eli's were wide in shock like a child hearing his first horror story by a fire.

"My God," Eli whispered.

"It sounds," John said skeptically, "as if you lost your mind in that forest."

"I have no doubt I did," Father Benjamin said sadly. "No doubt, indeed."

John wondered about his skepticism when he was still trying to fathom the wolf speaking to him.

"How do you feel now?" John asked.

"My head is splitting, my body hurts, and I feel nauseous," Father Benjamin replied honestly, "but I am alive. I feel blessed to still live."

"And you do not remember what happened with your clothing or what carved the wounds in your back?" John asked.

"I would have told you if I did."

"Why do you think your wife and son appeared to you in the states like you described?" John asked.

"Some things are better left unsaid," Father Benjamin said, glaring at John now.

"Is there anything more we can do for you?" Eli asked.

"More water," the priest said, "please."

"Of course," Eli said. "John, come with me. We will be right back, Father Benjamin."

The brothers walked out to the well, and Eli drew from it.

"What do you think?" Eli asked.

"About his story?" John said. "Insanity. Pure insanity."

"He seemed sincere," Eli said.

"I am not saying he does not believe that he saw or heard those things, but…"

"But?" Eli asked, setting the bucket on the wall of the well.

"Surely, there is an explanation," John said.

"And how do you explain the bloody drawing in the barn?" Eli asked.

"I am not sure," John said, "but there is a logical reason for everything."

They returned to the cottage and filled the priest's cup. He drank deeply and refilled it again before emptying it once more. On the third fill, he sipped slowly and sighed.

"I do not feel well," Father Benjamin said.

"You need to rest," Eli said.

"Yes, I think I must," Father Benjamin said.

"You can take my bed over there," Eli said.

"Are you sure?"

"Of course," Eli said. "Go. Rest."

"We need to get our daily chores done anyway, Father," John said. "Rest. We will come to check on you when we have finished. Then, we can ride with you back home. We have kept your horse here. She has been fed and watered. She is a good beast. Well-behaved."

"I thank you for looking after her," the priest said, closing his eyes as he lay his head down. "I would like an escort into town. That would be greatly appreciated."

"Certainly," Eli said. "We will come back later. Rest now."

The priest obeyed and fell asleep.

John and Eli went about their daily chores and occasionally checked on Father Benjamin, who slept soundly. Eli assisted John with some of the crop care and had earned a splinter for his help. John had to remove it since Eli seemed nervous by the idea. They began to walk across the farm back to the cottage.

"Shall we check on the priest then?" John asked.

Eli nodded, still fixated on the spot the splinter had been pulled from. They heard the horses behind the cottage squealing loudly. This only lasted a few moments before the whinnying ceased. They decided to check on them after Father Benjamin. They opened the door and entered. The priest was not in the bed anymore. He was no longer in the cottage.

"Father Benjamin?" John called out.

"Oh!" Eli exclaimed.

Father Benjamin stood just outside the doorway behind them. His body was bare. Blood drenched his pale skin, and the kitchen knife was gripped in his hand so tightly that the priest's nails dug into his palm, drawing even more blood. He stared at the brothers. John noticed that his eyes had become a pale, milky white color, as if he were blinded. John's own eyes widened.

"Hell cometh."

"Father Benjamin?" Eli asked.

The priest's head craned slowly and tightly as if he were in a struggle. He coughed painfully, and flecks of blood hit the door. He made a choking noise, then his head snapped around and faced John directly.

"Hell cometh."

John felt his muscles tense as he prepared to defend himself and Eli. Whatever had taken hold of the wolf in the forest had now taken over the priest. Father Benjamin then turned to stare at Eli. His head cocked to the side, agonizingly slowly, like a curious dog. Then, Father Benjamin, or whatever had taken control of Father Benjamin, smiled a disturbing grin to spread across his face as he observed the youngest brother.

The priest's head then shook, and he made more choking noises. John grabbed Eli and pushed his younger brother behind him. He watched the priest cough and sputter. His eyes flew wildly in all directions as they slowly regained color. A small crack came from the priest's back as he straightened out tensely. Words came from the priest in a guttural roar as he fought the hold of what controlled him.

"You. Will. Not. Have. Me!"

"Priest?" John asked.

"RELEASE ME!" the priest howled.

Whatever had him under its power at last freed him. His legs shook violently as he regained feeling in his limbs. He looked at the brothers with tears in his eyes.

"Oh, boys," he said, voice wavering with shock and horror, "I fear I have done something horrible."

A loud, sickening crack echoed through the farm grounds as the priest's spine bent backwards in half at the base of the vertebral column. The knife was dropped immediately. He collapsed to the ground and screamed. John rushed to the priest's side. Father Benjamin continued to wail, and tears flooded his face like violent rivers. John held the priest's hand in his own.

"What is happening?" John asked, terrified.

"I angered it!" Father Benjamin cried.

Another gut-wrenching crack came from the priest's brittle body. John saw his ribcage begin to spread open, as if something were pulling it apart. The priest's mouth filled with blood, and his cries for God's help went unanswered. A couple ribs pierced through the priest's torso and blood saturated the dry ground.

"Oh my God," John whispered.

Then, it stopped, and John looked into the priest's pleading, weeping eyes. John assessed the damage. Nothing could be done. He knew it. Eli knew it. Father Benjamin knew it.

"John," the priest gasped, blood spilling over his chin and cheeks.

"I am here," John said, letting his own terrified tears be released.

"Please... help me," he choked out.

"How?" John asked quietly.

"I... must confess," Father Benjamin said, "I must... tell you."

"Tell me what?"

"I am... I am not a good man," he said weakly. "I... saw my family in those woods. My son... my wife. It... it took me... it commanded me. The horses..."

"Try not to speak," John said, holding the dying man's hand tightly.

"It is over," Benjamin said. "I will leave this place soon... I must... I must confess to you."

John looked at the priest. His mangled body tortured him. John looked back at Eli, who cried quietly in paralyzing fear. His eyes pleaded with John to help in any way possible. John looked back at Father Benjamin and nodded. The priest's eyes softened and seemed to become almost peaceful as he confessed.

Chapter 10
Of the Priest's Confession

Benjamin looked out the window that Sunday morning and sighed. It was a beautiful sight to behold, and he thanked God for the glorious display to begin the day. He got out of bed and splashed cool water on his face. He smiled at himself in the mirror then donned his priest's frock. He opened the door to the family room where his wife, Mary, was getting breakfast ready for their son, Samuel. Benjamin took his place at the table and ate with his boy.

"Are you ready for today?" Mary asked.

"I am," Benjamin said, smiling. "I feel that God will move many hearts today. I feel He will speak through me. My words shall be His."

Mary kissed Benjamin lightly on his brow then kissed Samuel's head, though he tried to squirm away from her. She ate her breakfast with them and then cleared the table.

"You should hurry," Mary said to Benjamin sweetly. "You should prepare before everyone gets there."

"You are right, my dear," he replied. "I will go speak with the Lord and pray for His Spirit to shine on everyone this day."

Benjamin almost ran to the church, his spirits were so high. He smiled, waved, and greeted everyone he came across. Most everyone was friendly in return. He opened the doors to the church and entered. He knelt before the large cross at the head of the room and clasped his hands.

"Lord," he prayed, "please bless this town with Your words today. Make me a vessel for Your message and allow Your light to shine through me. Make me Your tool. And help my heart to be wreathed in humility so that I may give all the praise to You. Allow me none for myself."

He continued to pray a while longer then said "amen" before preparing his notes for the sermon. He opened the Bible at his pulpit and rehearsed what he would say several times. He practiced thumping the pulpit to emphasize his points for when the townspeople would be here. He would have felt foolish if anyone had caught him rehearsing as he did. But Benjamin was happiest here. He felt called to this town. He felt God had an important task for him: to lead the people here to His light.

The church bells rang, summoning everyone for the sermon. Mary and Samuel took their seats at the very front and smiled at Benjamin, who smiled back. Soon, all the people had gathered and were seated in the pews. He greeted them with a bright expression and prayed over them. They sang the hymnals from the books for some time until Benjamin asked them to be seated. He gave his sermon, and it was perfect, even the pounding of his fist on the pulpit. Women wept openly, and men's eyes misted at his words. Their reactions caused his chest to swell with pride.

"I am the Shepherd," he thought to himself.

When he prayed over them once more then dismissed them, he stood by the front door to shake everyone's hands and wish them well. Everyone praised his sermon. He thanked them and told most (not all) that praise should go to the Lord. Pride had made its home in his heart. Mary kissed his cheek.

"I know you have one more service to conduct," she said. "I will take Samuel for a picnic, and we shall see you at home."

Benjamin smiled. "I cannot wait. Son, we can finally go out and play as I promised, alright?"

Samuel grinned and nodded. He knew his father had had a long week preparing for this service. He knew his father would honor his promise to play when the sermons had been delivered. He hugged his father and held his mother's hand as they walked home. Benjamin watched them go and grinned again. He had a lovely family, a wonderful home, and the respect and admiration of the town. He had it all.

And it would all be taken from him.

When Benjamin and delivered the final sermon, he thanked everyone and shook hands with those departing. This time, he kept the praise of his sermon for himself. He prayed with those who stayed, who needed a personal prayer. The pride deepened as he left the church for home.

When he arrived home in the late afternoon, he found it empty. Neither Mary nor Samuel was present, and Benjamin assumed they were still on their picnic, enjoying the day outside. He began to prepare a meal, deciding to surprise his wife by making supper himself rather than leaving it to her, when he heard a commotion outside. Someone was screaming.

"Benjamin!" he heard. "Benjamin! Oh, God!"

Mary was running to the house franticly. Tears spilled down her cheeks as she wailed and screamed. Her dress was sopping wet, and her hair was soaked. Benjamin dropped the cutlery to the floor with a loud ringing sound as he bolted out the door to meet his wife.

"Mary," he said, holding her by the shoulders trying to calm her. "Mary, what is going on?"

"It is Samuel," she wailed. "Help... Oh, God!"

"Samuel!" Benjamin said. "Where is he? Where is the boy?"

"The lake," she howled, "Benjamin, the lake... Oh my God! Oh my God!"

The lake. The usual spot where the family picnicked. The place where Benjamin had begun teaching Samuel how to swim. He bolted. Mary followed from a distance, running much slower than her husband and still in a frenzy. It did not take long for Benjamin to reach the body of water. An abandoned picnic greeted him. Samuel was not there. Mary came up behind her husband.

"Where is he?" Benjamin asked as calmly as he could muster.

Mary was speaking unintelligibly through her wild cries. Benjamin gripped her shoulders harder than he would have liked. It hurt her, and he knew it.

"Mary!" he barked. "Where is Samuel? Where is he?"

She screamed and pointed at the water. Benjamin understood.

"SAMUEL!" he screamed before diving in, fully clothed.

The water was cold, but he ignored his initial response of shock. He swam to the depths. His son was in here. He kept his eyes open and barely could make out something large, enveloped in shadow, at the lakebed. He ignored his burning lungs and used his determination and love for his son to drive him deeper. It was Samuel. He wrapped an arm around his torso and kicked off the bottom with his boy in tow. He soon broke the surface, and his screaming lungs filled with fresh oxygen. Mary was still wailing at the shore.

Benjamin brought Samuel's still body to the shore and laid him on his back. He leaned close to the boy. No heartbeat. No breathing. Nothing.

"Samuel," Benjamin whispered.

He pumped Samuel's chest with his hands. After a few minutes of this with no change, he began to panic. His strong, flat-handed compressions intensified.

"SAMUEL!" Benjamin yelled.

Mary was now seated on the ground, crying loudly. Benjamin's hands turned into fists, and his hammer-like blows pummeled his son's chest with great force. He screamed Samuel's name over and over, hoping it would bring him back to life. Benjamin inwardly screamed at God for a miracle.

"Save my son!" he finally pleaded aloud. "Not my boy! Not my boy! God! God, please!"

The blows intensified still, and he heard Samuel's chest crack loudly as ribs began to break from the hits. Mary screamed.

"Shut up, woman!" Benjamin barked. "Shut up!"

She cried louder in response, and Benjamin felt a rage ignite within him like a wildfire. He stopped the compressions long enough to turn to Mary, looming over her crumpled, defeated frame, even on his knees. He grabbed her shoulders and shook her.

"Shut up, Mary!" He barked, "I cannot concentrate!"

"He is dead," she wailed. "He is dead. My boy!"

Benjamin went back to his compressions, trying to resuscitate Samuel, but it was in vain. After what felt like an eternity, his arms were weak. Samuel was gone. His prayers went unanswered. Benjamin wiped a tear from his eye. He looked at his wife, who was rocking back and forth, weeping silently. He glared at her. His grief and rage were released from their cage.

"How did this happen?" he asked, over enunciating every syllable.

"We were together," she said between sobs. "I went back to the house... to get some things we forgot. I... I came back, and he was not there."

"How long?" Benjamin asked in a quiet rage.

"What?"

"How long was he under there?"

"I..." she cried. "I do not know. I thought he was trying to hide from me... I thought he was trying to play a joke."

She began sobbing uncontrollably. Benjamin lifted her off the ground to face him.

"Stop crying, Mary!" he ordered.

She did not.

"STOP CRYING, DAMN YOU!" he yelled.

This had the opposite effect. And then, he did something he would regret the rest of his life. He hit her. He felt the rage bubble over, and his hand was quick, decisive, and powerful. The slap echoed over the water. The force knocked her back to the ground, and the shock of the act made the wails cease. She looked up at her husband towering above her. His breathing was shallow, like a hungry predator.

"How could you let this happen?" he asked her coldly.

"I was not strong enough to get him out," she whimpered.

"My boy..." Benjamin whispered. "My boy is gone. My precious son."

Mary began to cry again, but Benjamin slapped her hard on the face once more.

"No!" he said. "You will not cry again."

Her fear brought forth obedience.

The funeral was long and drawn out. The entire town had been present to support their priest. When Benjamin took his turn to speak, he had forgotten what he would say. He remembered he was supposed to deliver a message of hope. That his boy was now in the sweet embrace of Christ. He remembered he was supposed to quote the Apostle Paul in the book of Romans about rejoicing in suffering. But the words caught in his throat, and his anger and his mourning held back everything he had thought about saying. He remained silent and looked out over the many people who attended his church. He opened and closed his mouth wordlessly several times then sat back down, hanging his head. He cursed Mary. He cursed the people who had come and their pity. He cursed God. And Benjamin's heart turned dark.

The Lord did not answer my prayer to save the life of a child, *he had thought.*

Some weeks later, after delivering a hopeless message to his dwindling flock, he came home to find the house empty again. It did not surprise him. The death of Samuel had taken its toll on their marriage swiftly. They spoke very little. He slept on the floor or in the other room, not wanting to share a bed with her unless he wished to take his frustrations out on her sexually.

"Be a good wife for once," he would said angrily as he forced the sleeves of her dress from her shoulders.

The violent change in Benjamin's heart molded her spirit into one of submission. Her passivity brought her to a morose state so deep, a shining sun felt hidden behind black curtains in her mind. Her Benjamin was gone. Her Samuel was gone. And her despair would consume her, force her hand.

Benjamin paced the house, his hateful thoughts overwhelming him, until he decided to walk to the river in search of her. He thought of what he might do if he found her. Supper was never on time any longer. His belly groaned in hunger. He soon came to the lake, and he did not at first realize what he was seeing.

Mary was in the shallows of the lake, floating there without a care in the world, with her favorite dress on. His anger was fueled anew, and he marched toward her.

"So this is what I find?!" Benjamin yelled. "You bitch, you--"

Then he saw it. The blood. The bloody knife on the bank. The long vertical slits in her arms. The deep slits. Benjamin became himself again and ran to her.

"Oh, God!" he exclaimed. "Mary? Mary!"

He held her in his arms and cried in the water. Her lifeless body pressed against his chest, soaking his shirt with water and blood. He lost his mind and wept and growled and screamed. He cursed God and begged for His help in the same breath. He rocked back and forth with his wife.

"Oh, Mary!" he wept. "Oh, God..."

He buried her beside their son. He shut himself in his home and drank in private. When he had to go out to give his sermons, he was late and unprepared. The townspeople pitied him and offered their sympathies, which he rejected most forcefully and retreated home to find the comfort of his bottle. People would knock on his door to check on him, and he would drunkenly yell until they ran from his property. Soon, Benjamin could no longer take the emptiness of the house, the pity of the town, and the memories of Samuel's and Mary's deaths in this place. He fled. He fled to try and find a new life. He would eventually take a position at another church in a different colony far from his home. And though he kept his wrath at the Lord tucked away from the eyes of his congregation, he still cursed God in his private moments, his anger keeping him warm at night.

Father Benjamin looked tearfully into the eyes of John. He searched for the words to conclude what was in his heart.

"I did what Job would not," he said weakly. "I cursed God, and now... I have finally... paid for it with my life. I know He did not take... my son from me. But I was too enshrouded in my own grief... I needed to blame Him and Mary. I am a wicked man. I do not deserve... the light of His forgiveness. I was weak... and my spirit was shattered... When you asked me to pray over your farm, I did not know... what dwelled here... what was waiting to feed off my weakness. And whatever possessed me knew I was weak... and could not fight it off. It commanded me to do things... I killed the horses. I could not... fight it off."

"You did though, Father," John said softly, "you did fend it off in the end."

"John," Father Benjamin said, his voice growing weaker, "you must leave this place... You must take your brother and go."

"What?" John said. "Our life is here. We built this place. This is our life, our livelihood."

Father Benjamin looked at him fearfully, the tears streaming down his face. His end was drawing nearer.

"John," he whispered so quietly, it required the eldest brother to bring his ear to the lips of the priest, "my time is ended... I go to face the Creator... of Heaven and Earth... I will throw myself at His feet... and beg forgiveness. But you... you and your brother MUST flee... Run from this accursed place... I... beg you."

"I--I cannot," John said softly.

Benjamin looked at him, and John thought he could see a degree of understanding in the priest's dying eyes. He seemed to nod, and John thought he heard him say "God be with you" before his eyes slowly closed. The priest's hand relaxed in John's grip, and John laid Benjamin's arm over his lifeless, broken body. He felt fear. He felt sadness for the priest. John hoped that when he met God, Father Benjamin would be able to see his wife and son again, make amends, and that his soul would still be accepted into Heaven's light.

John stood and went to Eli. He held his brother, who shook uncontrollably. He was babbling softly and incoherently. John calmed him, took him inside, and helped him to his bed. They sat together. After a long while, Eli was able to speak in a whisper.

"What was it that took hold of him?" Eli asked.

"I do not know," John said. "I do not wish to know."

He stood up, and Eli remained seated.

"I will bury him," John said, "wait here."

Eli did not reply. His quiet shock took over once again. John left the cottage and observed the lifeless body of the priest. He then went around the back of the cottage and confirmed the priest's words. The horses were dead. Each one's throat was cut so precisely and deeply, their heads were barely attached.

"My God..." John muttered.

God had turned His face from the damned pit their home had become.

Chapter 11
Of the Carcasses and the Second Plague

John dragged Father Benjamin's bloody, mangled body across the farm to the general area where old Tom had been laid to rest. He grabbed the shovel and dug as quickly as he could. The sight of the priest's corpse disturbed him and increased his determination. He ignored the blisters forming on the callous-free parts of his hands, and even as they began to burst, he continued without losing a fraction of the effort he started with. Soon, Benjamin was placed carefully in the hole and covered with the dirt.

John went back to the cottage and peeked inside through the window. Eli still sat on his bed, staring into oblivion. His unblinking expression concerned John, but there was still a job to do: the horses. He picked up the knife that the priest had carried and knew what he had to do. He was not strong enough to carry even one of the horses away. He would have to dig their own hole and dismember them into more manageable pieces. A sickening dread filled him; why must he do this to such loyal and magnificent creatures? But the wolves would come if he did not accomplish this task quickly.

John dug the hole a good distance from the cottage. He worked as quickly as he could and as deep as the ground and his own aching muscles would allow. When he felt confident it was deep enough, he stuck the shovel in the mound and returned to the barn to begin the grievous task. He started with the horses' heads since the possessed priest had nearly managed to remove them. He completed the deed, carried the heads to the hole, and buried them. He dug another hole, lengthier and slightly shallower, for the legs he would soon remove.

John cut through the horses' legs, feeling sick to his stomach. These once-noble creatures deserved better than this. As he cut through the last bit of muscle and tissue of the hind leg of Eli's horse, he could suddenly feel eyes on him. The hair on the back of his neck bristled, and a chill ran through him. He told himself he was being childish and paranoid. He looked at the knife and stuck it in the ground forcefully before he took a long, calming breath.

The wind blew through the trees, and the leaves upon their branches sang their soft song. John focused on the sound. The peaceful thoughts that nature could bring allowed him to continue his task. He set the knife gently on the ground as it was finished. Soon, the legs were arranged in their own hole, and he shoveled the dirt over them. John looked at his hands and arms. They were covered in the blood of the horses, and he felt wretched.

"Such beautiful creatures," he said quietly.

After thoroughly washing the blood off his hands, John turned and went back to the cottage to check on Eli. He entered, and his brother had not moved; he was still as a statue. He sat beside Eli and placed a hand on his knee. Eli snapped out of the trance he was in and recoiled at his brother's touch. His eyes were wide and terrified, and a small yelp escaped his throat.

"Eli?" John said. "It is just me."

Recognition filled Eli's gaze as he looked over his brother, and he sighed.

"Forgive me," Eli said, "I was... lost in thought."

"It is alright," John said.

"How are things going?" Eli asked, unsure if he really wanted to know the answer.

"I buried the priest," John replied. "The horses..."

John thought a moment about how to respond. He did not want to give too much detail since he still felt dirty after dismembering the animals. Besides, he knew this would upset and disturb his brother. He settled on an answer after a few moments.

"The horses are almost taken care of," he finally said.

"Did they suffer?" Eli asked, placing his head in his hands.

"No," John said. "No, I do not believe so."

"That is... good," Eli said. "They were good to us."

"Indeed, they were," John said.

They sat together for a long time, sharing the comfort of each other's company. The light breeze outside sang a calming tune through the window, and for a moment, the two forgot their troubles and felt normal, if only for a moment. But it was a moment crucial to the brothers, both of them, as their minds had gone through such torment.

"Are you hungry?" Eli asked quietly after a while.

"No," John replied, thinking of the horses and of Benjamin, "I do not think I could stomach food right now."

"Alright," Eli said before sitting at the table with a small bit of bread.

Eli picked at the morsel and began staring off into nothingness again. His thoughts deepened. John stood.

"I will go finish," he said.

Eli did not respond. John exited and grabbed the knife in front of the doorway. The knife was stuck in the ground, and he pulled it free. He stopped dead in his tracks before he turned the corner.

Did he not leave the knife on the ground near the horses' remains? He wracked his brain of all his actions before going in to see Eli. He was *certain* he had laid it near the horses, not stuck it in front of the cottage. His fingers tightened around the handle, and he slowly crept to the corner of the cottage. He jumped out from behind the wall, and a sight of pure horror greeted him.

The carcasses of all three steeds at been expertly cut from the breast to the lower abdomen and split open. They were all emptied of their intestines, and the blood that soiled the ground was all that remained besides the torsos themselves. John gasped and looked around frantically. No animal could have done that so quickly, so precisely, and without making so much as a sound. The grip on the knife grew ever tighter. He crept over to the defiled carcasses. He surveyed his surroundings once more. His fear only grew. He dragged the empty corpses out into the woods, one by one, away from the cottage. Each time, he fled from the forest as he dropped one off, like a child running from a dark room out of fear of what lurked inside. When he returned to Eli, he composed himself as best he could.

"All done?" Eli asked.

"Yes..." John said, not mentioning what he saw. "Yes..."

It took three days for the brothers to even think about starting their normal routine again. During those three days, they usually remained together inside, talking very little and eating less. Whenever they needed to go outside to relieve themselves, they went together to watch out for the other. Eli only went to see the cow once every day: when the sun was at its brightest to keep any evil thoughts at bay. He also did his best to wash away the rune on the wall of the barn, but it had long been dried. He instead elected to grab a wooden plank and hammer it over the rune.

On the fourth morning, after much thought, John was the first to speak up about their situation of being shut in.

"I think I should check on the crop," he said. "I have been neglectful. We cannot survive without it. We should return to our routine. This place cannot run itself."

"I agree," Eli said, though hesitantly. "Perhaps a return to normalcy is what we need?"

John nodded.

"If you require my help," Eli said, "just ask."

"I shall," John replied.

The brothers slowly settled back into their usual routine. John went back to tending the crop and was occasionally assisted by Eli. Eli spent more time with Beth, talking to her; spending time with her eased his mind and no doubt helped her mood, as well (as well as a cow's mood can be aided, that is). Eli often looked at the empty chicken nests but did his best to remove any memory of the sickness that plagued the hens before they could dampen his spirits. However, the memory of the rotting, yet living, fetus always slipped through the net he created in his mind, frightening him and darkening his disposition. Helping John served as a good distraction from those thoughts.

The next few days passed by without incident, save for a visitor from town on horseback. He was a young man, perhaps nineteen, who arrived at their farm from the distant road. He greeted the brothers out in the field and provided them with his name, and they politely offered theirs in return. He had come asking about a missing priest, saying that the town was worried and had sent out volunteers to see if their was any sign or news of him. Eli remained silent and stared at the ground, and this allowed John to speak.

"Have not seen a priest around here," he lied (though he did feel a twinge of guilt about it). "If we see him, we shall inform someone in town immediately."

"Please do," the young scout said, looking around carefully, "he has not been seen for quite some time. We all fear for him. He is an older gentlemen. Goes by the name of Father Benjamin."

"We shall certainly keep a lookout for you," John said confidently.

The young man smiled from his horse and lifted his hat in farewell. John waved, as did Eli. When he had galloped out of sight, Eli turned to John, slightly upset at his older brother's dishonesty.

"Why did you lie?" he asked.

"Would you rather tell him of the priest being possessed, being broken open, and dying on our doorstep?" John asked simply.

"No," Eli said, feeling foolish.

"No," John said matter-of-factly. "Besides, do you think he would believe such a story? Next thing you know, we are on trial for the murder of the town priest, and what do we have to offer to defend ourselves? 'No, we did not do it; an invisible force of evil did'? Be wise, Eli. Now, run along, and go see to Beth. You have not tended to her since yesterday."

Eli nodded, and John returned to the crops.

Eli, a couple days later, entered the barn and took hold of the milk bucket. He walked to Beth's pen and smiled at her.

"Hello there," he said kindly. "May I?"

The cow did not respond, but Eli entered her pen anyway and set the stool up beside her. He placed the bucket below her udder and pat her on the haunches lovingly.

"You are a good girl," Eli said, as if to a young infant, "are you not?"

Beth mooed.

"That is right." He smiled and took hold of one of her teats.

He pinched and pulled, and a small amount of milk came forth. Eli talked to the cow soothingly as he always did, and that normally caused the milking process to become that much easier. He spoke gently, and Beth responded with her usual, soft moos. Eli looked down to see how much progress they had made. The sight made him stand up quickly, knocking the stool over, which upset the cow.

The bucket contained a great deal of blood mixed with the milk. Eli frowned and furrowed his brow. He pet Beth's neck and spoke gently.

"Are you alright?" he asked her, knowing she could not give him a proper answer.

He took the bucket, cleaned it thoroughly, then returned and set the stool up properly once again. He sat, gave the cow's haunches a pat, and began the process again as if nothing had happened. He looked down at the bucket after a while and saw the milk had come out curdled. The smell hit him the moment he saw it, and he gagged.

"Beth," he moaned, "what happened, girl?"

She mooed.

"Okay," Eli said. "Maybe just... Maybe just rest and eat and feel better. We will try again tomorrow."

He took the bucket. The image of a rotting hatchling flashed through his mind, haunting him. He took the bucket of curdled milk and dumped it away from the cottage. The smell was horrendous, so he took the shovel and piled dirt over the puddle of sour dairy to mask the scent. It helped, if only a little.

The next day, Eli visited Beth, and he found that she had gotten thinner. Not by much, but it was certainly noticeable. Regardless, he continued his normal routine with her. He spoke calmly about his evening and his dreams, and he pretended she understood. The bucket was soon filled, not with milk but with blood, and Eli cried out. He angrily took the bucket, ran to the road, into the wood, and dumped it. He returned to the cow and stroked her gently.

"You are not well," Eli said sadly. "You cannot be sick, Beth. You *cannot* be. Please get better. Please get better."

The next day, Beth had become even thinner, and Eli felt himself becoming emotional. He held back his tears and did not bother setting up the stool or the bucket. He knew she would only provide him blood. He stroked her again and spoke softly, his voice breaking every so often from his emotional state. She licked the side of Eli's face tenderly, and Eli looked into her eyes. He thought he saw sadness in them. Sadness and pain. He wept for her pain. He stayed with her for a while and stroked her as she rested.

"What is going on?" John asked from behind him. Eli had lost track of time.

"Beth is not well," Eli said, his voice wavering.

"What do you mean she is not well?" asked John with a hint of anxiety.

"Her milk is bad," Eli said. "She is losing weight."

"She does look thin," John said, observing the cow. "You have been taking good care of her, have you not?"

"Yes, I have," Eli said.

"Feeding her and everything?"

"Yes," Eli said, "she is just... sick."

John cursed softly.

"Do not curse," Eli said, patting the cow, "she doe not like it."

"I am cursing at myself," John said, perturbed. "She did not seem to be affected by whatever the chickens had, but it looks like I was wrong. She finally got it. I am a fool. A damn fool."

"It is not your fault," Eli said.

"I should have been smarter," John said, his temper rising. "I never think these things through. I am stupid. He was right."

"Who was right?" Eli asked.

"No one," John said, realizing his error. "No one. I just..."

John left the barn abruptly and left Eli alone with the cow. He went to the crops and forced himself to work. His feeling of foolishness grew.

YOU STUPID, INSIGNIFICANT, LITTLE SHIT! YOU ARE A CURSE UPON ME!

John felt his eyes well up, and he wiped at them furiously. He would not let his father win. He had built this place. He had become self-reliant. He had proved his worth.

He was going to be more than his father ever was. He cursed him over and over and over until the words from his childhood passed. Then, he sat down and held his face in his hands, allowing himself to let the emotions spill for just a few moments. Finally, he got up, washed his face, and began a different task to keep himself busy, distracted.

Eli visited Beth the next day, and she was on her side in her pen. In a great deal of pain. Tears spilled over when he saw that she was so thin, her ribs were clearly visible through her hide. Blood seeped out of the udder, and flies flew around her. The smell did not deter Eli from staying. She licked at his hands when he sat with her.

"Oh, Beth," he cried. "Oh no, no, no, no."

By midday, she had passed. Eli cried openly for he loved the beast. John came inside, saw the scene, swore, and stomped to the cottage where he pounded his fists into the table until his knuckles split and bled. Eli remained at her side, speaking gently to her and stroking her hide. After he had said his goodbyes, he kissed her neck and left, closing the barn door behind him.

He entered the cottage, tears still stinging at his eyes. John was at the table, wrapping his knuckles. Eli sat across from him and sighed. John grunted.

"So she is dead?" he asked.

Eli nodded.

John cursed. "This is not good, Eli. This is not good at all. We rely on her, the money we make trading her milk."

Eli watched his brother processing the whole situation. He watched him think on what they would do.

"I do not know what we should do," John said. "We are low on money after the chickens. And a new cow will not be cheap. I will also need to build a new barn and dismantle the old one. I have to try and find the reasons for the animals getting sick. I just... Eli..."

John looked into his brother's tear-filled eyes, and Eli returned the gaze. Eli noted the look of unyielding fear and anxiety breaking through his brother's normally calm and controlled demeanor. John was now looking at Eli as if asking, *searching*, for answers on what to do from his younger sibling for the first time.

"I do not know what we should do, John," Eli said, his voice pained.

John exhaled sharply. "I need... I need to think."

Eli nodded and gently patted his brother's wrapped hand. John felt a small degree of comfort from his younger brother, which was a new feeling entirely.

Chapter 12
Of the Second Visitation

John knew the night would be long, but he had hoped, had prayed, that he might find some form of rest. None was found. As he lie awake, his anxieties weighed on him heavier and heavier with each passing hour. The cow, the chickens, the priest, the wolf, the runes, the future.

Hell cometh.

He tossed onto his side and shut his eyes tightly. He cursed his mind for betraying him with such thoughts. The future of the farm and the future of Eli and his livelihood were at serious risk. What if something happened to the crop? His eyes snapped open, and he turned onto his back once more. The crop was their final hope. It was the main source of income, and if something happened…

John forced himself to think of a brick wall. He would not allow himself to think of the ramifications of a failed crop. He focused on the imaginary wall and counted the bricks. He measured the mortar of the wall layer by layer. Then, the brick wall was smashed to the ground as he thought of alternative plans if the farm failed. He groaned and rubbed at the sides of his head with clenched fists.

They could sell the farm at a cheap price, sell most of their belongings, and start a new life. They would not be able to afford to live well, though. John knew he could always get work in laborious trades. Maybe he could work on a ship or find work in construction opportunities. But where would that leave Eli? His brother was not a strong man by any account, and his hands were those of a scholar. He was well read and educated, for the most part, so he might be able to assist in bookkeeping or other work of that sort.

John looked at his brother in the other bed. He slept, but it was not pleasant rest as he twitched and made an occasional cry in his sleep. His dreams haunted him. John put his head back down on the bed. He could not let his brother down. He would always keep his promise to him no matter what.

John slammed his trunk, carried it down the stairs, and left it beside the front door. He clenched and unclenched his fists as he stared at the knob. He was going to do it. He was finally going to do it. He flinched when he felt a tug at his sleeve. Eli stared up at him with his big, curious eyes. John towered over his little brother, who had just turned five some days ago. John felt a pang of guilt; he felt compelled to stay for his brother's sake. But John was an adult now, having turned twenty some months ago, and he knew he had to leave. He could no longer be a prisoner here, and he could no longer face the strangers who had dared to demand the respect of parents. John knelt before his kid brother so that they were level with one another.

"Hey, little brother," John said softly, feeling emotion swell within him.

"John," Eli said with confused tonality, "where are you going?"

"I... uh..." John felt the words catch in his throat, and he stared at his shoes, forcing the sadness down into his stomach. "I have to go, Eli."

"Go? Why?" the young boy asked.

"I have to make a life for myself," John said. "I have to go and find my fortune out there."

"Will you come back?" Eli asked, his little eyes beginning to well up, which caused John to feel a sickness in his gut.

"I do not know, Eli," John said, forcing himself to be strong.

Eli took John off guard then. He rushed John and wrapped his tiny arms around John's strong torso, burying his face in his vest. John could feel his younger brother weeping into the cloth, and he felt as though he may cry in response.

"Do not go, big brother," Eli wept. "Please... please..."

John wrapped his arm around Eli. His younger brother was so small and felt so delicate within his embrace, he feared he would crush him by accident. He cradled Eli's head with his other hand and felt his own tears fighting to be released.

"Do not leave me," Eli sobbed, his voice muffled by John's clothing, "I want to go with you."

John wanted to tell Eli everything would be alright. He desperately wanted to give his younger brother hope for the future, but he felt so unsure of his own, he could not find the words. But in this moment, holding his little brother in his arms and seeing him like this, an answer became clear, and his path was set. He gently, yet firmly, pulled Eli away from him, and they locked eyes through their tears.

"Eli," John said softly, "listen to me. No. Do not cry anymore. You must be strong. For me. Are you listening?"

Eli nodded, his face twisted in grief.

"Good," John said. "I will come back for you. I will. I will always protect you. I swear it. I will come visit when I can to check on you, but I promise you... I swear to you, I will come back for you. I will make sure that I can provide a life for us both. When I have gotten everything prepared, I will come back. We can live a free life.

I will protect you and watch out for you always. But I must accomplish this first. Do you understand?"

"I think so," Eli cried.

"You must be strong now," John said. "You will have to be tough. You will need to stand up for yourself when I cannot be there. You understand?"

Eli nodded, even though he did not fully understand. All the child knew as a certainty was that his big brother was leaving. He hugged John again, and John allowed himself to weep once more as he embraced Eli. After a moment, John pushed Eli away gently and grabbed his trunk. He opened the front door and almost ran into James, who stood there frowning and making sense of what he saw.

"Packed, I see?" James said with a poison tone.

"I am," John said, glaring at his father.

"And what do you think you shall do?" James asked. "Make it rich? Become a successful man of business? Someone like that would require a more... capable mind. Not a head filled with cobwebs and sawdust."

John felt the hatred rise in his chest, and his eyes narrowed. John saw the ghost of fear pass over his father's features. James had had that same look in his eye when John had finally found the nerve to become the man James said he never would be.

"I do not know what is going to happen," John said, "but I do know this: I will work hard. And I will put every ounce of will I have into making a life for myself outside of the Hell you created here. I will become more successful in my life than you could ever be in yours, in every aspect. I will be twice the man you ever could be, but..."

John looked his father up and down with a mocking look.

"I doubt that will be difficult."

The fear turned to rage in James's eyes, but he did not dare strike. Not again.

"You have always been an ungrateful curse upon me," he said, "after everything I have done for you."

"Which was very little," John said, temper rising even more so. "I will not throw myself at your feet and ask for your parental teachings. That is one thing I have promised myself. Should I ever become a husband and father, your examples set in those areas will be just standards on how not to act."

James smirked.

"And one more thing," John said, stepping forward so that his face came within a foot of his father's. "Should I return, and make no mistake, I shall make visits without your blessing and without granting you knowledge of it prior, if I come to find out that you have enacted the same 'strategies' that you chose to employ on me as a child--"

"You mean discipline?" James interrupted.

"Do not interrupt me again, James," John said with a calm fury. "If you do to Eli what you did to me growing up... I shall return, and by God, I will kill you. Do you hear me? I will kill you."

James did not respond nor make any expression, but John knew the effect of his words had not been ignored.

"Understand?" John asked.

James snorted and stood aside, extending a hand out to the world.

"Go then." James smirked. "Go and make a name for yourself. You have always been a scourge upon this house. It will be good to finally have you gone."

John glared at his father once more then took a tight hold on his trunk. He felt his arm twitch, and a desire to swing the luggage at the man's head became a strong urge that took great willpower to *fight off. As he walked down the path from the house, he took one last look at his kid brother, who was crying quietly in the open doorway and waving at John. John waved back and then faced the world ahead. The determination to keep his promise grew with every step, even as his father renounced him as a son from the porch.*

"Touch one hair on his head, 'Father'. I beg you," John whispered to himself through gritted teeth.

"I promise to take care of you, Brother," John whispered to a sleeping Eli.

John ran a hand through his hair, pinched the bridge of his nose, and silently begged for the exhaustion to overtake him. He looked out the window for a moment before laying his head back down. He would always take care of Eli. He could not let that little boy down. He closed his eyes.

"Everything will be alright," John said quietly. "Everything will--"

His eyes snapped open. He thought he had seen someone by the well when he looked outside but was too lost in his own reflection, it did not register. He shot up in bed and looked out the window. She was there. The thin woman in rags was standing by the well, staring at the cottage from under the hood she wore.

John felt the fear attempt to drown him as he stared at her. The darkness seemed deeper than normal this night, and the moon's light did not aid his vision as he scrambled out of bed and grabbed the hatchet from his bedside table. He stood at the window watching her. She did not move a muscle, and he felt her eyes boring into him from the shadows of her hood.

"It is you," John whispered.

He could feel it in his bones that this woman, whoever she was, was responsible for the chaos on the farm. The death of old Tom, the death of the chickens and the cow. He knew she was responsible for cutting open the horses and taking their entrails. He knew that she was responsible for what had happened to Father Benjamin. He could not explain it to himself, and if Eli were to ask, he would not have any words for why he knew. But he knew nonetheless. He tightened his grip on the hatchet. Everything he had built here was at stake. And he found the source of their misery.

He went to the door and opened it wide, ignoring the panic in his mind and the fear in his heart. He would cure the farm's disease this night. He ran outside, hatchet raised to strike, but when he stepped foot outside, she was gone. John ran to the well regardless and searched for her.

"Come out, hag!" he barked.

No answer. John peered into the barn and circled the crops and the well. She was nowhere to be seen. John still felt her presence, though, and her eyes were drilling into the back of his head from every angle he searched. John looked back toward the cottage and saw something through the window, something like a curtain moving in the wind. But it was further in the house, closer to Eli. And they did not have curtains. John's eyes widened. The woman was in the cottage.

"ELI!" John screamed as he charged toward his home.

It took him several moments to make it to the cottage, and when he did so, he burst through the door and swung the hatchet blindly. In his blind but strong swing, he lost grip of the hatchet and sent it hurling into the wall above Eli's bed. There, it stuck with a crack of the wood. The woman was gone again. John looked around frantically. Eli was awake after the hatchet had embedded itself in the wall above him, and he cried out.

"John!" he yelled. "What is happening?"

"She was here, Eli!" John shouted as he went for the hatchet.

"Who?"

"That woman!" he barked. "That woman from before. In the rags."

He wrenched the hatchet free, and splintered wood showered over Eli's head.

"Where is she?" Eli asked.

"I do not know! Grab the knife, and help me look!"

"John, I am scared!"

"You have to be strong now!" John ordered. "You have to be strong for me!"

Eli nodded, grabbed a knife, and helped look, but the woman was nowhere to be found. They searched for the better part of an hour but never dared to step into the forest.

"She cannot have just disappeared," John said quietly.

"Where was the last place you saw her?" Eli asked, truly not wanting to hear the answer.

"She was in the cottage with you," John said, "and I was out here looking for her."

"Oh, God," Eli whispered.

"She must be here," John said. "She has a lot to answer for."

"John, what if she--"

"Eli, I cannot explain it, but... she has to be the reason for everything! She must be. What happened to Tom and the chickens and Beth and..."

"And?"

"Father Benjamin."

"She was not here when Father Benjamin died," Eli said.

"Eli, I know it sounds crazy, but it has to be her. It *has* to be. The wound in Father Benjamin's back. The drawings on the walls of the cottage and in the barn. They matched."

"Right, but how do you know it was her?"

"When we first saw her," John said, "I got a good look at her. In her arms and her legs, those same drawings were carved into her skin. She was bleeding out of them."

"We both saw what happened to Father Benjamin," Eli said. "She was not here to do it! The man was... possessed. Humans cannot possess people."

"What if..." He could not finish the thought.

"What if what, John?"

They were both silent as John thought to himself. Eli watched his older brother shift through his thoughts. As he did so, Eli glanced around to try and catch a glimpse of her. He saw nothing.

"Eli," John said, finally breaking the silence.

"Yes?"

"Humans cannot possess people."

"Right," Eli said, "that would be insanity."

"What if she is not human?" John said.

"John... please," Eli said. "Scary stories? There is no time for this. We have a madwoman running around here somewhere. We have to find her."

"It all connects, Eli," John said. "Those runes connect everything. They were *carved* into her. They were on the priest. In the barn. For God's sake, they are still in the cottage."

"So what is she, do you think?" Eli asked. "A witch?"

"A witch," John said, "some servant of the Devil. I do not know for sure, but she is not of good intent, Eli."

"So we are putting forth the notion that she is one of Lucifer's cohorts?" Eli asked. Though his skepticism was voiced rather quietly, when he muttered the name of the Devil, the brothers both seemed to wince slightly.

"Just..." John began, staring at his brother.

"Just what?" Eli asked.

Hell cometh.

John felt his body tense up completely. His brother's nightshirt hung open slightly, and in the pale moonlight, he caught a glimpse of something. He felt the fear rise from his loins and up into his chest. His legs felt like jelly.

"Eli, take off your shirt," John said.

"What? Why?"

"Eli," John said, voice wavering, "take off your shirt right now."

"You are being foolish, brother," Eli said.

"*Now!*"

"Alright!" Eli said. "Take it easy!"

Eli slowly pulled his nightshirt off and gripped it by his side. He then extended his arms outward in a display of his skinny frame.

"There," Eli said, "are you pleased?"

"Eli," John said, voice trembling, eyes wide with fright, "she marked you."

"What?"

"She marked you."

Eli looked down at his chest and saw a rune, not unlike the one that had been carved into the priest, scratched into his chest, small and shallow. A miniscule amount of blood trickled from it. Eli looked to his brother, and panic hit him in full force.

"Dear God," Eli murmured. "John. Oh, John. Oh, God. Oh, God!"

John grabbed his brother by the shoulders and tried to calm him to no avail. Eli began to babble and weep. John felt fearful, too, as the brothers both imagined a fate like Father Benjamin had suffered happening right now.

"John," Eli blurted with tears streaming down his cheeks, "help me. John, for the love of God, do not let it get me."

"Come with me, now," John said and grabbed Eli by the wrist, forcefully leading him to the cottage.

"What is going to happen?" Eli cried out. "Oh, God, help me…"

"I promised to take care of you, Eli," John said, determination swelling within him, "I swore it."

"John?"

He led Eli to the table and ordered him to lie on it. Eli obeyed hesitantly. He lay on his back upon the supper table and whimpered. John took Eli's shirt from his grasp and twisted it until it became tight like a length of rope. He handed it to Eli.

"What are you doing?" Eli asked.

John did not respond and placed the hatchet on his bedside table. He went to the window again and peered outside. She was not there.

"John, I am scared," Eli whimpered.

"I know, little brother," John said, summoning his courage, "so am I. But we must be brave."

Hell cometh.

He looked into his brother's eyes.

"You trust me, do you not?" John asked.

Eli's eyes welled with fresh tears.

"Eli, I promised I would always protect you," John said confidently. "I need you to trust me now. Will you?"

"I will," Eli sobbed.

John had no idea if what he had planned would work, but he had to try. For his brother's sake, it had to be done. He would not suffer like Benjamin had been made to suffer. He would not see Eli turned into the puppet of some vile force. *No.* He had made an oath. He would protect his little brother. John grabbed Eli's free hand and held it firmly, staring into his eyes.

"I will protect you," John said. "Do you believe that?"

Eli began to cry harder but nodded.

"Good," John said, letting Eli's hand go. "Then, bite onto that shirt."

"John?"

"Bite the shirt, Eli," John ordered.

Eli obeyed. John finally fetched the hunting knife, and Eli's terrified eyes finally understood what was going to happen.

"Do not move, Eli!" John ordered, though his eyes pled for forgiveness. "Trust me."

Eli obeyed and took several frantic breaths before John laid a strong arm over Eli's chest just above the wound, holding him down, and began to cut.

Hell cometh.

Chapter 13
Of the Removal of Tainted Flesh

John cut around the wound as quickly as he could without sacrificing precision. Eli was doing his best to remain still, and he bit down the shirt forcefully to distract himself from the pain he was experiencing. Still, John heard Eli's muffled screams from under the shirt, and his tears mixed with the heavy sweat upon his face.

John noticed that the runic wound was now bleeding profusely while the cuts around the area were not. It worried John, but he kept at it, slicing around the wound in a crude, almost circular, shape. The evil marking had to be removed.

"I am almost done, Eli," John said as calmly as he could, "I promise. It is almost done."

Eli kept screaming under the shirt and fought the urge to thrash around. The cut that John was making was not afflicting him, though he still felt it, of course. The wound that the hag had created, however, was causing him excruciating pain. It seemed to know what John was doing and was punishing Eli for it. Soon, when John had reached about halfway, it became too much, and Eli began to kick and writhe on the table.

"Eli!" John yelled, yanking the knife away as to not cause further damage.

John then noticed that the rune began to bleed even heavier than before, and a greenish pus was leaking from it. He had no time to think about it. He threw an arm over Eli's clavicle and fought to continue the cutting. Eli's screams were no longer held back as the shirt fell from his mouth. Eli gripped John's shoulder, and his nails sank into the flesh ever so slightly. John ignored it and continued.

"ELI!" John barked. "You must stop thrashing!"

Eli screamed louder, and John almost lost his handling on the knife. He regained it in time to just barely avoid causing further and unnecessary damage to his younger brother. He was able to make one unsteady inch of progress before Eli's knee twitched in self-defense and knocked the knife free from John's hand.

The rune felt like it was burning and slicing further and further into Eli's chest. He felt it reacting angrily to John's attempts at eradicating it. The wound seemed to have a will of its own.

John went to grab the knife, and Eli thrashed uncontrollably until he crashed to the floor. His head struck the ground hard, and his screams subsided. Darkness took him.

It had been a good day. Nothing very special had occurred, but nothing had happened that would cause distress either. It was his birthday. It was as normal a day as ever, and for that reason alone, it was good. Eli was thankful. He had gone to school that day, and while he was mocked and teased for the better part of the learning day by the other boys, he was away from home, and for that, he was thankful. It made their teasing a welcome addition to his day.

The school itself was open only to the upper class in the area. Since his father had a great deal of wealth as a financier and merchant manager, Eli was sent to school instead of to an apprenticeship on his mother's request. He enjoyed school a great deal and desired to make his own fortune. He wanted to go into business with his brother one day. He would daydream sometimes about when John would return, never forgetting the promise that was made when Eli was barely a child.

During breaks, he would walk by himself, skip, hum, and would occasionally see how far he could throw a stick or a rock (which was not very far, given his lack of strength), and this would entertain him. The girls at his school recognized his youthful beauty and giggled whenever he would walk by. Eli did not notice this, thinking they were just entertaining themselves, but the other boys, fueled by jealousy at the attention, would mock him and sometimes hurt him.

Several times, the teacher had asked where he got his bruises and black eyes. Eli would not speak up. He chose silence over tattling. This only made him all the stranger in the eyes of his peers, but he would simply sit quietly and wait for the teacher to begin educating again. He loved to learn. Everything the instructor would throw at him, he seemed to absorb like a sponge. Writing and basic mathematics were not troubling. His religious studies were handled easily enough, though some things confused him (which he would never dare speak of or ask about; it allowed seeds of doubt to be planted, and those seeds would grow as he became a man). He was the student of every teacher's dreams.

Eli turned ten that day, and he was not surprised by the lack of interest in his birthday by his father or mother. He went to school believing that the day away from home would be gift enough. He walked by himself to the schoolhouse that morning, and the boys in his class were waiting for him. Eli expected this as the day before, he had made a wise remark about Martin being too frightened to look Anna in the eye when she said hello. Eli had asked why he was so scared of a girl but took no shame in bullying smaller children.

"Well, look who it is. It is our friend, Eli," Martin chuckled with his friends, who followed his lead. "Having a good morning?"

"I am," Eli said. "It is my birthday."

"Is it?" Martin asked with a sinister grin. "And what do birthday boys get on their special day?"

"Left alone, I should hope," Eli said. "If you are planning on terrorizing me today, I suggest you get on with it. I would like to get ready for class. I am very interested in the mathematics lesson we will be doing today."

"Can you believe him?" Martin laughed with his friends, who followed suit.

"Who does he think he is?" one of Martin's friends remarked.

"Do you think you are tough?" Martin asked.

"Not particularly," Eli said, "but I do know I am tougher than you when it comes to speaking to women. Especially when it comes to acknowledging them when they deem you worthy of some acknowledgement."

Martin's pride took a hit, and his face turned red.

"Perhaps you will leave me alone if I fetch Anna," Eli offered. "I know you will be petrified at the sight of her. It is odd what infatuation does to children."

The beating was swift but less intense that morning. And even though Eli walked into class with a cut lip and bruised ribs, he smiled, knowing he had won not with brawn or muscle but with his mind and his wit. Martin and his cronies were cavemen, destined for nothing more than farming or blacksmithing or being the heavy-lifters for a ship's cargo. Eli expected he would own a company they would work for and that he could terrorize them in ways more devious than that of a simple pummeling.

When the class was dismissed, Eli gathered his belongings and went outside into the fresh air. Martin and his lackeys took no interest in him (probably from being so confused about how to perform basic arithmetic, he thought), so he sat underneath the big oak tree. He leaned against it and enjoyed the fresh air, his mind bursting with knowledge from the day's studies.

"Hello." A timid, friendly voice broke through his thoughts.

Eli opened his eyes. Anna was smiling at him, the sun was shining just above her head. In that moment, he thought she was an angel, and the sun was her halo. This notion surely came from what had recently been discussed during their religious studies.

"Beautiful," he said quietly, staring at her. A boyish grin spread across his cheeks.

She giggled.

"You are Eli," she said.

"I am," Eli replied. "And you are Anna."

"Yes, I am." She smiled.

"Well, how can I help you?" Eli asked, not unkindly.

"I heard about what happened this morning with Martin," Anna said.

"Oh?"

"Yes," she said, "I heard you said that he was scared of me. Because he is infatuated with me."

"I did say that," Eli said proudly. "Do you notice how he cannot seem to speak to you? He likes you very much, it would seem."

"You believe so?"

"I know so," Eli said. "I can understand why. I thought you were an angel a moment ago when you approached."

She laughed. "An angel?"

"And the sun was your halo," Eli replied. "You were radiant."

"Thank you," she chimed.

"You are welcome."

"I have a question for you," Anna said, "if you are okay with me asking."

"Please," Eli said.

"I was wondering if I might walk home with you," Anna said carefully, weighing her words. "I know you live on the way to my house."

"Well..." Eli said hesitantly.

"It is alright if not!" Anna said quickly, trying to hide the embarrassment in her voice.

"Will we not make Martin jealous?" Eli asked with a chuckle.

"I would imagine so," Anna answered with a smile.

"He really likes you," Eli said.

"Yes, but that does not mean I return the feeling for him," Anna said. "He is... brutish. I see what he and his friends do to you. It is terrible."

"It is alright," Eli said. "One day, they will get theirs."

"I suppose so," Anna said quietly.

They were silent for a moment before Anna spoke again.

"So will you walk with me, Eli?" she asked.

"I must," Eli said confidently. "It would be shameful of me not to escort a lady home."

She giggled. Eli felt his chest swell. He, too, secretly felt anxious talking to a girl like Anna, but he had never let that dictate his actions. Unlike Martin, he felt confident and secure that he was better than the other boys he was forced to call "schoolmates".

He and Anna walked together at the end of that school day, discussing various topics such as their lessons and their interests. He shared with her how much he desired to go into business with his older brother, John, and live a noble life. Anna offered some trivial gossip and told him what her life at home was like. Then, she asked Eli a question he was not prepared for.

"What is your family like?" she asked, smiling.

Eli stopped walking and frowned. Anna did not see him stop at first and continued for a short distance before she turned around. She saw him staring at the ground, rolling a small pebble beneath his shoe as he pondered the question.

"Eli?"

"I am sorry," Eli said, "I do not really know how to respond."

"You do not know how to talk about your family?"

"Yes," Eli said.

"Well," Anna said, "start with your parents. What are they like? They must be proud to have a son like you."

Eli felt a pang of sadness.

"No," he said softly, as if an uninvited listener were nearby. "No, I do not think they are."

"What do you mean?"

"Well," Eli began, still toying with the pebble, "my father. My father is a drinker. A mean one. He never says anything pleasant. To me or my mother. He drinks too much, and though he does not cause me any harm, I know he... I know he wants to. I think."

Anna watched at him in silence, respecting Eli's desire to finally confide in someone.

"My mother has suffered being his wife. I know he is cruel to her, but I do not know to what end. She is very protective of me. I think she, too, believes my father would hurt me given the chance, so in her eyes, I have become less of a son and more of a fragile possession to be kept safe."

Anna took Eli's hand in hers with a delicate touch. Eli looked into her eyes, and they shared a moment of compassion. Though they both were young in age, their spirits were both matured well beyond their years.

"I am sorry to hear this," Anna said sadly.

Her eyes told the depth of her sadness, and Eli knew that she felt for him. It was a new feeling to feel cared for by someone else, other than John. He had not seen John in some years, so to finally feel a connection with someone was strange. A good strange.

"It is alright," Eli said, forcing a smile. "One day, my brother will come for me, and we will make a new life."

"Maybe one day, I could be a part of that new life," Anna said.

Eli's eyes widened. He felt his cheeks flush. Anna smiled, and she quickly kissed his cheek before starting off down the road with a laugh. Eli brought his fingertips to his cheek, and he smiled. When he regained his senses, he saw that he was standing in front of his house already.

He did not notice, however, Katherine's disapproving glare staring down at him from the upstairs window.

Eli awoke on the table again. His chest pained him greatly, and he groaned.

"You are awake!" John exclaimed from beside him. "What a relief!"

"What happened?" Eli asked.

"You fell off the table and passed out," John said. "I was able to finish while you were unconscious."

Eli noticed the bloody rags on the table. He looked at his chest and saw a crude circle carved around where the rune used to be, now gone. The new wound was seared shut. It hurt but not as badly as when the rune was still on him.

"I cauterized it while you slept," John said. "You did not even stir when it happened. I guess that hit to your head helped a great deal."

Eli rubbed at the lump that was forming beneath his hair.

"I suppose it did," Eli said.

"And how do you feel?" John asked.

Eli decided against telling John of the dream he had awakened from.

"Aside from the bump on my head and the cauterized hole in my chest," Eli said, "I feel alright."

"Good," John said. "The bit of flesh where that hag touched you... It is strange."

"What happened?" Eli asked.

"It... caught fire in my hand when I finally cut it free," John explained with a frown. "I had to throw it outside, and it is nothing but ash now."

"And the woman?" Eli asked. "Did she come here while I was out? Try to stop what you were doing?"

"I have not seen her," John said, "but we must keep an eye out."

"Of course," Eli said.

That night, the brothers discussed what to do. With the woman still out there, they thought it best to take turns on watch while the other slept. John had insisted on taking the first, but Eli declined.

"You have done much for me," Eli said. "Besides, after I hit my head, I got plenty of rest. It is your turn. I will wake you in a few hours."

John did not want to argue, but since it was his little brother, he made a halfhearted attempt to convince Eli to give him first watch.

"No," Eli said rather firmly, "I do not feel sleepy. You need rest more than I do."

"Alright," John said, "but wake me the moment you feel tired. Or if you see her."

"I will," Eli said.

"You remember how to fire that?" John said, pointing at the musket.

"I remember well enough from when you last tried to teach me," Eli said.

"Just... be careful, alright?" John said.

"Stop worrying," Eli said. "Rest! Now!"

"Alright!"

John settled into bed as Eli pulled the chair next to the window. He grabbed the musket and laid it across his lap. He doused the lantern and allowed his eyes to adjust to the darkness of night. Thus began his watch that evening.

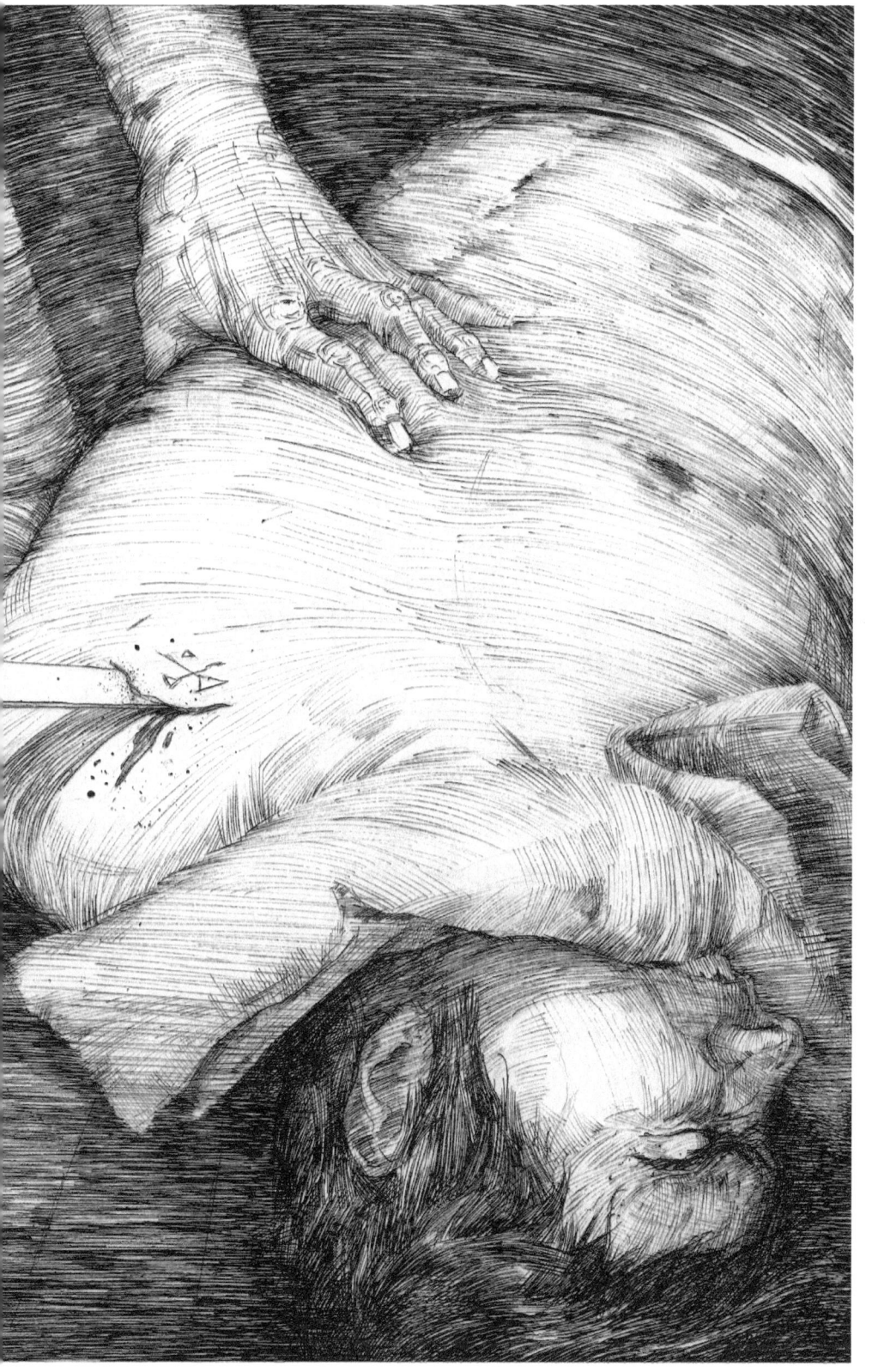

Chapter 14
Of Eli's First Watch

Eli's finger twitched involuntarily, creating an erratic rhythm against the trigger guard of the musket that otherwise lay undisturbed in his lap. He was not sure how long it had been since he began his watch, but time seemed to pass at an agonizingly painful speed that he compared to an exhausted snail. The darkness brought forth a torrent of persistent anxieties, and at times, his mind played tricks on him. A number of times, he thought he saw the hag at the edge of the farm or darting between the well and the crops. Other times, he thought he could feel her long, hideous fingers tracing the back of his neck. He did not turn around immediately when he felt this but instead would wait a few moments to pluck up his courage before turning to see if she indeed was behind him. She never was.

Eli leaned back in the chair and placed a cold hand against the cauterized wound on his chest. The coolness of his fingers felt nice against the tender flesh. His mind told him a moving branch was the hag, and his hand swiftly returned to the musket. He was not confident in his ability to fire the weapon. The last time he had touched the musket was during a hunt with John. The recoil, the sudden burst of smoke, and the loud bang had surprised Eli so greatly, he had flown backward with a girlish squeal before landing in a muddy ditch. John had laughed heartily (and continued to laugh about it even now). Eli had not.

Still, confident or not, Eli felt a sense of duty to protect the farm and his brother's work. He would make the musket do his bidding this time if it came to it. He knew what to expect from the musket this time. He just prayed that his muscles would obey him if he did need to fire it. When it mattered the most.

The night dragged on, and even with a heightened sense of danger, Eli was lulled into a feeling of dullness. He was not tired, nor did he feel any need for sleep. Instead, his eyes stared into the abyss, and the world seemed to disappear around him. He stared into the dark, and it stared back. He was alone with his thoughts. And his thoughts soon drifted from a wide-open nothingness to a sea of memories he wished to leave buried. But night changes one's thoughts, and even when Eli desired not to remember, the dark brought them forth, ugly and exhaustive. Eli shuddered and his fingers gripped the musket as his mind was sent back in time.

"Speak the truth," Katherine barked.

"I am, Mother," Eli said. "She is just a girl. She wished for me to accompany her home from the schoolhouse."

"Her name," Katherine said.

"What?"

"Her name, boy! What is her name?"

"Anna," Eli said hesitantly, feeling small.

"I saw what that harlot did," Katherine said in a calm yet venomous tone.

"What?"

"Do you not know that I was observing from my bedroom window?" Katherine asked. "Do you think she is good enough for you as you allow her to kiss your cheek?"

"Mother..." Eli began but decided against it.

"Listen and understand me now, Eli," Katherine said, leveling her eyes on the young boy with a disturbing gaze. "She is common filth. She probably plans to sink her claws into you so that when you both become of age, she can marry into your money."

"Mother, what--"

"DO NOT INTERRUPT ME!"

Eli fell silent.

"Would you like that?" Katherine asked. "To be used for your wealth? To be a tool for her own gains? You really think she cares about you?"

Eli knew it would be unwise to answer the question, so he stared at the floor.

"You are both young and foolish," Katherine ranted. "You are too young to understand, Eli. She does not care for you. She only wants what will come to you when your father passes. She will use you then discard you. Is that what you desire?"

Eli did not respond. Katherine slapped him.

"Answer me when I ask you a question," Katherine snapped.

"No, Mother," Eli said quickly.

"No, what?"

"No, that is not what I desire," Eli said.

"Wise boy," his mother said. "She is a temptress. She is not good enough for you. No one is good enough for you. Understand?"

"Yes," Eli said, masking his glumness.

"If you are to wed, she will be of high class, and she will be of my choosing." Katherine smirked. "Now, I do not want you to associate with her again. Do you understand me?"

"But Mother--"

This slap was more forceful than the previous. His cheek stung viciously and caused Eli's eyes to well up.

"Do. You. Understand. Me?" Katherine said, each word dripping with poison.

"I understand," Eli said.

She slapped him once more.

"That is so you never forget," Katherine said quietly. "Love is for fools, Eli. You would do well to remember it."

Eli nodded in forced agreement. He rubbed gently at his stinging cheek. He blinked the tears away.

"Good," Katherine said. "Now, go get ready. We shall go to market to pick up some things. I can keep my eye on you if you are with me."

"Yes, Mother," Eli said in a monotone.

They went to the market where Katherine watched Eli closely, all while purchasing various breads, cheeses, and wine. Eli never saw her drink wine. Not at supper or any other time. He kept close to her so as to not upset her. The sting on his cheek served as a reminder not to wander off.

As Eli and his mother walked along the market square, some young girls with their family took notice of Eli and began to giggle amongst themselves. They were struck by his charm and dared to think that he might even speak to them when he saw them. They were pretty. Two of them were even a little older than he was. Eli let a small smile play on his face, and this made them blush. Katherine saw the exchange, and her fury was instant. She grabbed his hand and marched up to the girls' father.

"You should teach your daughters to have a little more respect," Katherine said to him.

"I am sorry, madam?"

"As you should be," Katherine hissed. "Perhaps with a firmer hand, they will learn not to behave like common street trollops. My boy is above all of you."

She led Eli swiftly away from the shocked and confused family. The girls burst into tears, and their father tried his best to understand what had occurred. Eli and Katherine soon went home, where they found James asleep in his favorite chair, an empty bottle nestled in his lap. Katherine sighed.

"Go to your room," she told Eli, "and remember what I told you. You are better than those ill-bred whores we saw today."

Eli went to his room and saw his mother go to hers. He thought the wine bottle in her hand was already uncorked.

Eli broke from the trance and looked around frantically. How long had he been daydreaming? Too long. He looked toward John, who slept undisturbed. Eli sighed then looked back out the window. The darkness was still deep, but he squinted through it. His stomach turned, and he felt his hands become sweaty. Someone was wandering near the well. They took slow, lazy steps. Eli took up the musket and stared at them. It was not the hag as the figure was taller. Their clothing was not made of rags. Even so, Eli felt frightened by the uninvited visitor and went to wake John.

"What is it?" John mumbled sleepily.

"There is someone outside," Eli whispered in a panic.

This got John's attention, and he leapt from his bed. He went to the window with Eli, but when they peered out, no one was there.

"Do not toy with me," John said.

"There was someone there!" Eli said. "Just a moment ago."

"Was it that woman?" John asked.

"No," Eli said, "but--"

"Look, if you wanted to switch, you just had to say so," John said, perturbed. "You do not need to fabricate a story. You have been at it long enough."

"But I swear it, John!" Eli said. "I did see someone!"

"Alright," John said and went outside, musket in hand.

He returned soon after.

"Nothing," John said.

"I would not lie about this," Eli said.

John nodded. "Still. Being up so long, the darkness, our situation, and what has already happened tonight... Probably best I take it from here. Get some rest, Brother."

Eli nodded. He did wonder if maybe it was his imagination. He did think he saw the hag earlier (multiple times, in fact), and even though he felt her presence, none of that had been real. She had not turned up. He shrugged and got into bed. After all he had experienced recently, he was amazed he had not gone completely insane. He turned onto his side and faced the wall next to his bed. He gasped when he thought he saw a rune, scratched faintly into the wood, but when he blinked, it was gone. Another trick of the mind.

"I am tired," Eli said to himself. "I am simply in need of some rest."

He closed his eyes.

Chapter 15
Of the Third Plague

Eli awoke, stiff and uncomfortable. He stretched, and when he finally opened his eyes, he saw John was not in the cottage.

"John?" Eli called out.

That is when he heard John yelling outside. The worst came to mind as Eli shot out of bed. The hag had him. Something had him. He was under her control. Eli threw open the door and ran outside. John was standing by the fence that normally circled the crops. But now, Eli noticed the crops were gone. *Entirely* gone. John broke the hoe over his leg and was cursing horribly. Eli approached hesitantly.

"What is wrong?" Eli asked. "Where did the crop go?"

John looked at Eli, at the barren land that once contained their livelihood, then punched the wooden fence and cursed loudly.

"John," Eli said, "tell me what is happening."

"It is lost," John said, "All of it. It is all lost."

"How?" Eli asked.

"The crop is lost!" John roared.

"*How?*"

John hurdled over the fence and knelt. He dug into the dirt, shifted it around, and returned to Eli. He held his hand open and showed his brother what lay inside.

"What is that?" Eli asked.

"Look closely," John said.

Eli peered closer. A small grasshopper-looking insect was in John's palm. John flung it to the ground in disgust.

"Locust," John sighed angrily.

"What?"

"A locust, Eli!" John yelled at his brother. "The crop is gone. We have nothing!"

John swore again, and Eli flinched from his brother's anger. John leaned against the fence and groaned. Eli stood watching him a moment.

"How is this possible?" Eli asked. "It looks like they just ate the crop. The grass around the fence is untouched, it looks like."

"That is exactly it!" John said, panicked. "It does not make any sense! They consumed the crop but nothing around it. Not the grass. Not the trees. Not the bushes. Just that which we make a living on! Just our survival! Damn it! Damn it all!"

Eli attempted unsuccessfully to calm John down.

"Go, Eli! Just... just leave me. I need to think."

Eli sighed and then nodded before returning to the cottage. John slid down the wooden fence and sat in the dirt, playing with the dead locust between his fingers. He pondered what to do. He wrestled with his anxieties. He did his best to fight off his own pride and instead deal with their new reality. Replant the crops? But so much time had already been lost. Living off of the money from the animal products for the remaining season was not an option either; they did not have enough to get through even a month.

John tossed the locust away. He knew what had to be done. They would have to sell what they could and find work elsewhere. They could not stay here. John got up slowly and went to the well to get a drink. He lowered the bucket and pulled it up slowly. When it came to the top, a horrid stench came from inside. It made John retch. He looked in the bucket.

Instead of water was a diseased, sludge-like liquid. Flies buzzed around it. Bile crept into John's throat as he saw the half-decomposed corpse of a small animal in the bucket. John recoiled from the septic liquid, and it toppled over the edge, spewing upon the ground. It seemed to stew and bubble, tainting the grass. The flies that landed in the filth died, and John thought he saw an eel-like creature flop out from the muddy substance. John vomited. He got to his feet and wiped his lips. The truth was now firmly fixed in his mind: the farm, **his** farm, was cursed. Plagued. A dead place. And no matter how much he desired to save the land he had built with his own hands--the monument he had made to show his father that he was worth something, that he could make his own way, that he was no scourge--it must be abandoned.

Then John saw her. The woman in rags was standing at the edge of the forest, watching him. John's eyes widened as he noticed her. Her limbs were covered in locusts. They slowly, almost obediently, crawled up her neck and then disappeared into her hood.

"You," John whispered. "You did this."

The woman did not react. She did not move. From under her ragged hood, John could feel her eyes piercing him. He felt that she knew his next move, but regardless, his rage overpowered him, and he darted for the musket leaning against the fence. In one swift motion, he had it cocked and readied against his shoulder. He swung it around to aim at the woman. Her back was now turned to him, and she was walking lazily back into the forest. She dared him to fire. And John accepted her challenge.

The musket fired, and the pellet struck the woman in the shoulder. Blood painted a nearby tree. The woman did not react in pain, but instead, she stopped walking. Her opposite hand went to feel the wound. She then turned and stared at John, who felt petrified after wounding her. They stared at one another for a few moments.

"John!" Eli called out as he ran toward his brother.

John did not reply, still staring at the hag.

"I heard the musket fire, and--" Eli said. He then saw the woman standing at the tree line.

Her ragged clothing was darkening. The brothers both thought they saw black smoke seeping from the wound, mixing with the blood, but they were unsure if it was smoke from *her* or from the musket shot. A locust wriggled out of the bullet hole, expanding it to escape, and began to eat away at the crone's bloodstained fabric before it died. The runes carved into the woman's body seemed to glow, and the brothers prayed it was a trick of the light.

"John?" Eli asked in quiet fear.

"She is hurt," John whispered.

She stared at them and cocked her head slightly like a curious dog. Then, she screamed. A high-pitched, shrill scream that seemed to command the winds that carried it. The winds became gusts of a hurricane, and their power blew the brothers off their feet and onto their backs. The scream became louder, and the brothers covered their ears, crying in agony. John's head felt like it was splitting, like it would tear itself apart.

Wolf.

Father.

Locust.

Horses.

Father Benjamin.

Images were conjured inside his head in a furious display of death and horror. John's own scream tore at his throat, and yet, he still could not hear himself over the hag's shrieking. The images came faster and faster, threatening to throw him into insanity. The shrieking turned into words for John: the words he heard from the wolf.

Hell cometh.

"OH, GOD!" John thought he yelled.

HELL COMETH!

Over and over, it assaulted his ears. John began slamming his head into the ground to try and knock himself out, but the hag seemed to know what he was doing: the release of unconsciousness eluded him.

Eli could not decide between covering his ears or scratching at the pain in his chest. The screams made his ears bleed, but at the same time, a violent burning erupted where his cauterized wound was. Eli interchanged his hands from ears to chest with no means to escape torture. The hag's shrieking brought forth an image of Father Benjamin. The possession he had gone through. He prayed that John's craving of the rune would block out any attempts of control over him.

Please... Eli thought. *Make it stop.... Please....*

Katherine materialized in Eli's mind. Then, old Tom's brutalized corpse. The cow, Beth. And Eli wailed in agony. Tears flowed from his eyes like burst dams, and finally, at the peak of his most intense pain, he fell unconscious.

John rolled on the grass and howled like a wounded animal. Suddenly, the hag's shrieks ceased, and when he opened his eyes, through their haziness, he saw the hag standing over him. The runes carved into her flesh pulsed and bled. The glint of eyes, red, yellow, and milky white, came from beneath her hood. Blood from her extended arm dripped onto John's face, and he quickly realized that he could not move. His arms and legs did not respond to his commands. His ability to speak was removed. The hag held power over him now.

Just kill me, John thought. *Why not just kill me?*

"In due time, Johnathan." His father's voice came from under the hood.

"You still wish to live," the growling, inhuman voice of the wolf then said.

God, please. Save me. He thought.

"He cannot hear you," the wolf's voice said.

"He does not heed the cries of those already in Hell," his father's voice said.

Then, the woman crouched nearer to him, and he shut his eyes. He did not want to see what terrors she would inflict on him. He began to weep. The fear, the pain, became too much. He tried to focus on something pleasant without success. And soon, he fell into a tormented sleep from which he could not escape.

Chapter 16
Of an Attempted Exodus

He knew what would come. The moment he opened that front door, his father would be waiting. He knew what his father would do. He knew what his father would be upset about. He knew what was about to happen. The question that John asked himself again and again in the moments building up to entering the house was how he would respond. John could hear his baby brother crying just inside the door. John loved Eli the moment he saw him and vowed to himself that he would take care of the boy. No matter what.

"Make him quiet!" James's roar burst from inside.

"I am trying, James!" Katherine yelled. "Screaming about it will not help things."

"Make him quiet, or I will!" James shouted.

A rage built inside John, and his reluctance to enter the house disappeared immediately. Eli would not receive the same treatment as John. He vowed this the moment he threw open the door.

"You," James said over the cries of Eli, eyes filling with hatred for John.

John did not reply.

"Outside," James said. "Now."

John obeyed and went out to the backyard. James followed behind him. He slammed the door shut, which quieted the baby's cries immensely. James stood looming over John, which normally terrified the boy, but something was different now. John did not know what it was, but something indeed was different. Was it his turning sixteen? Was it that he felt responsible for his baby brother?

Perhaps a combination of these and more. But once he no longer felt fear toward his father's anger, he stood taller and knew what to do.

"I heard an interesting bit of information about you," James said, words dripping malice. "Would you like to hear?"

"I would love to," John said, almost bored.

The tone John used then further intensified James's rage, but he did not let his fist fly. Not yet.

"I heard you have been seen with Abigail," James said.

"Abigail?" John asked, feigning ignorance.

"My superior's daughter?" James growled. "Do not play the fool."

"Oh," John said. "Yes, I remember her."

"Of course you do," James said, glaring, "and it has come to my attention that you were together. Fooling about."

"She is lovely, Father," John said. "If speaking in passing is 'fooling about', then sure. We were."

"Do not get smart with me, boy," James said with quiet maliciousness. "Do you have any notion would this could do to me?"

John did not reply.

"You are not up to her standard," James said. "If you insult her or cause her any distress, do you understand what could happen to my livelihood? We could lose everything!"

"The only thing you would lose is your drinking money, I suppose," John said quickly and without hesitation.

The blow landed just as swiftly as John's retort. John put a hand to his cheek and felt the all-too-familiar ache that sent pulse after pulse through his brain. John knew that that was coming because his father was predictable, but something snapped inside him this time. He noticed that his father was only a head taller than he was now. John also realized that his father's job, which lacked in physical labor, made James weaker with every passing year. John stood to his full height and looked his father squarely in the eye.

"Do not hit me again," John said daringly.

"Feel like a man now, do you?" James asked with a sneer. "Think you can hurt me? Think you have the gall?"

James hit John again with tremendous force. John did not cry out. He barely reacted. The blood that began pouring from his nostrils fueled a rage that he bitterly realized was inherited from his father. Without thinking, John clenched his right fist and swung upwards at his father's jaw. The blow connected with great power and precise accuracy and sent James reeling backwards from the sudden shock. Blood flooded James's mouth: he had bit into his tongue.

"You little bastard!" James roared.

John's father rushed at him, and John felt his body leave the ground as his father picked him up. John threw wild punches at the back of his father's head as he was tackled violently to the ground. A flurry of hammer-like blows drilled into John's face. John used the strength of his torso to lift his father, which caught James off guard, allowing John to squirm out from under him.

"Little boy thinks he is a man now!" James yelled.

John, still wriggling away, delivered a well-placed kick that hit James in the side of the cheek. Blood splattered the ground, which only infuriated James. John stood up shakily. He was dizzy and felt altogether wrong. But he screamed at his father with the fury of a wounded warrior making his last stand.

John then threw himself at James and, for a moment, had the upper hand as he sat on his chest and lashed out once, twice. Seeing his father bleed by his hand fueled him. The tables had turned. The father, whose hand had caused the son to bleed, was now experiencing the same torment. An eye for an eye. John knew things *would be different now. He would fight back. He would defend himself from this monstrosity he called "Father". He was no longer the voiceless little child who cowered in the corner as his father's belt cracked upon his flesh, leaving welt after welt. He was no longer the terrified boy who silently accepted his father's fists, which gave him bruises and abrasions that never healed properly. He was not scared anymore, and one day soon, his father would come to understand that.*

James finally deflected one of John's punches and countered with one of his own. A sickening crack echoed from John's jaw, and blackness crowded his vision, threatening to swallow him whole. James yelled with rage in John's face as his blows continued.

"You are killing him!" John heard his mother's voice scream. "You are—"

James's fists and Katherine's cries dissolved into nothingness as unconsciousness finally, mercifully, took him.

John woke and groaned loudly. His head was throbbing violently. He looked around. The woman was nowhere to be found, and the soft wind was the only sound that greeted his ears. John cursed as his brain pounded intensely. Eli was still unconscious nearby, breathing steadily. John slowly got to his feet, and as he did so, he noticed something. His chest was bleeding slightly. He removed his shirt and looked. A rune had been carved into his chest, much like the one Eli had had.

"Damn," John moaned.

He knew what he had to do, remove it in the same way as Eli's, but he also knew something that was far more pressing. They needed to leave the farm.

Now.

John put his shirt back on, making sure it covered the mark properly. He would not admit to his own fear of the rune nor would he admit the fear of cutting it away. He had cut Eli's because he was the older brother, but he was also wiser. More experienced. Perhaps nothing would happen to him. Perhaps it only affected weaker men.

"I am stronger than Eli and Father Benjamin," John said to himself. "Maybe... maybe I will be fine."

He secretly dreaded having to experience the pain Eli had gone through to remove the tainted flesh. He calmed himself. It was not hurting him. It was just a scratch from that witch. He would be fine. He assured himself of this over and over with each step he took closer to his brother.

"Eli," John said urgently. "Eli, wake up."

Eli immediately jerked awake and scrambled away from John when the elder brother placed hands on his shoulders. Tears spilled from Eli's eyes until recognition filled them.

"John?"

"It is alright now," John said kneeling, "it is alright."

"She... that... what?"

"Calm down," John said, "she is gone."

Eli quieted.

"Eli," John said softly, "we must go. We need to leave."

"Yes," Eli said quietly, as though he may cry again. "Yes, we do."

"We are going to grab only the essentials, and we are leaving," John said firmly, as if to convince himself more than his brother, "understand?"

"I do," Eli said.

"Alright. Make sure to grab the money you have tucked away. We will need it."

"John?" Eli asked.

"Yes?"

"What will we do?"

"I started a new life with nothing once before, dear brother," John replied, "and I can do so again. Trust me."

This answer brought a certain peace to Eli, and he nodded.

The brothers gathered a few of their belongings before setting off. John grabbed the knife and hatchet and tucked them into his belt. He also loaded the musket and tied the bag of powder and ammunition to his belt, as well.

"In case we run into her again," John said.

Eli tried to convince John of bringing some of the sellable items left in the larder, but John forbade it.

"We do not need to be slowed down with a bucket full of milk," John said. "Besides, I do not think you will enjoy carrying it the miles we must go to get to town. The horses are dead, remember?"

Eli winced at John's directness then nodded, following his brother out of the cottage and onto the dirt road. The pair walked slowly along as they both kept an eye out for signs of the hag. The idea of running into her on the path set them on edge and caused John to cock and uncock the musket several times as they went. Eli would occasionally look behind them, thinking he heard the shuffling of footsteps or a twig snap, but there was always nothing. They continued along, anxious and fearful.

"I hurt her," John said.

"What?"

"I hurt her," John repeated. "I shot the witch. Right in the shoulder. I saw her bleed."

"So, she can be harmed then?" Eli asked, "But when she screamed... Those screams--"

"Do not think about it, Eli," John said.

"Did she fill your head with things, too?" Eli asked.

"Yes."

"What did she show you?" Eli asked.

"It is best not to think on it, Brother," John said. "Do not give her a place in your mind. That is how she becomes more powerful, I believe."

"Alright," Eli said softly.

They trudged onward. Each step seemed slow and agonizing for them. Neither brother could describe it, nor did they mention it aloud, but they each felt as if they dragged a great weight behind them. They felt tired, and their feet began to ache. It had been awhile since they had left the farm as the sun's positioning changed. Though the pit of fear remained, they both felt more weary than terrified now.

"What will we do now?" Eli asked.

"Start anew," John said. "We have little choice. I could take a job in construction or loading ships at port. You could find work as a bookkeeper? You have a head for numbers. Or maybe you could mend clothing? You do well with a needle considering how many times I have torn a hole in something."

"Will we be together still?" Eli asked.

"What do you mean?"

"Can we... can we still live our lives together? I enjoy having you around, John."

"I enjoy your company, as well," John said with a reassuring smile. "You are my little brother, after all."

"I have always remembered your promise to me," Eli said quietly.

"My promise?"

"Yes," Eli said, "the one you made when I was a boy. Before you left to go work."

"Ah," John said, slightly embarrassed, "you remember that? You were very young back then."

"And yet, I still remember it so clearly," Eli said.

"I hope I have fulfilled it," John said. "As best as I can, anyway."

"You have," Eli said softly.

"I swore that our drunk father would not harm you. And I saw to it."

"You think he would have?" Eli asked.

"I *know* he would have if I had not made certain he would not," John replied. "He was... very fond of drink, I am sure you remember."

"He did not hurt me," Eli said. "He drank. Often. But he did not hurt me."

"Then, I have kept my promise," John said. Then, almost as if he were ashamed to be so open, he hesitantly said, "I swore to myself I would protect you, no matter what. Our mother was unkind and neglectful, but she could not harm a fly. So I did not worry about her. But father? He was..."

John was quiet. He thought about how he should conclude his statement without revealing to Eli the constant pain and distress the memories of his father still provided. Eli was quiet himself. He listened carefully to everything John said and held back his emotions so that his brother could finish his thoughts.

"He could be cruel," John finally said.

"Did... did he hurt you?" Eli asked.

John was quiet then. He did not speak until they passed by a large oak tree beside the road. John stopped in his tracks and looked around confusedly then frantically.

"We... wait, this cannot be," John muttered.

"What is it?" Eli asked.

"Wait, wait, wait," John said to himself, "no. I must be losing my mind."

"What is wrong, John?"

"Did we not pass this oak tree already?" John asked Eli.

Eli studied the tree John indicated to the right of the road as well as their surroundings. There was something familiar about it, but Eli was not sure. He had not been paying attention to much of anything as they had gone along.

"I am not certain," Eli said after a moment.

"I swear we passed this tree already," John said.

"John?"

"Let us just continue," John said. "And be mindful."

Eli obeyed his brother's command. As they went along, the time seemed to crawl by. John felt as if they should have at least come across a landmark. Even on foot, reaching town did not take this long. He went onward, trying hard not to alert Eli of the panic that was brewing within him. That bush to their left looked familiar. But it could not be the same bush from the start of the road. The rune on John's chest began to ache, and he felt the wet stickiness of blood begin to soak into the worn fabric. An oak tree on their right caught Eli's attention.

"John?" Eli said timidly.

"What?" John said, already knowing what his brother would say.

"Was that not... the same oak tree?"

John stopped, and Eli followed suit. Terror took hold of their hearts. John looked into the sky. The sun had not changed position in the slightest. It was still midday, and yet, he felt as though it was later. *Should* be later. They had been walking for hours. He knew this. He felt it in the soles of his feet.

"Let us keep going," John said.

"John?"

"Not now!"

They went on. Everything about their surroundings was familiar. They followed the road, a road they had ridden on time and time again to town. John felt his desperation begin to seize his will as they reached a point where he thought that same oak tree may appear.

Do not be an oak tree. Do not be an oak tree. Do not be an oak tree, John thought, *prayed,* fiercely.

An oak stood looming over them to their right. John felt a cold sweat form. Eli began whimpering softly.

"This is not real," John said aloud. "This cannot be right. We *cannot* have gone in a circle."

Eli did not reply, his fear controlling his ability to speak.

"And the sun? The sun has not moved an inch..."

Eli looked behind them. A presence made him feel uneasy. The hairs on his neck stood up: no one was there. But what he did see almost brought him to tears of complete insanity.

"The road does not fork off," John muttered to himself, "it is just *one* road. We have taken it dozens of times--"

Eli made a noise, trying to alert John of what lie behind them.

"What is going on?" John asked himself. "Eli?"

Eli was noiselessly opening and closing his mouth. His eyes were wide in shock. John looked at his younger brother and then followed his eyes to what they were taking in. When he saw, his own eyes widened in response. The pain on his chest intensified, and his head was forcing a dull ache to the forefront of his skull.

"What in God's name...." he whispered.

Their farm was before them. Just the way they had left it. It was as if they had never abandoned it in the first place.

Chapter 17
Of the Return to the Farm

"I cannot believe it," John whispered. "Did we not leave hours ago?"

"We did," Eli said just as quietly.

"But how did--" John began, not knowing what to say.

The brothers stood there, staring at the farm. Their mouths hung open in disbelief. Neither dared take a step forward. John looked behind them. The road was as it was when they first set off, no oak tree beside the path.

"I--" John tried again then stopped, unable to process what they had experienced.

"She put us in a kind of... loop," Eli said, pondering what had happened himself, "a cycle."

"You think that woman, that witch, did that?" John asked.

Eli looked at his brother, brow furrowed at his brother's inept question.

"Who else? Better yet, *how* else do you explain this?" Eli asked with a slight shake of his head.

John nodded, understanding his own foolishness of asking such a question. The pair remained rooted to the spot, still staring at the farm.

"So, what do we do now?" Eli asked.

"I do not know," John said quietly.

The fear they thought they were leaving behind returned.

"If we try to leave, she will just put us in that cycle again," Eli said, "I am sure of it."

John swore, and anger mixed with the fear. He felt trapped. He felt like he was a child again, being cornered by his father. The rune on his chest was burning, and it felt like the familiar whip of his father's belt. John groaned.

"John, are you alright?" Eli asked.

"No."

"What are we going to do?" Eli asked.

"I am not sure, Eli," John said, rubbing his chest gingerly, "but we are her playthings now. But, if she can bleed, if we can hurt her, then perhaps..."

John trailed off.

"Perhaps what?" Eli asked.

John did not reply immediately as he toyed with the idea in his head. He did indeed wound her, which sent her into a frenzy of sorts. What if it had not been her shoulder he wounded? What if he had taken a more deadly aim and struck her somewhere more vital?

"Perhaps," John replied softly, "she can be killed."

It took awhile for the brothers to summon the courage to move from the spot they had been frozen. It took John's cautionary footstep forward to snap Eli from his trance. They went to the farm, slowly and carefully. Each footstep felt like a dare for the witch to come back and finish them off. Together, they walked back to the cottage and took many precautions in case she was present. But, when they entered, she was nowhere to be found. The cottage was in the exact state as they had left it.

John placed the musket on the table and removed the hatchet and knife from his belt, laying them delicately beside the firearm. He admired each weapon and allowed himself to imagine a scenario in which he could kill the hag with any of them. A hatchet swing that removed her head with one, clean swipe (or multiple chops that ensured the job was done brutally). The knife plunging into her evil heart. A well-aimed shot from the musket that turned her brains into porridge. John dismissed these visions when Eli spoke.

"What will we do?" Eli asked.

"There is no doubt she has power over our land," John said. "Over us, even. If we try to leave, she will put us into a loop again."

"So, we need to break her power?" Eli asked.

"I think that is our only option at this point," John said. "Straight at the source. I think we need to kill her."

"You propose a hunt, then?" Eli asked.

"Better than waiting to die," John suggested finally, resigning himself to his fate.

"We should have left sooner," Eli said.

"In hindsight," John muttered, "yes. Yes, we should have. But there is nothing to be done about that now. Come."

John picked up the hatchet and replaced it on his belt. He picked up the musket and, with one hand, leaned it against his shoulder. He then picked up the knife and held it out to Eli. Eli shook his head.

"Do not argue," John said, "you need to defend yourself."

Eli looked into John's eyes and felt like a child again, the younger brother pleading for the big brother to protect him and keep him safe. But John's eyes held a strong resolve. He was no longer protecting him from the natural world.

From bullies or their father. This was something evil. Supernatural. Something from Hell itself.

"I do not know how to fight," Eli said softly.

"I will do my best to make sure you will not have to," John said, still holding the knife out, "but if I fail, you have to try and defend yourself."

Eli nodded and hesitantly took the knife from his brother. John then placed a reassuring hand on Eli's shoulder.

"If you can," John said with a small, teasing (though nervous) smile, "just stick her with the pointed end there. Make it count."

Eli nodded and tried to look brave like John. Although he wore a mask of courage, John felt the same sick anxiety like a pit in his stomach. John gave Eli's shoulder a reassuring pat as the young man put the knife in his belt like a knight of the medieval days sheathing a sword. The brothers then walked outside the cottage and surveyed the farm. Nothing seemed out of the ordinary. The sun was moving again, which alerted them that time was no longer standing still. That meant they only had a limited period if they wanted to find her before dark. But John felt that she would be difficult to find. She had only revealed herself when she wanted to be seen. He prayed that the hag had become overconfident in her toying with them and that maybe, just maybe, they could make her pay for it.

"Are you ready?" John asked Eli.

"No," Eli said, "but what else is there to be done? Let us go."

John nodded, and they walked toward the forest.

Chapter 18
Of a Past Reborn

When they entered the forest, they felt uneasy. Quiet dread flooded their veins, and they expected to see the witch behind every tree, thinking every shadow was hers. Their paranoia did not cease, and several times, John almost fired the musket at one of the many surrounding trees. Eli followed John and jumped whenever one of them accidentally stepped on a stick that snapped underfoot. He trembled uncontrollably as if the air was filled with a winter chill he had not prepared for.

"Do you think we can make it to the other side of the forest?" Eli asked, trying to keep the fear from being heard in his voice.

"If she can cast a spell like she did on the road, what would stop her from making the forest endless?" John asked.

"But what if--" Eli began.

"There are more dangers in this wood to be mindful of, Eli," John said.

He thought of the wolf beside the stream. Of its milky white eyes that pierced his soul. Its voice that disturbed him each and every moment he gave it consideration. John felt the rune on his chest begin to ache. He massaged it gently.

"Are you alright?" Eli asked, noticing his brother's irritated look and the rubbing at his chest.

"I am fine," John said, "pay attention."

They went on. The afternoon was transforming into dusk when they turned around to head back to the farm.

Better to rest in the familiarity of the farm than in the darkness of the woods. As they turned back, Eli noticed something near a tree.

"John... John, look."

John turned his attention to where Eli was pointing. He squinted at the tree Eli indicated and saw it: crows. A murder of crows, at least twenty or so, were perched, staring at the brothers in silent interest. When John moved slightly to the left, half of them followed his movement while the other half remained fixated on Eli. Their unseeing, white eyes bulged from the sockets. Terror filled John as he thought they might speak. The thought of what they might say and the sound they could produce when communicating prompted John to act quickly. The crows' heads cocked sideways with curiosity. John leaned in closely and whispered in Eli's ear.

"They are hers," John said quietly, almost breathing the words like an exhale.

"What?" Eli asked.

"The crows," John whispered, "they are hers."

"What do we do?"

John looked at the murder again, and they stared back. Their eyes were almost popping out at the brothers. John shivered and turned to whisper to Eli again.

"Back to the cottage," John said, "but *calmly*. Try not to spook them."

Eli nodded and trembled as he turned in the direction of the farm.

"I am scared," Eli said to himself.

"Go slowly," John said, "we will try to--"

The crows cawed then. John's and Eli's heads snapped to their perch, and their eyes widened. The crows were now hovering above the tree branches in an odd circular pattern, still staring at them with those terrifying eyes. Eli took another step in the direction of the farm, never tearing his eyes from them. They cawed in unison, and the sound of their displeasure echoed throughout the wood. Eli almost gave in to panic, but his brother placed a strong hand on his shoulder.

"Run," John whispered to him. "Run to the cottage."

"What about you?" Eli asked quietly.

"I am going to buy you some time to make it there," John said.

"John..."

"Run!" John then shouted.

Eli took off and sprinted in the farm's direction. The crows' squawks were amplified and thundered through the trees. John rushed in their direction. It felt as if a hot iron was searing the flesh of his chest. The runic wound began to bleed again. The crows then darted toward John as he advanced.

Hell cometh!

John fired the musket at the murder, and one bird burst into a mess of feathers and blood. The discharging smoke from the firearm blinded him as he ran toward the possessed birds. When they closed in on him, he swung the musket wildly, occasionally making contact with one, which would screech loudly. They pecked at him in turns, making passes to tear into his flesh again and again. The rune in his chest burned enough to make him scream out in pain, and the lacerations from the crows' incessant pecking wounded him further. He swung the hatchet frantically and was able to take down two of the possessed creatures with furious swipes. The crows then hovered above him and watched as the cloud of smoke cleared around him.

John's clothing was torn, and his arms, neck, torso, and face were badly bleeding. He cried out as the pain erupted in his skull. He looked at the murder above him.

"Three less of you now," he groaned.

They cawed before attacking once again. The pain became overwhelming for John, and he slowly succumbed to the pain. He fell into the dirt and the dead leaves, unconscious.

Hell cometh for thee, John.

Eli tore through the woods in the direction of home. His lungs were burning, but he never slowed. He heard the firing musket ring out in the distance and knew that John was in danger. But he obeyed without question. He ran faster when he heard his brother's screams mix with the squawking of the crows. The sounds were so loud, he thought they were directly behind him, but he knew he could not turn back.

He heard other shouts ringing through the forest, but they were not from John: it was a woman's voice. He did not slow down. He needed to reach the cottage.

"Look at me!"

"No!" Eli shouted back automatically.

"LOOK AT ME, ELI!"

Eli blinked frightened tears away and continued on. He would not face whoever called out to him. The voice was familiar, but even so, it was a voice not belonging to John, and that fact made him run faster.

As he cleared the forest, he bolted straight for the cottage and saw that the last rays of daylight were dwindling. He opened the door and slammed it closed. He looked out of the window and saw them. The crows were flying above the tree line, watching him. They did not come any closer to the farm as if either a barrier around the house or a leash tying them elsewhere restricted them from getting closer. They cawed loudly several times and then withdrew into the forest. Eli looked desperately for any sign of John, but after a long while, he felt the dread that his brother was not coming back. He felt frightened that he may die alone or in some unspeakable manner, but that did not stop him from dragging the supper table over to barricade the door.

Night came, and Eli sat looking out the window, waiting for John to return or for the witch to come and seal his fate. The hours dragged on, and neither John nor the hag came. Eli held the knife in his sweating palm, turning it over and over with his other hand, still remaining watchful. Sleep was the last thing on his mind.

"Where are you, John?" Eli questioned the darkness.

"Wake up, boy."

A voice rang out, clear as day. John stirred in the dirt. His eyes opened, but he saw nothing. Just darkness.

"Wake up!"

"I am awake," John replied.

"Then get up. Now."

John reluctantly did as he was told. He stood and felt the pain coursing through his body. It helped him to chase off the drowsiness. The inky darkness around him was unnerving.

"How do you feel?"

"Fine," John replied.

"Can you see me?"

John squinted into the pitch black. Nothing could be seen.

"No," John said.

"Look harder, then."

John felt himself frown, but he obeyed and looked this way and that. Still, nothing.

"I do not see you," John sighed.

Something appeared: a light. Then, a shadow enveloped in a blurry light. It slowly began to take shape. A silhouette of a person began to appear, but John was unsure whether man or woman.

"I see someone," John said softly, squinting at the shape, the light somewhat blinding. "Is that you?"

"It is."

The silhouette began to walk closer to John, still wrapped in the light. John raised a hand to shade his eyes from its growing intensity.

"Who are you?" John asked.

"You know who I am."

"I do?" John asked.

The light then disappeared. John dropped his hand and began to look around for the illuminated figure. But the darkness overcame his sight once again.

"Yes. You do."

"It is so dark here," John said, "where are we?"

No response.

"Are you there?" John asked.

Nothing.

"Where am I?" John sighed to himself, his head still swimming in pain.

Then, James appeared before John with a wide, malicious smile that made John recoil in surprise. At first, he felt fear, then he felt rage and confusion. He did not immediately notice that his father appeared younger than he had remembered.

"YOU!" John shouted.

"Me," James said.

"But how are you--" John began angrily.

"Hush now, boy!" James interrupted.

John's mouth was firmly shut, not by his own choice. He felt... *something* covering it. Cold, slick hands in the dark were firmly clamped over his mouth. John's heart pounded in his chest. He could not see the hands nor did he see to whom they belonged. All he could see was James.

"It is good to see you again," James said, grinning.

John could not respond with the vulgarities he desired to use.

"I have no doubt you wish to say a great deal to me, John," James said, antagonizing John with his tone. "Perhaps you wish to even let some of your anger out upon me, release your rage and your fear with your fists."

John narrowed his eyes. While they suppressed his words, the hands he felt over his mouth could not stifle the rage he felt when he saw his father.

"Would you like that?"

John nodded slowly.

"Then what are you waiting for?" James asked. He then snapped his fingers.

John blinked, and when he opened his eyes, he was in the forest again. The moon in the sky was bright enough for him to see his surroundings. His blood was soaking the ground. The crows he had killed were surrounding him. He was back in reality. And yet, James was still before him. He was some yards away with that same unnerving smile.

"You know," James said, slowly turning his back to John, "I think I should go and pay a visit to your brother. It has been so long since I have seen him."

"You will not!" John yelled, his voice now unrestricted.

James turned his head to smile at John smugly.

"And is it *you* who will stop me?" he asked John with a chuckle.

John felt the rage boiling over.

"Your promises to protect him," James said with a laugh, "are very foolish. Naïve. But I want to see your dedication. So how about a race of sorts? I am going to go to your cottage. I am going to find Eli. Dear, sweet, precious Eli. Then, I am going to kill him. I am going to kill him as I should have killed you when you were first born. Burdens, the both of you, who deserved nothing more than to have your miniscule brains dashed upon the rocks. Try and stop me, John."

John was taken by surprise by his statements. None of this could be happening. He knew this. And yet, how could he deny what was right in front of his own eyes? At fist, John did not comprehend the full weight of James's words. That is until James took one more look back at John, grinned like a mischievous jester, then ran in the direction of the farm, laughing much like he did when he used to beat John after having too much to drink.

John ran after him. Anger spurred his legs faster and faster. Visions of what was to come flashed in his mind: James was going to crush Eli beneath his shoe. He was going to laugh as he destroyed his brother. This made John's mind snap, and he screamed at his father, who was running just a step ahead of him.

"I will kill you!" John roared.

Eli stared at the forest from the window, still playing with the knife in his hand. He had begun to wonder if maybe he should go and search for John, despite the dangers, when someone burst through the tree line.

"John?" Eli breathed.

John was sprinting from the forest, roaring as he did.

"ELI!" John screamed. "ELI, WHERE ARE YOU?"

Eli ran outside to meet his brother halfway.

"GET BACK INSIDE RIGHT NOW!" John yelled at him.

Eli looked around frantically in search of the source of John's anger and anxiety but saw nothing. No dangers. No witch. No monsters in the night. Nothing was following John either.

"John, what is--"

"INSIDE!"

Eli obeyed and ran back into the cottage. His knuckles turned white as he gripped the knife in hand. Eli went to the window and saw John alter his course. He no longer ran for the cottage but past it.

"GET OVER HERE!" Eli heard John scream from outside.

"John?"

"YOU DARE THREATEN MY BROTHER? YOU DARE?"

"John?" Eli asked as he crept outside.

He tiptoed out the door and heard a commotion. A vehement fight had erupted from behind the cottage. Eli felt his courage die when he dropped the knife, but still, he found the will to walk around the cottage.

"I WILL KILL YOU!" John screamed.

Eli turned the corner and saw what was occurring. John was violently punching the stump they used to chop logs for firewood. His hands were bleeding from his splitting knuckles, injuries that only worsened with each ferocious blow. John then grabbed the stump, as if strangling a man, and screamed at it. John was squeezing it so hard, his fingers gathered splinters. Eli ran to John and shook him. John ignored Eli's attempts to pull him away from the stump.

"I WILL KILL YOU!" John repeated.

"John!" Eli yelled. Eli then grabbed his brother around the neck and pulled backwards.

"You cannot kill me, boy!" James mocked.

John threw Eli off, returned to James, and continued beating his father's already bloody and mangled face. Eli wrapped an arm around his neck, and John found it difficult to breathe. What was his brother doing?

"*He* cares about his father!" James laughed. "If only he knew!"

John only tightened his grasp on James's neck despite Eli's attempts to pry him off. Finally, as Eli's grip was closing off his airway, John forcibly shoved Eli to the ground with a growl and returned to James, who was laughing loudly at the scene.

"Kill me, John!" James baited, still grinning despite the loss of some teeth and his swollen face.

"I INTEND TO!" John howled.

John went back to beating his father's face in until it was nothing more than a pulp. Even so, he could still hear James's laughter. His hands were gory, and he was sure his fingers were broken. Still, he did not stop. John ignored the pain in his hands and the pulsing headache that was like an erupting volcano in his skull. He had to protect Eli. He had to kill this man they called "Father". This was no man. This was an abomination.

Eli picked himself off the ground. He was terrified by his brother's episode of insanity. He gathered himself, took a deep breath, and charged at John. Eli threw his whole body at him and tackled him to the ground. John's head struck the side of one of the logs next to the stump. John rolled slowly onto his back and stared at the sky. He panted heavily and groaned.

"Eli," he murmured, "he needs to die. He has to."

"John..." Eli said softly.

John took a deep breath of air and struggled to his knee. Eli was already standing above him, ready to spring again. Terrorized tears filled his eyes.

"Why are you defending him?" John asked.

"Defending who?" Eli asked in a broken voice.

John looked to where James should have been. Only the stump was there. The blood from his hands had painted it red. Confusion ran over John's features, and he looked around frantically.

"Where did he go?" John asked loudly.

"John--"

"He was here!" John yelled, now on his feet, looking and running around wildly. "He was just here! He could not have--"

John then looked at Eli, who was standing in quiet confusion and sadness.

"Who is it you speak of?" Eli asked softly, trying to summon some form of composure.

John did not reply. He looked at the stump then at his hands. The pieces of what had happened began to come together. Soon, John realized what his brother had witnessed. The sane part of him knew it could not have been possible. And yet...

"I thought..." John began softly. "I... I..."

"John, are you alright?" Eli asked.

"No," John whispered. "No, I--I do not think I am, Eli."

"Let us go inside," Eli said.

"Alright," John said.

Before he followed his brother inside, he opened his shirt and looked at his chest, which had been hurting him since they entered the forest. The runic wound looked more irritated, and a black liquid was slowly oozing from it. John closed his shirt, shook his head, and got to his feet.

Chapter 19
Of the Possession of John

They entered the cottage, and John took a seat. His breathing was heavy, and sweat poured down his face. He groaned through his panting, and when he managed to finally catch his breath, he looked at Eli, who sat by the window, staring out. Unblinking.

"What happened back there?" Eli asked, his eyes affixed outside.

John's chest throbbed in response, and he felt the ooze dripping down his clothed torso.

"The woman," John said, "that witch. She got into my head."

"Clearly," Eli said quietly. "What did you see?"

John thought about how to answer but remained silent.

"How are your hands?" Eli asked as he knew John would not tell him of his visions.

John held them out and looked carefully. They were bruised, bloodied, and broken. A couple of his fingers were out of place, but that was not the first time. It had happened before when he first built the farm. He gritted his teeth and set them back into place with sickening pops.

"They are fine," John grunted.

"Right," Eli muttered, rolling his eyes.

John's chest began to both throb and burn, as if fire was brushing his skin. The rune was growing restless, and his fear only grew. He felt pain and fear and exhaustion overwhelming him.

"I am tired," John sighed painfully.

"Rest, then," Eli said. "I can keep watch. Are you sure you will be alright? You really--"

John flopped into his bed with an agonized groan.

"Drop it," John growled. "Call if you need me."

Eli remained focused on the world outside. Though dark, his eyes had adjusted just fine, and he searched for any sign of the witch. He felt like a rat trapped in a cage. He felt as if he and his brother's fate was sealed, and he wondered what the hag was waiting for. Why did she stall (what felt like) the inevitable? They could not leave. They could not travel through the forest with the animals under her command. His mind flashed with vivid images of the crows and their bulging, white eyes. He shivered.

"What are you waiting for?" Eli asked the darkness quietly. "Why not come and finish us off if you want us dead?"

John forced his eyes closed. He did not know why he felt such irritation toward his brother. Perhaps it was a combination of the achiness coursing through his body, the fear in his heart, and the rune on his chest that pulsed with every beat of his heart. He fell asleep almost immediately, and he tumbled into a dream of the past once again.

It had become a new routine for John, almost ritualistic at times. After John had defended himself for the first time, things were different. His father never beat him during the day anymore. Now, he would wait for night, wait until he thought John could be asleep. But John did not rest until he knew for certain his father was asleep first. He would hear his father drinking sloppily downstairs. He would only grow louder and angrier, and he would start to rant and rave and curse everyone. When he had ranted enough, John would listen to him climb the stairs, knowing it was a fifty-fifty chance: he would either go straight to bed or come into John's room to beat him. Some nights, John prayed for him to just go to sleep so that John could rest himself, but other nights, John wished for him to enter.

John's door burst open this night, and James, in his drunken stupor, came at him. John leapt from his bed and squared off with his father. John raised his fists in front to his face and stared his father down. James was holding the silver candlestick with which John's back had been very quickly acquainted as a child.

"Clever boy," James slurred, "already prepared for my visit?"

John fumed in quiet rage. He desired sleep this night, but James impeded that. James chuckled then beckoned to John with the candlestick.

"Well?" he asked.

John stayed on his toes, silent, ready.

"COME ON, THEN!" James roared.

John bellowed and charged at James, who threw the candlestick wildly, just missing John. James backed up slightly but not enough to miss John's right fist as it crashed in a downward motion, striking near his temple. An inhuman, gasping squeal came from James, but John ignored the sound. He swung with his left fist and caught James squarely in the jaw. Blood filled James's mouth and dribbled down his chin. James began to retreat out of John's room, but John pressed forward.

"Come on, then!" James yelled again.

John screamed and launched himself at James. He tackled him to the floor and began to unleash a barrage of furious punches at his father. The blows to James's body caused satisfying cries of pain to erupt from his throat as one of his ribs cracked, which elated John. James cried out loudly then kicked John away from him. He found the strength to scramble away from John's clutches, and John stood and watched his father crawl to his own room. He was scared. Terrified, even. The son was stronger than the father now. James kicked the door closed. John followed, pounding at the door and roaring like a lion at the wooden obstacle.

"YOU CANNOT HIDE FROM ME!" John screamed.

Cries of terror came from behind the door and filled John with a determination to finally show his father what it had been like for him growing up.

"YOU HAVE BEEN A CURSE ON THIS FAMILY!" John roared. He began ramming his shoulder into the door.

James barricaded it with his own weight from the other side. This did not deter John. He rammed into the door again, and the wood cracked loudly.

"YOU WILL DIE TONIGHT, FATHER!"

The door gave way, and John watched his father scramble away. His back found the wall, and he stared up at John in absolute terror. James looked like a whimpering child. His mouth was bloody, and he had a hand clutched over his hurt ribs.

"Now you know what it was like for me," John said quietly.

"Wait, John!" James tried to plea.

"Face your sins," John said.

James lifted a hand to defend himself, as if shielding his eyes from intense sunlight. The cries that met John's ears were unlike anything he had ever heard from his father. It made him hesitate. But the rage he felt won over.

John used his right hand to grab his father's outstretched wrist, and he yanked it hard, away from his face. John then proceeded to use his left fist to beat his father into unyielding submission. Every memory of his childhood, every fearful moment, every lick of his father's belt, and every tear he had shed would be taken out upon the man responsible, here and now.

Blow after blow after blow slowed James's reactions, and soon, he stopped trying to defend himself altogether. He spat blood onto the floor and wept. Tears spilled down his cheeks.

"John," he cried, "stop... please..."

"No!" John roared. "No!"

His fist met his father's already-weakened jaw once again. John felt that even if he wanted to stop, he could not. He would not.

"John," James wept loudly, though his words were hard to understand with the blood that flooded his mouth. "John... listen to me."

"Listen to you?" John almost laughed.

He hit his father again, but the blow came less intense now that his own exhaustion was catching up to him.

"John," James cried.

John finally, for the first time since barging into the room, met his father weepy eyes. They were pleading. They were in agony. They were... innocent. They were not the eyes of his father.

John hit his father again, but this time, it was not by his will. It seemed like his fist flew on its own. He looked into James's eyes then.

"What?" John whispered, confused.

"John..." James whispered hoarsely, "you are hurting me."

"I--"

John looked at James. Something was wrong. He felt his body tense to strike again, but his mind overcame this impulse. He suddenly felt sick. His chest was hurting. He rubbed at it, and when he lifted his hand, it felt wet. Looking down at his chest, there was no injury, but on his fingers was a black, sticky liquid. He looked into his father's eyes once more, and the realization dawned on him.

"Oh, God," he whispered. "Eli?"

James nodded.

WHY ARE YOU STOPPING? *a hellish voice erupted through John's mind.* KILL HIM!

John felt his chest explode with a burning sensation that made him scream. It dropped him to his knees, and he wailed as it felt like fire was searing his flesh.

"HELP ME!" John screamed.

James rushed out of the room and soon came back with a familiar knife: the same knife that he had used to cut the rune from Eli's chest. James leaned closely to John, his face a grotesque, swollen mass. But his brother's eyes locked with John's, and John knew.

"Hold still," James said, though the voice that came out of his mouth now belonged to Eli.

John screamed as the knife began to slice at his chest. John's mind erupted with thousands of hellish voices. He identified and honed in on the voices of his father and of the wolf. They screamed over one another, and he felt his mind was splitting.

THERE IS NO RUNE, JOHN!

HE HIS KILLING YOU!

YOU WILL DIE HERE!

WE AWAIT YOUR SOUL IN HELL!

YOU CANNOT ESCAPE!

"The rune is gone!" John screamed. "You are killing me! You are killing me!"

"You need to trust me!" James shouted.

The pain was unbearable, and John tried to fight off the shadow of his father, who only pressed more of his weight on him and continued to slice into John's flesh. John grabbed James by the throat and began choking him with all of his might.

"GET OFF ME!" John heard himself yell.

James continued to slice at John's chest despite being choked. John then mustered the strength to throw James off of him and threw himself on top of James, strangling him now in the dominant position. James slashed at John's chest again, and John screamed. The pain was too much.

KILL HIM, JOHN!

HE DESERVES DEATH!

John was no longer in control of his body now. And he quickly realized that perhaps he never was. He felt himself squeezing the life out of his father, who gathered the last of his strength to lunge with the knife one more time. John's chest erupted in pain, and he retreated from his father; James began coughing and gasping for air, now out of John's reach.

SEND HIM TO HELL, JOHN!

KILL HIM!

John felt weak, and he ignored the voices in his head. He felt his body trying to attack James again, but John willed himself to focus on another voice that was fighting for his attention: Eli's.

"John," Eli said, though it was quiet and was almost drowned out by all the others that were yelling. "John, come back. Focus on my voice now. Come back."

Soon, the voices faded, then they disappeared altogether.

John opened his eyes and what he saw before him almost brought him to tears.

Eli's battered and bloody face came into view. His once-soft features were now grotesque, bruised, and swollen. John looked at his chest and saw that his shirt was torn open, the rune nothing more than a bloody gash. His chest hurt, but it was no longer a pain stemming from the supernatural. There was no longer black ooze, only blood from his body. He groaned and sat up slowly. He looked around. They somehow had gone into the barn. Eli tossed the knife aside and leaned against the wall of the barn.

"Who do you see?" Eli asked, pained.

John rubbed his eyes, squinted, and made certain that this was neither illusion nor dream. Tears filled his eyes at his brother's injuries.

"I see you, Eli," John whimpered.

Eli nodded and wiped the tears from his own eyes.

"Eli..." John began, but he knew there was no way he could apologize for what had transpired. This was unforgiveable.

He looked past his brother. The barn door was broken on its hinges.

"I hurt you," John whispered after a moment.

Eli met his brother's eyes through swollen lids and nodded. And in that moment, John's heart broke.

Chapter 20
Of John's Remorse

John and Eli sat quietly in the cottage. They had gathered spare cloths and created a makeshift bandage for John's chest that slowed the bleeding. When this was done, they sat next to each other in silence and stared out the window into the night. John could not bear to look upon his brother, so when Eli spoke (as difficult as it was for him, given his injuries), John remained fixated on the night sky.

"John?" Eli asked.

"Yes?" John replied hesitantly.

"Why did you keep it a secret?"

"Keep what a secret?" John asked, feigning ignorance, though he knew what the follow up question would be.

"The rune," Eli said with a heavy sigh. "The wound in your chest. It was the same as mine, so you cannot possibly have thought that it was nothing to be concerned about."

John sighed and then was quiet. No answer he could give would be good enough, and he knew it. There was no excuse for the cowardice that he had felt when he first saw it. There was no excuse for keeping it secret from his brother, and because of that cowardice and secrecy, it had been the hag's way of seizing control over his actions and mind. He felt that he would weep if he spoke, so he remained quiet.

"John," Eli said, "you need to talk to me."

"I know," John said quietly, voice filling with uncontrollable emotions.

They were quiet for a while as John thought about what to say. They stared out the window, still searching for anything or anyone who could cause more harm to them.

"I was scared," John said finally.

"You were scared?" Eli asked. "Of what?"

"When I saw that thing on my chest, I was petrified of what could happen," John said, his guilt now cascading over his features. "And after what I did to you when you received the same wound, I..."

John trailed off, and Eli allowed him to gather himself. John began to shift uncomfortably in his chair. They both felt a sickness in their stomachs over what John was about to say.

"I did not know if cutting it off of you would do any good," John said. "I took a chance on you. I did not want to take that chance with myself. And after seeing how much pain it brought you, I did not want to have to experience that myself. I was terrified. I thought maybe... somehow it would not affect me. That somehow I could resist. I was a coward. I was selfish. I--I put myself ahead of you, Eli."

John was sobbing now. Eli rested a hand on his shoulder.

"I am sorry," John wept, "I am so sorry."

Eli had already forgiven his brother the moment he came back to reality back in the barn, but he knew his brother. Eli would verbalize forgiveness after he had taken time to come to terms with it, when he would be able to accept Eli's forgiveness.

"I will keep watch tonight," John said through his tears. "Try to get some rest."

Eli nodded and did as he was told. When he was in bed, he looked toward John; a question had been nagging at him.

"John?" Eli asked.

"Yes?" John replied from the chair.

"What did you see?" Eli asked. "You called me 'Father'."

John was silent, and Eli wondered if he would ever receive a response. Then finally, John spoke.

"Get some rest," he said. "I promise I will try and explain tomorrow. I promise you that."

Eli closed his eyes, and despite his injuries, the excruciating pain that he was experiencing, and the fear of the hag, he found a way to sleep. And this time, his sleep would not be disturbed in any way, and in the morning, he would thank whomever listened to such a prayer for that bit of peace.

Chapter 21
Of the Musket's Retrieval

The morning came, and John gently woke Eli from his slumber. Eli recoiled from him with a gasp, half expecting John to attack him again. John retreated and sat down; he understood his brother's reaction, but still, his feelings were hurt.

"I am sorry," Eli said softly after seeing his brother's face fall, "I did not mean to--"

"No," John said, holding a hand up, "it is fine. I understand. I am sorry for what I did to you, and I do not expect you to just forget what happened."

Eli nodded and watched John's sad eyes avoid his. They shifted to the window and observed the dawning of a new day.

"I left the musket out there," John said after a moment of contemplation. "As well as the hatchet."

Eli did not respond, fearing what John was about to suggest.

"I would feel better if we were to get them," John said. "She is still out there somewhere, and those... would be a big help should she return."

Eli knew he was right, but the idea of going into the forest did not sit right with him. Then again, perhaps with the sun's light to guide them...

"Do you want me to go with you?" Eli asked.

"I think it would be best," John said. "I do not think we should split up."

Eli nodded in agreement. A nagging feeling came over him then, a precautionary warning of sorts that was brought to the forefront of his mind.

"Turn around, and let me look at you," Eli said.

"What?"

"Do not argue," Eli ordered sternly, which took John off guard. "Take off your shirt, and turn about."

John stood, removed his shirt, and turned in a circle as Eli observed him closely. Eli raised John's arms to double check; satisfied, he backed away.

"Alright," Eli said.

"What was that?" John asked.

"Checking to make sure she has not marked you again," Eli said almost bitterly.

John noted the coldness of Eli's tone but understood it. He nodded.

"Alright then," John said. "Shall we go?"

Eli carried the knife loosely in hand as they walked into the woods. He felt braver with it, especially after last night. They walked together, keeping an eye out for any signs of the witch or her spies. They both half-expected to see a flurry of crows with their bulging white eyes coming to peck out theirs, but nothing happened. Instead, what they were met with was the unnerving and unparalleled silence of the wood. The only sounds came from their footsteps. The brothers became so consumed by the silence they experienced, when Eli finally worked up the courage to ask the question that had been gnawing at him, they both jumped from the noise.

"Are you going to tell me?" Eli asked.

"Tell you what?" John replied.

"Last night," Eli said, "you promised you would explain what happened. I think… I think you owe me that much, at least."

"She got hold of me, made me see things, and I hurt you," John said quickly.

"No," Eli said. "No. That will not do, John. You promised me."

John looked into his brother's eyes. His face was still swollen, and the bloody welts had scabbed. Eli's once-beautiful face was now just a reminder of John's suppressed violence. The guilt stabbed John in the gut, and he looked away from Eli, debating what should be said. He had never told anyone about his childhood, not even Eli.

John knew, without a shadow of doubt, that Eli would not judge him. But when it came down to it, he felt scared and ashamed, that confronting, or even acknowledging, his past would make him seem weak or cowardly. He always wondered what would happen if he were to be asked about certain things from his childhood. He had already come up with excuses for a future wife. If she were to see the oddly-shaped scarring on his back and ask about them, he had come up with several stories about working on the docks and a cargo accident. He had rehearsed such stories over and over in his head until even John began to convince himself that these false events were the truth. A cargo or shipping accident sounded much better than having to explain how in his father's drunken rage, he had gone too far with the leather belt or thrown a bottle that shattered against his flesh; in that instance, John had had to pick the pieces out himself and keep the wounds from staining his clothing.

The lies he had created for himself never truly satisfied him. He was always reminded, either in nightmares or daydreams, the truth of these matters and his father's shadow were always there to remind him of everything that had happened.

John looked toward Eli again and gazed into his pleading eyes. Those eyes that begged for the return of his protective older brother. John opened and closed his mouth. He had no idea what to say.

"John," Eli said softly but firmly, "why did you call me 'Father'?"

John almost found the words. *Almost.* But James had appeared from the shadows over Eli's shoulder. A shade, a phantom of their father, stared blankly at John just a few feet behind Eli. John's mouth fell open, and his eyes widened. Terror mixed with rage flooded him, but he found a way to compose himself.

"What will you say, John?" James asked quietly.

Eli noticed John's gaze looking past him. He wondered if it was the witch or maybe animals under her possession. Eli turned slowly, cautiously, around. Nothing. Nothing but the trees and the leaves filled his vision.

"What are you looking at?" Eli asked, looking back at his brother.

"You do not see him?" John asked, still staring at his father, who had not moved even slightly.

Eli turned around again. A gentle breeze drifted past, picking up some leaves upon the ground, but Eli saw nothing. He shook his head. John's brow furrowed; puzzled, he pointed directly at James.

"Right there!" John said. "Right behind you!"

Eli looked once more but still nothing. Concern ghosted over Eli's disfigured features.

"He cannot see me," James hissed softly with a laugh, "only you."

John opened and closed his mouth like a suffocating fish out of water. He removed his shirt and checked himself for any visible runes in his flesh. Nothing. Eli began to back away from John.

"What is wrong?" Eli asked him.

John looked up and saw Eli taking careful steps backward. His hand was tightening on the knife's handle. James had disappeared.

"Wait," John said, "I am not crazy. I am not."

"What is going on?"

"I just need to think," John said.

"Alright," Eli said, not moving away anymore.

John could feel his father's presence behind him, but when he looked, no one was there. As soon as he turned again, the presence returned and hovered inches from his ear.

"What will you say, John?" James's voice whispered to John. "Will you tell him how you are not as big and strong as Eli has always been led to believe? How you are just a scared, insignificant runt without any hint of greatness to you? Your brother at least got himself educated. And yet, you dragged him down to your world. A farmer. Eli could have been something if not for you. There you go again, ruining the lives of your family, but... what else should I expect?"

John said nothing. Shame and guilt flooded his eyes as he looked at Eli again. His younger brother, who he had hurt so badly, stared curiously back at him.

"John," Eli said, "I just want to know the truth."

James meandered slowly between the two brothers. He smiled at John then began walking in circles around him.

"What will you tell him, John?" James asked. "Perhaps you should rehearse the cargo story again?"

John's heart raced furiously. His father's presence was not real. It could not be. The weight of the burden his father inflicted on him was so great, he felt his knees shake. John looked into Eli's eyes and felt the tears form. A single tear fell, and Eli stepped closer to his brother.

"John," Eli said voice breaking slightly, "what is wrong?"

John knew he could no longer carry this anymore. His mind was overwhelmed, and he could no longer hide it from his younger brother. If they were to die by the hands of phantoms or witches or demons, he would finally give some relief to his heavy-laden heart.

"He is here," John whispered.

"Who is?"

"Father."

"John," Eli said, "I do not understand."

"Eli... he is here. He is next to you right now, and he is laughing at me."

Eli looked but did not see anything.

"John, you are scaring me."

"Eli, please, just listen to me," John said. "I am trying, alright? I am trying."

Eli remained silent and watched his brother struggle to form words. He struggled to fight off the emotions that gripped him. John finally spoke.

"I do not know why, but Father is here," John said, "He is leaning against that tree over there. I do not know what devil magic this is, but he *is* there, Eli. For some days, I have heard his voice. I saw him the other night in the woods, and he is here again. He... he is the reason I hurt you last night, Eli. I thought you were him."

"Why would you hurt him?" Eli asked.

John felt a knot form in his throat. This was it, the moment he had tried so hard and for so long to run from. The truth. He found it difficult to speak, even more so as his father glared down at him, his eyes sinister and fiery, from a branch hanging above the brothers.

"I did not have a... good or pleasant upbringing, Eli," John said slowly with his eyes closed. "Our father--"

"YOU WEAK, PATHETIC LITTLE SHIT!" James roared in John's ear.

John recoiled slightly but focused on his little brother. Focusing on Eli, the one person he cared about, brought him an unfamiliar strength.

"He hurt me," John said, tears spilling down his cheeks. "He hurt me so badly, Eli."

Eli's eyes widened.

"When I was a boy, he beat me," John explained quietly through painful sobs. "He beat me into submission; I would cry, and he would laugh. He would say I was worthless and useless. A waste."

"DO YOU TRULY THINK THIS WILL BRING YOU PEACE? YOU ARE NOTHING! YOU HAVE ALWAYS BEEN NOTHING!"

"He would get drunk and wake me in the middle of the night to satisfy his anger," John continued, ignoring James's screaming. "I... I was so scared all of the time, Eli."

John cried then. Like a young child, John talked through tears, and Eli watched as his older brother hugged himself tightly, as if holding himself together. The sight made Eli's eyes wet. This was a sight unfamiliar to Eli, and he beheld it in silent shock. His older brother, who exuded such strength and confidence, was now this broken husk of sadness and despair. The ugliness of John's childhood spilled out in a flood of tears so uncontrollable, Eli thought he would drown in them.

"I just wanted him to love me," John cried, "I just wanted his approval. I wanted to prove I was someone. Something. I wanted to prove that I was not worthless."

"That is why you left," Eli said almost inaudibly, eyes widening further.

John nodded furiously, keeping his eyes firmly shut still.

"YOU ARE WORTHLESS! NEVER FORGET THAT, JOHN! YOU ARE NOTHING! YOU ARE LOWER THAN DIRT! LOWER THAN SHIT!"

"He made me afraid," John continued, "and nothing I did could ever make him see my worth. I was a burden to him. A curse."

John's legs gave out, and he collapsed to the ground. He sat, put his face in his hands, and wept.

"I was never his son," John cried. "I was always so afraid of him until I just could not take it anymore. I fought back. I wanted to hurt him like he hurt me. So, what I saw last night was something I had envisioned night after night when I was a boy. The witch showed me our childhood home. She made me see you as our father. And I did what I always wanted to when I was younger. I wanted to kill him, Eli. I wanted him to die so many times. She found that piece of myself and exploited it."

John wept and felt a comforting arm wrap around his shoulders. Eli was next to him now, weeping with him.

"I stood up to him once," John said, "but that did not help me get what I really wanted."

John took a deep breath and tried to calm himself. But when he finally realized what he truly wanted all those years, he felt himself begin to give in to his sadness again.

"YOU ARE NO SON OF MINE!"

"I just wanted a father…" John whispered then.

Silence settled over the wood. James was no longer shouting. Eli was beside John and was holding his older brother in his arms.

"I am sorry, John," Eli whispered, "I am so sorry."

John nodded slowly, eyes still shut. The shade of his father was gone now. When John opened his eyes, he felt the burden, the weight of his father's actions, was alleviated, in a sense. And when he looked around, he did not see James. He took a deep breath and slowly exhaled his demons away. He embraced his brother.

"I was scared to tell you," John admitted.

"Why?"

"I did not want you to think less of me."

"Less of you? You are my brother," Eli said, "and you could never be anything less than the greatest man I have ever known."

John smiled and blinked away the fresh tears. The brothers sat there together, and a blanket of peace settled over them. Despite everything that had happened, they felt that, in this moment, nothing could touch them. They separated then, and John wiped at his eyes. He looked around and spotted James off in the distance, further in the woods. His father stared the two of them down from afar. John pointed.

"He is there again," he whispered.

Eli's eyes widened when he followed John's gaze. He saw James now. Eli felt like a curtain had been pulled away from his eyes, and he saw James standing there, still as a statue, watching them. His brow was furrowed, and he seemed puzzled by the two of them. He looked down at the ground then slowly walked away, disappearing behind a cluster of trees.

"I saw him," Eli said, fear coloring his voice. "Why? How?"

John did not answer. But in his heart, he had a feeling, a fleeting feeling that passed almost as quickly as it had come, that their father would not come back to haunt him again. The weight had been lifted. He took a deep breath and stood then, helping his brother off the ground. The musket and hatchet lay waiting for them behind a nearby tree.

Chapter 22
Of Eli's Departure

John pulled in the reins of the wagon as he arrived in front of the house. He looked at his childhood home and felt the memories engulf his mind like a high tide. How many times had his father instilled fear into him in this place? How long had he silently accepted the undeserved punishment until he realized the son could overtake the father? John did not know these answers. But he was glad that this was the last time he would ever see this house and hopefully the last time he would see James.

John stepped onto the porch and raised a steady hand to the front door. He knocked three times. Hard. He waited patiently. No answer. He knocked on the door, harder, a few more times until he heard James's loud reply.

"ENOUGH! I am coming!"

The door swung wide, and John stared into the eyes of his aging father. Recognition soon filled James's eyes when he took in the sight of John, who was now taller and more well-built than when they last saw each other.

"So," James said narrowing his gaze, "you have come back. All grown up, it would seem. The world chew you up enough that you have come crawling back?"

"No," John said confidently, "I have been working. Doing anything I could to start making a life for myself. And now that I have completed what I set out to, I have returned for my brother."

James scoffed but did not say anything.

"Where is he?" John asked.

"ELI!" James shouted from the door without moving.

Slow footsteps came from behind him, and soon, Eli appeared before them. His face was downcast, and his eyes were gloomy.

"Yes, Father?" Eli asked.

"Your brother has come," James said.

Eli's head snapped upward, now registering John's presence. John smiled at his younger brother, who was now in his late teens and looking lovelier than he had remembered. Eli did not return the same expression, however. His eyes recognized his older brother, and they held a spark of joy seeing him; however, they also held a different look. A darker look. As if something had happened in John's absence.

"You alright, Eli?" John asked plainly.

Eli nodded quietly but averted his eyes from his brother's curious gaze. John felt the tension and brokenness rolling off of Eli; he grabbed James by the collar of his shirt, pinning him to the doorframe. A hot rage coursed through him.

"You did not take my warning seriously, did you?" John said through gritted teeth.

James's eyes were filled with terror for a moment, but they were also honest and true in his reply.

"I did not touch a hair on his head," James said, trying to shield his face from any incoming attack, "I swear it. I drank but kept to myself all these years!"

John turned his head to Eli, still keeping a tight grasp on his father's shirt.

"Is he lying?" John asked. "Be truthful. Did he harm you?"

Eli shook his head. John faced his father once again and looked into the now old and fragile man's eyes. There was no lie. James had not touched Eli. So why was Eli so different now? Probably because of the teachings of adolescence: he was no longer the young boy he once knew. Still, he had a promise to keep. John released James and turned to Eli.

"I have come back, little brother," John said with a reassuring smile. "I promised you, right? I said I would return, and so, I have."

Eli nodded blankly.

"I have a plot of land," John explained, "a farm I have begun to build and... if you still want to come with me..."

Eli looked up at his brother, and that childlike look of wonder and admiration he had when he was a boy flashed over his features, only for a brief moment.

"He will not," Katherine said, suddenly appearing as if out of thin air. "He will remain here with me. And your father."

John looked at his mother now. The ignorant woman who had never raised a hand to stop his childhood trauma now stood between Eli and his freedom, and John frowned at her. He had considered himself an orphan growing up, living in a house of strangers, and now, it was her that was going to try to stop him? John thought this odd.

"Interesting, Mother," John said, still frowning. "Why this sudden need for Eli to stay? Is it penance for never having been a mother to me?"

"Please," Katherine scoffed, "your younger brother is actually useful around here."

She rested her hand on the back of Eli's neck, and she seemed to give him a gentle caress. A slight shudder ran through Eli's body that did not escape John's notice. His brows furrowed.

"I see," John said. "However, I do not think it is up to you. Eli is his own man. You are what? Seventeen or eighteen now, is that about right? I think he can make his own decisions, do you not agree?"

Eli remained silent. Katherine scoffed again. The smug look on her face made John's blood boil.

"He is incapable of making wise decisions on his own, Johnathan," Katherine offered with a grin. "Besides... Mother knows best."

The way she said that made John's blood go from boiling to ice cold in a flash. Something was very wrong about what was going on here. Katherine had never cared, even slightly, for John growing up, so why the change of heart with Eli? And her smile, that damned smile, was something sinister, indeed. John looked at Eli, whose face was still downcast, and tried to put on a face his brother would recognize: the same look of intensity and compassion that he had displayed when he made that promise to him as a boy.

"Eli, look at me," John said softly.

Eli did so. His eyes were sad, pleading almost.

"It is your choice. Not his. Not hers." He indicated their parents. "And regardless of what she says, you are free to make any choice you desire. I have the wagon and the horses there. You do not even need to worry about packing anything. I made a promise to take care of you, and I intend to do just that. Now, if you have changed your mind, I will understand. As best I can, I will understand. But I will not be able to return or visit you often, even less so than I have these past years. I also will not say where I am going, so if you wish to come along..."

John trailed off as Eli meekly looked toward Katherine, who was glaring at the eldest son with a vicious guise that even John found off-putting.

"I think you should go, Johnathan," Katherine said sternly.

"That would be best," James muttered.

John locked eyes with his parents then with Eli, who was still unmoving, seeming like a petrified mouse: small and scared. John extended a hand to his brother, who shook it weakly.

"Farewell, little brother," John said sadly. "I... wish you luck."

He turned and walked dejectedly toward the wagon. He patted one of the horses and pulled his straw hat from its resting place on the seat. He looked toward the house once more and saw the front door slam. He took his place on the buckboard, put on the hat, and picked up the reins. He sighed and began steering the horses back toward town.

A million questions flooded his mind. That woman held blatant control over Eli, and he wondered what had happened to destroy Eli's spirit in such a way that rendered him effectively unresponsive. It terrified John to think of such things, but his brother had not argued her decision, so John would not argue either. He sighed again and gave the reins a snap. The horses began to trot.

"JOHN!"

John whirled his head around. Eli was sprinting toward the wagon. James was yelling from the porch, and Katherine was trying to run after him despite her heavy dress. She was screaming frantically at Eli like a banshee.

"JOHN!" Eli shouted again.

His little brother was crying as he dashed for the wagon.

"GET BACK HERE!" Katherine shrieked.

Eli reached out as he neared the front; John grabbed his frail arm and pulled. His own strength surprised him as he easily swung his younger brother onto the platform. Katherine was still sprinting, shrieking, at their backs. John lifted the reins and gave them a hard snap that sent the horses into a fierce gallop. Katherine was screaming obscenities that fell on deaf ears. Adrenaline coursed through John. He looked to see if she was still trying to follow, but *that would not matter soon as the horses took them further and further away. Behind him, he thought he saw Eli sobbing into his hands. He reached back and ruffled his hair.*

"Do not worry, Eli," John said, "you are safe now. I will keep you safe. You will never see them again."

Chapter 23
Of Eli's Phantom

The brothers returned to the farm without hindrance, save for the unnerving quiet. The silence around them as they walked back seemed to be an adversary against their minds in its own right. John was lost in the memory of when he and Eli abandoned their childhood home (if he dared to call it a home); so enveloped in his own mind, he gave no thought to his surroundings. Eli mostly stayed alert to the environment, constantly looking this way and that for any sign of the witch or anything under her command, but no threats appeared to stop them.

They entered the cottage, and John set the musket and hatchet on the supper table then sat on his bed, resting his head in his hands. The emotional impact of his confession had drained him. He began removing his shirt with a yawn.

"Are you tired?" Eli asked.

"I am," John said, tossing the shirt to the floor and rubbing at his puffy eyes.

Eli studied his brother. Questions about what he had just learned plagued him.

"John?" Eli asked.

"Hm?"

"May I ask you something?"

"Of course," John said, laying down and closing his eyes.

"Everything you told me," Eli said, "about our father. It is all true?"

"Every word," John sighed.

"So those scars..." Eli said softly. "Those were not from building this place, were they?"

John was quiet a moment and then answered, "No."

"Father is responsible for all of them?" Eli asked.

"Yes," John replied simply.

"You did not have to lie about how you got them," Eli said.

"I was not ready to tell you the truth, Eli," John said. "I did not believe I ever would be ready to tell you the truth. But seeing our Father and hearing his voice in my head... It was like a plague, Eli. And to be honest, I am not certain that I will be spared of his presence from now on. But if we are to die here, I would rather you know the truth. Why I hurt you, what that witch has been making me see. I did not want my history to consume me. I had to tell you. More than that, I *needed* you to know... I feel better. Not healed from it, by any means, but I do feel more..."

John was quiet, and Eli waited for him to finish his thought.

"What, John?" Eli asked. "You feel more what?"

John opened his eyes and looked at his injured brother. He gave him a small smile.

"I feel more free," John said, a glimmer of relief in his eyes.

John then closed his eyes and fell asleep almost immediately. Eli grabbed a chair and sat by the window to keep watch.

Eli sat there for a long while contemplating much of what had transpired. In the forest, how was it possible for

John to see their father? How long had he been experiencing shades and phantoms of him and keeping it secret? Too long, it seemed. And why could Eli suddenly see him? Even if for the briefest of moments, Eli knew he had seen their father in that forest. But Eli could only see him when John finally released his demons.

His thoughts wandered as he stared at the wood. His mind went to the witch. She was out there *somewhere*. He wondered why she bided her time. Why was she hiding from them? To cause further torment, surely. Or to starve them out? Eli did feel the pangs of hunger stab at his stomach and wondered how long it would take to die from starvation. What if that was her plan? Starve them to the brink of death and then do... God knows what? He was constantly afraid that she would come back to the farm, but if there was no escape for them, why must she wait? If death was to come to them, better to face it sooner than later and put them out of their misery.

This dark train of thought held sway over Eli. John eventually stirred in his sleep, and the noise made Eli's head snap in his direction. He half-expected John to rise from the bed, visions seizing control over him. Terror thundered in his heart for a moment, but when he saw John settle back into a deep sleep, Eli exhaled in relief. He turned back to the window and felt a scream catch in his throat. The chill running down his spine was like an icy tundra, and Eli felt he would collapse.

His mother was wandering near the well. Her skin was pale, and the dress she wore was dirty and torn. She was barefoot, sauntering through the fields. Eli felt his legs shake and his lower lip tremble. She strolled around, looking around aimlessly as if confused by her surroundings.

"J-John," Eli whispered urgently.

Katherine's head snapped in Eli's direction. Her eyes pierced his soul, and Eli felt he might relieve himself.

"J-John," Eli whispered as Katherine took a slow step in the cottage's direction, "wake up."

She came closer. Each step was slow but determined, and Eli's heart hammered within his chest.

"John, please..." Eli whispered his plea.

John remained undisturbed in his slumber. Katherine stood some ten feet from the cottage window and locked eyes with Eli. He thought he would pass out as a smile stretched across her lips.

"Hello, Eli," she cooed. "Are you ready?"

Eli trembled so violently, his knees knocked together. He shook his head. This response wiped the smile from Katherine's lips. She took another step.

"Why do you look at me like that?" she asked. "Are you not happy to see me?"

Eli wanted desperately to cry out for John to wake up, but the words caught in his throat as his mother approached. Eli was petrified and remained rooted to the spot. As she moved nearer to the door, she disappeared from his line of sight. Still, he knew she was now standing just outside the door. A cold sweat beaded on Eli's forehead. The door creaked open slowly, painfully slowly, as if relishing in his agony. Eli prayed for something, *anything*, to intervene on Katherine's entrance, but nothing came.

Eli stood facing his mother. She watched him closely. The unnerving smile returned, and Eli's mouth hung open, unable to scream. She took another step closer. The floorboard that normally creaked did not make a sound under her bare foot.

"My beautiful boy," she whispered with an eyebrow raised.

"No," Eli choked out.

Katherine then removed the sleeves of her garment at the shoulders. Her dress cascaded to the floor effortlessly, and she stepped over the discarded heap. She then stood mere inches from Eli, nude and smiling. She ran her tongue over the edges of her top teeth and looked at her youngest son like a predator would its prey.

"You do not want to disappoint me, do you, Eli?" she asked as she removed the pin that held her hair in place.

Eli tried to shut his eyes tightly enough so that when he opened them, she would be gone. But when he opened them, she was only leaning closer to him. Her hair flowed past her shoulders and encircled her breasts.

"Mother," Eli whispered, pleading. "Mother, please, no."

"Hush now," she whispered, "do not speak."

She placed her hands on either side of his cheeks and then kissed Eli's lips softly. Urine ran down his legs and soiled his trousers. The demon he thought he had rid himself of had come back.

Chapter 24
Of Eli's Shame

She was gone. Eli did not know how long she had been there. His mind had automatically gone elsewhere. Drifted away to something happier. He usually imagined he was with Anna. He imagined they were under a tree, laughing together while they exchanged stories as if no time had passed between them. That was normally what he would think about, and although his subconscious mind knew it was only fantasy, it helped pass moments like these with Katherine.

When he snapped out of his dazed state, he watched her walking from the cottage. Her nude form disappeared into the trees of the forest. The dress had vanished from the floor and was nowhere in sight, as if the cloth was a figment of a disappearing nightmare. Eli sat down, placed his face in his hands, and wept. His stomach somersaulted violently, and he swallowed down the rising bile in his throat.

"Oh, God," he wept. "Oh, God. No, no, not again."

John awoke to his brother crying into his palms and immediately rushed to him. He placed a gentle hand on Eli's shoulder and knelt before him.

"Eli?" John asked. "Eli, what is wrong?"

Eli wept harder and did not reply. Disgrace held his tongue in check. John assumed that the stress of their situation had taken its toll on his little brother, so he allowed him time to himself. John walked outside and gave Eli privacy. Even from outside, his little brother's sobs reached his ears in scattered, tortured fragments, and his heart broke for him, even though he had no notion of what exactly had caused his distress.

After some time, Eli came outside, wiping the tears away from his black eyes. They had grown puffier from his tears, and the sight was pitiful. John saw the dark, wet stain of Eli's urine-soaked trousers. He did not ask.

John stood up from the ground and brushed the dirt off his backside. John reached out to offer a reassuring embrace, but Eli recoiled slightly.

"Please," Eli said softly, "do not touch me. I do not want to be touched."

"Alright," John said, taking a step back to give his brother space, "that is alright."

"Can we go to the stream?" Eli asked. "In the forest?"

"I do not think that is a good idea," John said, shaking his head.

"Please," Eli said.

"No," John said, "the witch is still out there, and we--"

"If she wanted us dead, we would be dead already!" Eli snapped. "What is stopping her from ending us here or there? Nothing!"

John was taken aback by his brother's outburst.

"I just want to get clean," Eli said. "And we need water. I am thirsty. Are you not?"

John had not thought about his thirst, but once Eli made mention of it, he became very aware of how dry and parched his throat was. The water of the stream would be refreshing and slake their thirst, surely. But the dangers present in the woods made John pause.

"Are you sure?" John asked.

"I will go without you, John," Eli said firmly.

"No, hold on," John said. "Just let me grab the musket and the hatchet. Might as well see if I can find us something to eat while we are out there."

Eli nodded, and John entered the cottage to grab the supplies. Once armed, they walked to the forest edge and entered. John led, and Eli trudged behind him. Eli stared off into space, hardly blinking. His silence was somehow different to John.

The sun was still in the sky, and though the trees blocked much of its rays, John found it light enough and simple to navigate. However, the air around them was thick with gloom and anguish; it weighed on John's heart. He stayed on the lookout, always expecting to see that witch around every tree or shrub. He even convinced himself the shade of his father was following them, but it was just anxiety beguiling his mind.

Eli, on the other hand, had a very different experience.

The sky had grown dark in his eyes, but John seemingly did not notice. He wanted to ask his brother what he was seeing but instead remained quiet. Eli's mind dwelled on his mother's visit. He trembled and thought he might cry again. He bit his lower lip until the welling tears dried. John occasionally looked back at him, but Eli would avoid his concerned gaze each time. He turned away from John's prying eyes and stared into the collection of trees to his left. Katherine was walking stride for stride with them some yards off. Eli's heart lodged in his throat. A strangled gasp escaped, and John whirled about.

"What?" John asked intensely. "What is it?"

Eli stared at Katherine, who stopped and leaned against a tree, watching him with an expectant stare. Her smile was hellishly devious, and Eli turned to ice as she ran two of her fingers over her lips, her tongue flicking between her lips.

"Eli?" John asked. "Eli, are you alright?"

Eli did not reply. He did not move. He did not blink. He stared in horror as Katherine's fingers traced lightly around her breasts. Her smile grew.

"Eli?" John asked. "What is it?"

John looked in the same direction Eli was staring but saw nothing. He took steps in that direction, looking around the trees, and still, nothing came into view. No witch, no wolf, no James: just the wood. He turned around and faced Eli, who looked past him, entranced.

"Eli," John said urgently, "I need you to talk to me. What is going on?"

"Do not say a word to anyone, Eli," Katherine whispered. "If you do, they will hurt you for being of ill mind. They will kill me. You do not want that, do you?"

Eli shook his head. John frowned and stepped in front of his brother. John blocked the view of Katherine, and Eli seemed to snap out of his terrorizing stupor. He looked John in the eye.

"John?" Eli said.

John nodded, concerned.

"I think she is here," Eli said. "I think she is tormenting me."

"How so?" John asked. "I do not see her, what are you seeing?"

Eli shook his head.

"Are you hearing things?" John asked.

Eli hesitated then nodded.

"Noises or words?"

"Words," Eli said solemnly.

"What is she saying to you?" John asked.

Eli shook his head.

"Keep an eye out," John said. "We are almost to the stream. I will protect you, but you need to tell me if you spot her or anything that she might use against us."

Eli nodded, and they walked on. They arrived at the stream shortly thereafter, and John and Eli both knelt beside it. They each cupped their hands in the water and drank, their eyes ever open and alert. Eli dipped his cupped hands in the water to drink again. When he brought the water to his lips, he noticed Katherine sitting directly across the stream from him. She toyed with the dirt between her thighs suggestively, and her eyebrow was coyly cocked. Eli choked on the water and coughed, falling backwards.

"Eli, are you alright?" John asked.

Eli blinked, and Katherine was gone as quickly as she appeared. He took John's hand and allowed himself to be helped up off the ground.

"What is it?" John asked.

Eli stayed silent.

"You keep seeing something, yes?" John asked.

Eli nodded hesitantly.

"*What is it*?" he repeated urgently.

No response. This frustrated John.

"Eli, you *have* to tell me what is happening with you," John said firmly "You *must*. Let me help you."

"You cannot help me," Eli said softly enough that John could not hear.

"What?"

Eli did not repeat himself, removed his shirt and trousers, and stepped into the cold waters of the stream. He began to shiver as he cleaned his clothing as best he could, then he rubbed at his own body as hard as he could with his knuckles. John watched Eli angrily scrub at himself, a frantic determination in my eyes. He shook his head, confused, then started walking upstream to give him privacy.

"Call out if you need me," John said. "I will do the same. I will try to find us something to eat."

Eli did not reply, continuing to scour his skin. No matter how much and how hard he scrubbed, the shame he felt remained. He should have known this by now as it became routine after so many years in that house with Katherine, but he had forgotten how crippling the humiliation could be. Fresh tears spilled over Eli's cheeks as he felt soft hands caress his shoulders and back.

"My beautiful Eli," Katherine whispered, her words tickling the hairs on his neck.

Eli shuddered but not from the water's cold. He turned slowly and saw Katherine bathing herself before him. She laughed airily when Eli tried to cover himself and look away. Darkness surrounded them; the trees had disappeared, and the sky was now a black abyss. The water slapped against the rocks along the riverbed, and Eli tried to focus on the sound in an attempt to return to reality. But it did not aid him as Katherine stepped closer.

"Why do you avoid me with your eyes, Eli?" she asked, tracing a finger along his chest and encircling one of his nipples.

Eli inwardly screamed for release from this hell. He told himself to wake up. He began to pray, but just as he did, he felt her press her thigh against his groin. His eyes snapped open, and she smiled at him.

"Please," Eli croaked, "I do not want this. Leave me alone, *please*."

"You never objected back home," Katherine teased with a laugh.

"John!" Eli tried to call out, but he could only muster a smothered whisper.

Eli shut his eyes and tried to imagine something happier. Anna and her carefree laughter. The farm when he and his brother first arrived and experienced the freedom of a new life. The thought of never being near that cursed house ever again.

"Do not ignore me," Katherine hissed.

Eli's eyes opened reflexively, as if invisible claws pried the lids apart. Terror filled him as she breathed into his neck and placed a tender kiss at his throat.

"Please, stop," Eli whispered, unable to move.

"Do not speak," Katherine whispered.

"JOHN!" Eli finally screamed.

No response. Katherine chuckled.

"We are alone," she said quietly, "it is just us."

Her fingertips ran down his chest, down his sternum, down his abdomen.

"You do not want to disappoint me, do you?" she murmured.

John filled his pockets with as many of the wild berries as he could carry. It was no protein, but something to eat was better than an empty stomach. He ate directly from the berry bush until he was sick of the sweet juice. John made sure that no berries would fall from his pockets before heading back toward Eli. He looked around, feeling the unpleasant sensation that something was amiss, but when he saw neither apparitions of James nor any sign of the witch, he continued onward.

John realized as he went how much lighter his heart felt since he had told Eli of his childhood. He did not know why, but the weight, the burden, of his experiences was much easier to bear now that Eli knew. He felt that, maybe, he did not have to rely on himself so much anymore. He felt that he was much more clear-minded than he had been in many, many years. Perhaps if they made it through this--

John found Eli sitting in the stream. His clothes were tossed in a soaked heap on the dirt bank. Eli was staring at the sky, eyes wide and horrified. His arms were hanging limply on either side of him, like a marionette severed from its strings. John leaned next to Eli and heard his younger brother's quick, ragged breaths. His cheeks were tearstained.

"Eli?" John asked.

Eli blinked the shock from his gaze, recognized John, and cried violently.

"What is it?" John asked as he sat in the stream beside his brother, not minding getting soaked himself.

Eli only replied with sobs and buried his face in John's shirt.

"I should never have left you alone," John said, beginning to feel his own emotions overwhelm him.

"She is here," Eli said through his cries.

"Where?!" John said, reaching for the musket and looking frantically for the witch.

Eli sobbed further as John left his side, got out of the stream, and paced the area in search of her.

"Eli, where did she go?" John asked. "What did she do to you?"

Eli did not respond. John looked back at Eli as his brother went back to scrubbing roughly at himself with his knuckles. He dunked his hands into the water and rubbed at his chest violently with the tips of his fingers. He then used his nails, scratching feverishly at his raw skin. He continued this same pattern to the whole front of his body, even to his genitals.

"Eli, stop that," John demanded, "you are hurting yourself."

Eli's body shook with sobs as he collapsed and viciously raked his back against the stream floor. Rocks scraped at his back. John rushed to Eli and yanked him from the water.

"I am not clean!" Eli yelled. "I am not clean!"

Eli twisted free from John's grasp, leapt into the water, and scratched at his arms below the surface. Blood began to trickle free. Eli saw the blood and finally regained his senses. He stood up and looked at his brother, who was watching him in confused horror. Eli took a moment to collect himself and calm his breathing. He then exited the stream, picked up his clothes, and dressed himself. He wiped his eyes and stood wordlessly before his brother.

"Eli," John whispered, "what happened?"

Eli said nothing.

"If something happened... if you were in trouble..."

They stood quietly for a long while.

"Why did you not call for me?" John asked.

Eli then stared at his brother. Anguish filled his eyes. Anguish, numbness, and mortification flashed through his expression, and John saw each shift. Eli took a deep breath.

"I did call, John," Eli whispered in a vacant voice.

John saw no dishonesty in Eli's eyes, and a wave of guilt passed through him. Eli wiped his nose with the back of his hand, sniffed, and nodded. He trudged past John, his eyes fixed on the ground. John followed, unable to find any words.

Chapter 25
Of the Dinner of Berries

It was cold, and the night had fallen. The light breeze caused the trees and grass to sway gently to the south in a hypnotic dance. The darkness was deepening, and the light of the moon did little to aid any sense of sight. But It did not need light. It saw everything It needed to.

Its hand rested upon the tree trunk near the tree line. It carefully, silently, watched the two brothers in their cottage. One candle lit their abode, and It observed as they ate the berries they had found in the woods. It was glad, or something close to the feeling (for It did not know what that word truly meant), they had gone to the stream. It had purposefully allowed their safe passage to the water source. What delight could It take in watching them die of thirst? None. It needed to feel their fear: their despair was intoxicating. The ghosts of their pasts caused them such distress, It had become drunk upon their suffering. But the older one, the one called John, had finally become stronger than It had anticipated.

Why did he confess his past to the younger one? Why did he release his sorrow? His anger and fury? Surely, he did not have faith in the younger one to carry these truths alongside him. And yet, It saw that his heart was... lighter. The fear of his father's phantom was no longer present. It growled in Its throat and scratched absentmindedly at the bark of the tree. The nails of Its vessel, the girl It had taken, broke against the wood, and the hand bled. No matter. It would have a new vessel soon. A new puppet.

It breathed in. The vessel needed oxygen. It began planning what was to come next. It could no longer use the phantom of the father as the older brother had opened the younger one's eyes. They both would see. The plan to drive the one called John into madness had backfired. It cursed him to the darkest of pits from where It had been birthed.

It watched the younger one, who was seated silently at their table. He ate quietly and never looked up from his helping. His mind was plagued with what had happened at the stream. With his childhood memories. With the constant feeling of shame.

It moved closer to the cottage. The humiliation, the fear, was an intoxicating aroma that wafted into the sky, visible only to It. It breathed it in deeply. Not with the vessel but with Its own sulfur-filled lungs. To smell it, to smell something other than the noxious pits of Hell, made Its senses somersault with glee. The cloud of anxiety surrounding the young one tempted It to strike then, but It knew It must wait. Now was not the time. It needed them to separate. It needed to break the young one further to make resistance that much more difficult. It watched the older brother then and smacked Its lips. His soul would be delicious. The idea of feasting on *both* of their souls sent It into an exhilarated frenzy. It just needed to break the will of the one called Eli. It sensed that that was close.

A stirring sensation snapped It from Its thoughts, an odd feeling It had not felt in some time. It made It feel nauseated. It retreated to the woods again and used the vessel to pick up a sharp stick from the ground.

You should be asleep! It thought at the girl.

The stirring, the feeling, the nausea flooded Its senses. It forced the vessel to hold the sharp end of the stick against her carotid artery. The feeling was stronger than it had been in years.

"**How are you awake, my dear?!**" It called aloud.

She was yelling. She was crying out. Not the vessel itself but the will of the one who had once occupied the body. The girl. She screamed at It.

Leave them alone! her will cried out.

Now, now! Do not come between a predator and its prey!

They did nothing to you! her spirit screamed. *Release them! They do not deserve this demonic torment!*

"**Silence, my dear!**" It thundered aloud with a laugh. "**Go back to sleep!**"

It forced the vessel to carve a rune into the girl's flesh, another addition to her already impressive collection. Fresh blood flowed down the body of the girl. The stirring of her presence began to subside. The girl quieted down and soon slumbered once more. It sighed. She was growing more impulsive. Stronger somehow. Why did she feel this way for perfect strangers? Why did she impede Its desires? No matter. She slept now. But It knew that the power It possessed over the vessel was dwindling. With each of her attempts to regain control of her body, It felt Itself losing the grasp of the vessel. Soon, the body would die. It knew this. It knew It needed to find a new puppet to host and soon.

John sat in the chair in front of the window and took up the musket. He looked behind him at Eli, who still sat motionless at the table. They had eaten enough berries, the ones that had not fallen from John's pockets, to get by, but the situation seemed grim. Eli had not spoken since the stream, and John, despite his best attempts, could not get a word or response in any form out of him.

"I swear, I did not hear you call," John said softly for the fifth time since arriving at the cottage.

Eli did not respond nor look up. Instead, he stood and went to his bed. He placed the candle beside his bed, crawled under the blanket, and turned his back on his older brother. John heard painful sobs, but they slowly began to die down. Eli cried quietly to himself until he mercifully found sleep.

Despite not understanding what was happening, John felt a small twinge of guilt. What if Eli had come to harm at the witch's hands? Would "not hearing Eli's call" be a valid excuse for his brother's death? John sighed and tightened his grip on the firearm. He knew the guilt would be too much to bear if something did happen to his younger brother. He looked at the musket and knew that if anything happened to Eli, John would find himself staring up at the sky with the barrel of the gun under his chin.

Chapter 26
Of the Brief Separation

John's leg danced madly as he felt the call of nature. He did not want to leave his brother alone but did not want to make a mess either. His bladder screamed at him, and he knew he would have to relent sooner than later. He looked at Eli, who slept soundly. The candle flickered near him, and John made up his mind. He would leave for just a moment, relieve himself quickly, and be back just as quickly. He stood, picked up the musket, and opened the door out of the cottage. It creaked loudly enough that John was almost certain Eli would awaken: he did not. John closed the door gently behind him and walked out to the closest bush. He sighed gratefully as the warm sensation flowed from him.

Eli stirred. He had heard something but was not sure what. He opened his eyes and looked around the cottage. It was empty. The candle still flickered on the bedside table, but where was John? Most likely outside relieving himself, Eli concluded. He settled back down and closed his eyes again. Another noise captured his attention. It sounded like someone had blown air from their lips. When Eli's eyes snapped open, the candle was extinguished.

Eli looked around frantically, fear and anxiety flooding his nerves. The darkness was too much. Eli got out of bed. He tried to find the flint to light the candle again. His blood ran cold when he felt a presence in the room. A soft and steady breath came from somewhere in the dark. He shut his eyes. He knew that she had returned.

"Eli," Katherine whispered, "it is time."

"No," Eli whispered, eyes clamped shut. "No. Leave me. Leave!"

He felt her icy fingers clamp down on his shoulder, her nails digging into his flesh like talons. He cried out. Her strength, unnatural and dominant, allowed her to flip Eli onto his back on the bed. He whimpered in the dark. Tears escaped through his closed lids. He felt Katherine's warm breath tickle his face, and he flinched away from it as if it pained him.

***

John situated his pants back into their proper place and took in a deep breath. The night air was cool and crisp, and inhaling it brought John rejuvenation, clarity of mind. He began sauntering back to the cottage with the musket in hand, using it as a kind of walking stick. As he approached the door, he heard a sudden shout from Eli. John then sprinted for the door. He rammed his shoulder into the door, but it did not open. Instead, the force from his charge was repelled back at him, and he was sent flying.

"What?" John exclaimed, sprawled out on the ground.

The door was not barred nor was it barricaded. John got up quickly and began slamming into the door at full force. Eli screamed.

"Eli!" John called.

The door did not budge in the slightest. He ran to the window in the hopes that he might be able to squeeze through, but he found that the supper table was now blocking his entry. He tried to push the table away, but it was as if the table had been turned to stone, it was so heavy. He threw his body at it, and still, he could not move it even a bit. Eli's cries, though muffled, pierced the air.

"Eli!" John shouted, pounding the door again.

"John?" Eli cried. "Help me, please."

"Open the door, Eli!" John shouted.

"He is busy! Leave us!" an unnatural voice hissed from inside.

John's eyes widened as the voice reached his ears. The witch was in the cottage. John roared like a wounded beast and threw his body at the door again and again. The wood cracked and splintered against his violent attempts. When his shoulder felt like it would give out, he instead attacked the door with the butt of the musket.

"ELI!" John shouted. "I AM COMING! HOLD ON!"

Hell cometh.

Eli wept in the darkness. He felt everything. The indignity, the helplessness, and the hopelessness were like a cold tundra blasting through his flesh. His mind tore at itself as his mother's face engulfed his vision. She smiled. The smile that had torn his mind asunder for so long. Her face melted and twisted into some corrupt, demonic thing. The blood from newly-carved runes in the flesh above her glowing, violet eyes dripped down her cheeks. She screamed in wicked ecstasy, and he howled in terror. His mind filled with perverted memories of his adolescent years. He was a prisoner to her torment. He was her slave. A slave to a depraved mind, a sick mind.

Katherine's warped features began to resemble a feral wolf, her eyes hungry and rabid, as she loomed over him. Eli cried. The door burst open, and John rushed to his brother, who tried to slap him away.

"Eli! It is me. It is just me!"

"Oh, God! No, go away!" Eli cried.

John tried to restrain him but underestimated his younger brother's strength under panic-induced fear. Eli shoved him to the floor, flung himself from the bed, and backed against the wall. John found the candle and lit it with the flint. The flame flickered to life, and the lit wick bathed the cottage in warm light.

John saw that the supper table perfectly blocked the window, but the door had not been barricaded. They were alone. The younger brother was babbling through his tears as he looked around wildly. John inched closer to him and tried to reach out, but Eli cried and smacked the hand away.

"Eli," John said softly, "it is John. Your brother? John."

Eli's eyes slowly focused on John's face. Recognition soon replaced terror, though it was only a mask (and a frail one at that).

"John?" Eli whimpered.

"Yes."

Tears welled again in the Eli's eyes.

"She was here," Eli managed to choke out. "She was here."

"She is gone now," John said.

The terror slowly returned to Eli's eyes, and he mouthed wordlessly.

"No," Eli finally said quietly. "No, she is not."

John looked around and saw the cottage was empty. He set the candle down and looked under their beds. No one. John went to the table and set it back in its typical place with relative ease. The outside was visible once again, and nothing else seemed amiss.

"She is not here, Eli," John said, turning toward his brother.

Eli was pointing at the window, wide eyed. John whirled around to face it. Nothing. John looked back at Eli, brow furrowed. Eli was still pointing, but he had slumped to the floor and seemed to be trying to retreat backwards, despite there being no room for him to move. He was sobbing quietly to himself.

"Eli?" John asked.

"She is there!" Eli said.

John looked again. Nothing had changed. No creature, no person, no witch, nor demon was present.

"Eli, there is no--"

Eli wept and dropped his hands to his lap, as if defeated. John knelt by his side, and Eli recoiled from him. John was saddened by the reaction but did not press.

"Eli," John said quietly, "you need to tell me what happened."

"She was here, John..." Eli whispered.

"The witch?"

Eli did not respond.

"Eli? Where did she go?"

He wept silently, and John found himself losing patience. He grabbed Eli by the shoulders, and Eli screamed.

"Stop!" John shouted. "Eli, stop!"

"Let me go!" he wailed.

"Eli!"

"Let go!"

John slapped Eli, hard. Eli's cheek stung viciously, and he held on to that pain as it slowly led him back to reality.

"John?"

John nodded.

"You... you hurt me," Eli said, softly touching his cheek.

"You gave me no choice."

"She was here, John," Eli whispered again.

"You keep saying that, but where did she go?" John asked urgently.

"I do not know," Eli said.

They were quiet for a while, then Eli mumbled something.

"What?" John asked.

"You left me alone..." Eli muttered again.

John was quiet and contemplated how to answer. There was no answer to give.

"Why?" Eli asked.

"I was relieving myself," John admitted. "It was quick. I did not go far."

"Far enough," Eli said softly. "She came for me, and you were not here."

"I am sorry," John said.

The two were quiet for a long time. The wind outside whispered against the cottage, and the two sat there listening to its tune. Then, Eli broke the silence between them.

"You broke your promise," he said, finding the courage to finally say what had plagued his heart.

"What?" John replied.

"You broke your promise," Eli said.

"Eli, that is--"

"You cannot protect me," Eli said in a flat voice. "You cannot protect us from her."

"Eli, I have done everything I can to--"

Eli glared at his brother, and John fell silent at the willful gaze. Eli felt the shame and fear overwhelming him, but a deeply-rooted rage was also burning him from the inside out. He spoke firmly and evenly, despite the tears in his eyes.

"You could not protect me, John," Eli said. "I cannot blame you. You made sure Father would not harm me, I know that. I remember. He had been drunk before and told me that if it had not been for you, he would have beaten me within an inch of my life. His hand was stayed because of you. I know this. But, John..."

Eli's voice cracked. His emotions were on full display.

"John, you could not protect me from everything."

"Eli," John said, tearful himself, "I do not know how to fight such a monster."

"John, listen to me," Eli said eyes glistening, "I do not blame you. This is beyond us both. But you have to listen to me. I cannot bear it any longer. I... I cannot."

He struggled to find the words. He fought with himself, trying to say something, *anything*. John was silent, knowing that whatever he was about to say was impossibly difficult for him to admit.

"I have to tell you something," Eli said through gritted teeth. "I have to."

"Okay, Eli," John replied gently, encouragingly.

"And I do not know how to say it," Eli offered. "Just... hold on."

John sat with his brother as he fought with his emotions. Guilt and mortification forged an anchor in Eli's gut. Eli felt the need to vomit, but nothing came up when he gagged. He took a deep breath and exhaled slowly, deliberately, expelling his fear of judgment.

"John," Eli said, "you told me what happened between you and Father."

"Yes," John said. "Yes, I did."

"I have to tell you now," Eli said, forcing the words out. "I have to tell you."

"What did he do?"

"It was not, Father," Eli said.

"Then, who?" John asked.

Eli was silent. He shook his head.

"Eli?"

Eli held a hand up and tried to summon the words. A lump formed in his throat, and the anchor in his stomach rocked violently to and fro. He clenched and unclenched his fists.

"I am here, Eli," John said gently. "I am here, and I will always be here."

Eli nodded.

"Who was it?" John asked.

Eli stopped fighting his tears. The lump felt like a boulder in his throat.

"Mother."

Chapter 27
Of Eli's Confession

It had begun simply. She had always been controlling, but she gradually became more... possessive toward him. She demanded to know his whereabouts when he arrived home late or when he went to visit a friend. She demanded to know who his friends were and took an especially great interest in knowing if they were male or female friends. He eventually learned never to speak of girls he fancied or thought were pleasing to his eyes. She only flew into a rage when he spoke about matters like that.

Shortly after she caught Anna and him walking home from school together, she located Anna's home and threatened the girl. Anna never spoke to Eli after that, and soon, Katherine began escorting Eli to and from the school. By the time he turned eleven, she had pulled him from the school entirely and instead insisted upon schooling him herself.

So began his torment.

Katherine noticed Eli was stepping into adulthood. His sweet, boyish face was becoming more handsome than pretty, and his physique, while not as chiseled and defined as a statue, was now more toned and masculine. He was such a beauty to look at. Katherine found herself admiring her youngest son. She realized just how much she enjoyed looking at him.

She had not felt this way about James in a long while. Ever since Eli's birth, he never touched her nor looked at her the same way. She knew where he would spend his evenings, and she knew where he had come from as he stumbled home in the early mornings in such a state of dishevelment. She could smell it on him. But she never pried. She never demanded an explanation for his lies and deceit. Instead, she allowed his neglect to conceive a vile seed that she watered and cared for herself with every smile and lingering glance at Eli.

The darkness of her mind caused her to have an array of imaginings; she often wondered what kind of lover Eli might be. What his soft lips could be capable of. She did not dismiss these thoughts as unnatural. The corruption of her heart and mind instead welcomed her fantasies.

And soon, when it had become unsatisfying to daydream of her son softly kissing her or running his tongue upon her breast, she knew she had to act.

"Eli, it is time for your reading," she called.

They read from one of Eli's texts, sitting together on one of the wooden benches in their common room. As Eli read, he felt his mother shifting closer to him. He ignored this and continued reading aloud, trying to absorb the information displayed. Then, he felt her touch upon his thigh. Again, he ignored this, at first stumbling over a word before regaining himself and continuing. Katherine's touch then turned into a gentle caress, slow and methodical. Eli stopped reading. He felt uncomfortable sitting so close to her, and when he turned to look at her, he realized just how close she was. Her eyes pierced him as if he were looking into the eyes of an unsatisfied lioness. A chill ran down his spine.

"M-Mother?" Eli asked.

She used her other hand to put a finger to his lips. She shook her head to silence him. Her responding smile would haunt him forever. The hand that caressed his thigh traced slowly inward. His thigh twitched involuntarily.

"Eli," she whispered.

Her hand was now lightly grazing his inner thigh near his crotch.

"It is time I taught you... other things," she whispered.

She inclined her head, and he felt her steady breath next to his ear. Her hand massaged him. He was not sure if he had felt her kiss his neck softly. Eli suddenly became aware of his arousal, and he leapt from the sofa in shock and confusion.

"What are you doing?" he demanded.

"Come back here," she said coyly, patting the cushion beside her.

Eli shook his head, and feeling the discomfort of his groin, he held the book over it, appalled, ashamed.

"You do not have to be embarrassed," she said. "It is only natural."

That word would become a subject of debate in Eli's mind for years to come.

"No," Eli said. "No. I do not... I do not know what--"

He stumbled to find the words. He knew that what she was doing was wrong. He knew that something was very wrong about the situation. About Katherine.

"Do not disappoint me, Eli," she whispered.

Eli frowned. He watched as Katherine slipped out of the sleeves of her gown; she smiled as she revealed herself to him. She stood up, the dress falling around her feet. Eli looked away.

"Mother, you are naked," he said dumbstruck.

"Very observant," she teased with a laugh.

She approached him, and Eli shut his eyes, trying to think of something else. He could feel her hot breath on his neck. He flinched from it.

"What are you doing?" Eli asked.

"Open your eyes, and find out," she whispered.

Eli did not want to. The book that covered his humiliating arousal was removed from his hands, and he heard it as it was tossed aside.

"You are becoming a man," Katherine whispered.

Her warm hand pressed against the base of his stomach and trailed downward into his trousers.

"A young man has needs," she said.

A moan-like whimper escaped Eli. Katherine chuckled, as if pleased with his reaction.

"I... also have needs," she said softly.

"I do not think Father--" Eli began.

"Enough," Katherine whispered. "Do not speak of him to me."

He felt the warmth of her hand fondle his groin, and he retreated quickly. His eyes snapped open. He was suddenly furious.

"NO!" Eli shouted.

Katherine stood in shock at his angry and commanding voice. She had never heard this tone from him before. Eli, for the first time, displayed defiance.

"Do not touch me," Eli said.

"How disappointing," Katherine said.

She moved to her gown and dressed again. She smiled at him before tearing the sleeve of her dress. She then slapped herself viciously several times until welts appeared on her cheek.

"What are you doing?" Eli asked.

She grinned sadistically.

"Your father has not touched me since I became pregnant with you," she growled. "Not once has he shown any love to me. When you were born, I became like a disease to him, and now..."

She trailed off. Eli watched her quietly. Her eyes met his, and she gazed intensely at him.

"You WILL do what I tell you," Katherine said, her eyes glistening now, "or I go to town like this. And when the people ask why I cry as loudly as I do, I will be forced to tell them the truth."

"The truth?" Eli repeated quietly.

"That my son has become a tool of the Devil," she said, smiling through feigned tears. "How his heart has filled with unholy lust, and how he tried to... to..."

She began to cry. A convincing act that would have fooled even Eli if he had not known that he was the subject of such accusations. He understood now.

"They... They will not believe you," Eli said uncertainly.

"And why should they not?" Katherine asked. "Why did she insist on homeschooling her son? Perhaps she knew that he was uncontrollable around other girls. That his mind was filled with thoughts from the Devil. Katherine was only trying to protect others from her son, the monster."

"What?"

"And so, he turned on her, and, unable to control himself, he took his own mother forcibly," Katherine continued. "The monster. The abomination. They will surely hang you."

"No," Eli said, his mind screamed at him to flee.

She approached slowly.

"First, they will try you, and when they see me in tears, terrified of your very presence, they will have no choice," she cooed with a grin. "When I go to your father in my state of undress and he sees how you have hurt me, he may just kill you himself. But everyone will know what you are. And what you did to me."

Eli's young mind could barely process what she said. His breathing became shallow and quick. He needed to leave this place. But where could he go? He did not have any friends. He did not know where John was. He could not survive on his own in the wilderness. A chaotic string of thoughts overcame him, and soon, he felt her hands tighten over his wrists.

"So," Katherine said, "you can either obey me, or..."

Eli did not hear the rest. His mind raced, and as she touched him, he went limp and silent. He shut his eyes and began to count in his head. He allowed her to lead him to her bed, and he felt himself sit down. Fear flooded his body. He kept his eyes shut tight, not wanting to see what she would do to him. He tried to ignore his body's betrayal and instead imagine a paradise away from her bedroom. He imagined sailing the ocean with John. He imagined riding horses and flying over forests. But as she caressed him and he felt his arousal, the fairy tale concluded, and he was forced into Katherine's own sick fantasy. He wept as she climbed on top of him, but this did not deter her as the demon in her heart had taken hold. Its talons had sunken too deeply for her to be steered away from her disturbing course.

After that day, Eli retreated into himself. His mind was dark and clouded with thoughts that no boy should have. He found himself confused and guilt-ridden. Guilt that his own mother had bathed him in. He would lie awake at night and watch the door to his bedroom. Sometimes, it would go untouched, but other nights, Katherine would come. In the darkness of his room, he could not recognize her, and he would desperately try to think of other things or imagine another woman. But of course, he always knew in his heart who was truly there. He felt crippling terror every single night, for he knew that what was occurring was sinful and disgusting. While he did not give much credence to what the churches said, he knew that if God were all-knowing and all-seeing, judgment upon Katherine and him would be harsh.

Several years passed with this burden weighing on his heart. Katherine's visits became more frequent as his father aged. Eli had become quiet and obedient to her demands when she came in the night. He no longer groaned or whimpered or cried. He was as still as a statue until she commanded him otherwise. His eyes were empty and had lost the spark of the inquisitive boy he had once been. He did not eat much, and his body became frail. When she came to him, he would turn off his mind. When she tried to speak to him during her vulgar acts, he would respond in a monotone and despondent way.

"Is this not pleasurable?" she would moan.

"Yes, Mother," Eli would respond automatically.

When she left to return to her room, he would return to his proper senses. He would weep. The guilt and shame would become too intense. He would not sleep the rest of the night. His eyes became perpetually bloodshot, and dark circles encased them. When he bathed, he tried to scrub her smell from him. He would scrub so hard, he would break skin, and it was not until this happened that he feel clean. He would sit in the tub and cry quietly to himself.

He longed to be rid of his mother. He longed to leave this house. He longed to be reunited with John. But he had not seen John in years. This made his tears turn bitter.

"You lied..." Eli sobbed.

John had sworn to come back for him. To protect him. Where was he?

"You lied..."

John stared in disbelief at Eli. His younger brother sat against the wall, knees tucked against his chest like a frightening, fragile boy. His cheeks glistened as he fell silent. John became aware that he, too, was crying. John tried to find words, any words at all, to bring some form of comfort to his brother, but what was there to say?

"I prayed for you to return every night," Eli said quietly, staring at the floorboards.

"And she did that to you... for... years," John managed to say, almost inaudibly, as he came to terms with everything Eli had said.

Eli nodded.

"That is why you cannot sleep," John said.

Eli's lower lip trembled, and he nodded. John bit his lower lip to keep from crying again, and he nodded in silent understanding.

"I..." John began, and he felt his eyes well up. "I am sorry."

The brothers were silent for a while. Then, John began to sob angrily.

"I am so sorry," John wept. "I tried. *I tried.*"

"John?" Eli said, confused by his brother's display.

"I tried, Eli," John cried. "I tried to protect you! I could not."

"John--"

"I thought it was our father who would harm you," John continued. "I tried to stay his hand. I tried to make sure you would not go through the same Hell I did, but... I did not think... our own mother..."

John buried his face in his hands. He felt like a failure. Despite his best efforts, he could not protect his little brother. Not from the witch, nor his parents, and not even from himself. John then felt an arm around his shoulder, and he looked up. Eli sat beside him and locked John in an embrace.

"This is not your fault," Eli cried. "You cannot blame yourself. You could not have known."

John embraced Eli in return.

"You *did* stay our father's hand," Eli said tearfully. "You *did*."

They held one another tightly until the tears began to subside. They looked at one another.

"I am sorry I never told you," Eli said. "I did not know... where to begin with it. I just... I was scared."

"Of what?"

Eli began to get teary-eyed again. "I was scared you would find me repulsive. A... monster."

"No," John said, "you are my brother. And I love you. It was her fault, and nothing more. She was sick, *she* was the monster. You cannot blame yourself."

Eli nodded, and John hugged his brother once more.

"Thank you for listening," Eli murmured into his brother's shoulder. "I feel... better... Not good, but..."

"Better," John finished for him.

They separated, and John stood up. He looked around the cottage and saw the light from the slowly-approaching dawn brighten the room. He felt that the air around them was lighter. The weight on both their hearts, while not altogether gone, had been lessened. John looked outside, and his mouth fell open. Katherine was standing beside the barn, watching him. Eli saw John's face and looked where he did. He saw Katherine, as well. Her phantom stared at them both.

"You can see her?" Eli asked.

John nodded.

"Her shade... How long has she been visiting you?" John asked quietly.

"The past couple of days," Eli replied, stunned that John could now see her.

John grabbed the musket and aimed down the sight. Katherine glared at John and then moved behind the barn, out of sight. The two brothers watched carefully, John's finger resting on the trigger, waiting for his target to appear. Instead, the small, frail form of the witch peeked around the side of the barn. It was light enough for them to see the still-bleeding runes that decorated her limbs. John considered firing but hesitated. His fear of her power after the last time he wounded her stayed the impulse. They could hear a whisper carrying over the wind, and they did not know whether it was something truly audible or just their minds playing some devilish trick. But they both heard it.

Hell cometh.

In the blink of an eye, she had moved to the forest, still watching them carefully from beneath her tattered hood. Blood trickled down her stick-like legs and dripped almost in a rhythm from her fingertips. Then, she turned and walked slowly into the cover of the trees.

"Why does she wait?" Eli asked. "How long must we endure her?"

"Not long now," John replied simply. "I have a feeling that she will return for us very soon."

Chapter 28
Of the Diminishing Puppet

It cursed them. It hated them. And It knew that Its host was weak. It used her to lean against a tree. Small puffs of smoke seeped from the open, runic wound, and It exhaled. It cursed the brothers with all the horrors of Hell. Its time was running short. The girl was waking up again, and her will had grown even stronger. But It knew that It needed a despondent heart, a weary and accepting soul, if It were to find a new host. However, the two brothers, Its prey, had found solace in one another, had bolstered each other's spirits. Their resolve was impressive, and this only angered It further.

Leave them be, her spirit whispered weakly, as if from afar.

It forced the host to sit, and It forced air into her lungs. It felt, for the first time, exhausted. The power It had summoned, the shades of their pasts, had required much from It. It tried to stand but found that the legs were barely responding to Its commands. They lay limp on the ground, twitching sporadically. It grew angrier. The host was indeed weak but more so than It had anticipated.

Leave them be, she whispered again.

Enough! It ordered.

You are losing control, she said faintly. *They are finding their resolve.*

"**Be silent!**" It barked aloud.

Her will chimed with laughter, a chuckle that carried through the air and shattered the dimensions of any shred of confidence and strength that remained for It.

You are scared, she whispered, *I can feel it.*

"BE SILENT!" It roared, the host body quivering with the force behind Its spoken words.

She became quiet, and she withdrew from Its presence once again. It knew It had a small window of opportunity. Its control over the girl was diminishing, and time was running out quickly. It knew that the time for a new host was long overdue. It needed a heart that would accept It. A dark heart, a heart consumed with despair and sadness. It knew It needed to kill one of the brothers so that the other would lose himself to the darkness. Only then would It be able to manifest Itself within the heart.

But It grew afraid. It knew the laws that were passed down at the dawn of man. The balance of the world of Adam had to be maintained, and It knew that directly killing either of them with the powers from the Abyss would only bring about the wrath of more graceful beings to send It back to the Pit. But It yearned to remain on this plane of existence. To live as the seed of Adam. To breathe like them. To walk like they walk. To be one of them. But the laws were clear, and It knew that those same laws would have to be broken that night. But if it meant just one more minute, nay, just one more second, living as one of them, then It would be pleased. Not satisfied but pleased, for at least one fleeting moment.

It forced Itself to use the tree as a crutch and lifted Itself back onto the frail legs of the host. It felt sadness, or something akin to the feeling, for It knew that Its own time was just as short as the two brothers.

Chapter 29
Of the Confrontation

The crow perched atop the barn without a sound. Deep down, it desired to make its presence heard with a warning caw, but the sound was trapped in its throat. Its eyes, milky white, bulged, and the creature was forced to stare at the two men who sat in the cottage. They seemed exhausted, hungry, and weak. The crow attempted to break free of what controlled it but to no avail. It remained fixated on the two brothers, relaying what it saw to the master that enslaved it. The brothers were talking very quietly, too quietly for it to hear anything. The crow's master urged it to find a place where it could hear, but the crow remained.

One of the brothers stood and walked out of view. The other brother, the one with the battered face, was now staring at the raven. The cottage door burst open, and the larger man pressed a long, thin object to his shoulder, pointing it at the crow. Before the crow could take off, a thunderous echo rang through the air. A large cloud of smoke erupted from the object, and the raven felt it being released from its master's control. The pain was momentary, but then, it slipped into the warm embrace of death without a sound.

John waved the cloud of smoke from the musket quickly to clear the air. He went back inside, closed the door, and took his place in his chair, preparing the musket to fire again. Eli looked outside and watched the raven's still form slide off the barn roof and flop lifelessly to the ground.

"Excellent shot," Eli said, impressed.

"It was one of hers?" John asked. "You are certain?"

"The eyes told all," Eli said. "It was the same kind of crow as the forest."

"Then, she is sending spies," John said.

"Why do you say that?" Eli asked.

"Is it not obvious?" John asked with a grunt as he packed another metal ball into the musket's barrel. "She is coming. Soon."

It growled. The brother had shot Its spy, and It knew It did not have the power to spare to send another. It looked at the sky. The night would come soon, and then, It would strike. The idea of feeling human in a more suitable, less miserable state, if only for just a moment, was a mouthwatering temptress. Tonight, It would strike. It summoned the host's strength, and It moved carefully through the woods toward the farm, just a silhouette among the darkened shadows of trees as the sun dipped from view.

John ran his thumb along the edge of the hatchet, and as he determined he was satisfied with the blade's sharpness, he tucked it into his belt. He handed the knife to Eli, who accepted it without much hesitation.

"I am scared," Eli said simply.

"As am I," John replied, "but with you by my side... I think we will be alright."

Eli looked at his older brother and saw a light in his eyes. A hopeful gaze that Eli returned. He nodded to John, and John gave him a sad smile. He pulled Eli in and embraced him tightly. Eli hugged John in return.

"I love you, Brother," John whispered.

"You too, John," Eli said softly.

John looked over Eli's shoulder out the window and saw the witch at the tree line. She stood there like a statue, watching them. John released Eli gently and looked at Eli, who had taken notice of her presence, as well.

"Ready?" John asked.

"No," Eli said, "but how *can* I be ready after what we have already been through?"

"Too true," John said and, to Eli's surprise, chuckled softly.

"What is funny?" Eli asked as he stared at the witch.

"I am not sure," John replied. "I just found that... humorous, I suppose."

They exited the cottage and walked slowly but determinedly toward the witch. The sky was growing dark, and the moon would become their only source of light soon. Still, this did not deter them, nor did their fear and anxiety slow their steps. The source of their torment would be confronted now and, in some ways, had already been dealt with.

It watched them come ever closer to It. Their anxiety was written all over their faces and their reactions as they fidgeted nervously, looking at the host's blood-encrusted runes. It looked over each brother as they came nearer and could not decide which one It would enjoy manifesting more. The young one? Or the strong, older one? It weighed Its options. It lusted for both of their hearts and greedily toyed with the idea of how It might over the both of them. But It knew a decision had to be made and quickly.

John and Eli walked past the well and stood side-by-side some twenty feet from their aggressor. They observed her infirm frame and fragile-looking limbs covered in runes, both fresh and scarred from a time long ago. The brothers both noticed two glowing, yellow eyes, like luminescent orbs, fixated on them from beneath her hood.

A low and sinister hissing was released from her throat. With every exhale, a serpent's call was carried through the air. The brothers' minds were briefly granted an image of a snake offering a tasty-looking fruit from a tree to a nude woman, who ate it greedily.

John shook the image from his head and glared at the witch. Eli's hand tightened around the knife. His fear coursed down his spine like a river of thawing ice. John felt his palms grow sweaty against the musket.

"You are not welcome here," John said, summoning all of his courage.

Hell cometh.

"You have caused enough trouble," John said. "You have caused enough harm to my brother and me."

She stood there. Her head cocked slowly to the side, like a curious dog.

"BEGONE!" Eli commanded with a hateful ferocity that surprised John.

She did not move. The silence around them was deafening. The night sky seemed to grow even darker, and the forest around them seemed to disappear in the abyss of the gloom.

It stood there watching them. They were brave, It granted them that much. Perhaps It had pushed them too far. Perhaps It had truly driven them to madness if they had the audacity to address It in such a way. And the young one? Who was he to command It? How *dare* he?

"Did you not hear me?" Eli said, taking a step forward. "Depart from here and leave us alone!"

It sensed the fear behind the young one's bold words. It could taste his bravado in the air. It hissed low and deliberately. It decided that while the youth of the younger brother was tempting to It, It wanted to feel the strength of the elder. It wanted to consume him. It desired him more than anything in that moment. That look of pure hatred in his eyes reminded It of Its Lord in the Abyss. And so, It made the choice. The young one, Eli, would die so that John would despair and open his heart to Its call.

Leave them alone! the spirit of Its host cried from some distant place.

The brothers watched the witch raise a shaky hand to its opposite wrist. Using a long, talon-like nail, she carved something into herself. Another rune. Fresh blood dripped into the dirt. John and Eli took a hesitant step backwards upon seeing this. John cocked the hammer on the musket and prepared to fire, but how would he know when the time was right? He had to make his shot count. Even when he was truly focused and at his quickest, it would still take far too long to reload the weapon if things went awry.

It felt the girl's presence lethargically drift away and knew that her silence would not last. It heard the click of the musket's hammer cock into place and snapped Its head toward John, who held the weapon with both hands at his waist, relaxed. It noticed a look in the brothers' eyes then: determination, undeterred even by Its presence. For the first time, a new feeling hung in the air. It tasted Its own uncertainty. This confused It.

John made direct eye contact with the witch's yellow eyes and slowly raised the musket to his shoulder. He knew what happened the last time he had wounded her. He could still hear her high-pitched shrieking in his head.

But she *could* be wounded.

"Final warning!" John ordered. "Depart from here. Leave us and allow us to leave, as well!"

It sounded more threatening than he thought he could muster, but John finished his command by taking careful aim at her chest.

Who were they to command It? They were but men. Seeds of Adam. Flesh and bone. Did they truly expect It to obey such empty threats? It hissed and growled at them. They did not move.

"Hell hath come!"

The darkness of the night had reached its peak, and in the gloom, the brothers could only see the witch's silhouette and her bright yellow eyes. John and Eli both focused on those eyes, and John aimed the musket at the space between them. Time seemed to stop, and the silence and the darkness became like looming entities themselves. John gazed into the witch's eyes and seemed drawn to them. He began to see nothing but those glowing orbs, the forest around him dissolving. Her silhouette disappeared, and the moon's pale light seemed to fade. His mind began to race. A thousand thoughts erupted within him, and he feared he would be unable to react if she attacked him or Eli, her power over him rooting him in place.

Take the shot, John!
Shoot her!
She is going to kill you.
Eli is in trouble!
Where is Eli?
John!
Is this Hell?
YOU ARE GOING TO DIE JOHN!
YOU WILL BOTH DIE THIS NIGHT!
John then heard her shriek.

It screamed at them. It knew that their ears would be damaged from the noise, and so, It seized Its chance to catch them at their most vulnerable. Enough talk. Enough play. It was no longer a cat playing with a ball of yarn. It was a predator, and Its prey had willingly served themselves up to It.

It was loud, even to Its standards, and It knew that this would puncture their eardrums, causing them to bleed and rupture. They stood there. It was confused. The young one had his hands over his ears, but they were not dropping to the ground in pain or crying out. They were unfazed by the shrieking somehow.

John heard the screaming through the mass of cotton stuffed in his ears. He looked quickly at Eli, who had his hands over his ears, but he, too, was fine. Uncomfortable, but fine. They had learned from their last encounter and knew that if she was to screech, they did not stand a chance. So, they had cut into their own beds and made use of the material to create suitable plugs for their ears.

The musket boomed and kicked against John's shoulder with great force. A flash illuminated the brothers' darkened world. The moon's light returned, and he saw the silhouette of the witch come back into view. She stared at him disbelievingly. Her eyes were filled with fury and Hellfire. The shrieking stopped as she took unstable steps backward. In the moonlight, they could see the musket's shot had hit her on the left side of her chest. She brought a hand to the wound, and her fingers returned bloody. Her rage was an almost tangible aura as she regained her footing and took slow, seemingly cautionary, steps closer to them.

It could feel the host becoming rapidly weaker. The older brother had shot the host, and It felt her lung collapse. It flew into a rage, knowing Its over-reliance on the host's decaying body could be Its downfall this night. It tried to shriek again, but It could not. Raspy exhales were all the host's remaining lung could muster. It watched as the brothers removed masses of something from their ears and dropped them to the ground. It finally dawned on It what they were: wads of cotton. Its rage boiled over. It had had enough of their games and lunged at Eli.

John saw the witch go after his younger brother and tried to intercept her halfway. He swung the musket like a club but felt it suddenly halt on the backswing. James was holding it tightly behind John.

"Hello," James said with a laugh and pulled the musket in a downward motion.

John was caught off-guard by this and was yanked to the ground on his back. He hit the dirt hard and wheezed as the air was swiftly knocked from his lungs. He did not have time to catch his breath as his father mounted him and began to pummel him with his fists.

With each blow, violent memories flooded John's head. Memories of his childhood. Time slowed down within these moments. He saw his childhood self, cowering in his room. The belt whipping at him callously. The tears of an unwanted son. The undeserved consequences of a father's sins. John felt his eyes brim with tears as another fist hammered him.

Eli watched as the witch rushed him. He stood his ground but felt his courage melt away as she drew nearer. He raised the knife and swung wildly but missed. He felt her nails tear into his side like burning razors. He whirled around and saw her dart behind the barn. Eli then heard John's cries and looked in his direction. James was on top of John, battering him, who did his best to defend the blows. The shade of their father, the one who had tormented John to the brink of insanity, would kill his brother if this continued undeterred. Eli took a deep breath and charged at James.

"LEAVE MY BROTHER ALONE!"

John heard Eli's shout and then felt his father's weight leave his chest. The blows ceased, and the memories they brought cleared momentarily. He dizzily looked around and saw that Eli had tackled James to the ground. Eli was stabbing blindly at him with the knife and punching with his free hand. John got up on one knee and looked around in a daze. The musket lay nearby, and he clumsily reached for it, still searching.

Where was the witch?

It felt the girl stirring. She had awakened at an inopportune time. It could feel her presence, her resolve, gathering strength. Her influence was like a cloud hanging above It. Like a fog that was beginning to close in. It scratched a hasty rune into the host's neck and felt her spirit diminish. Nonetheless, she remained, and It could hear her still, though she seemed further off. It just needed more time.

Eli stabbed James and heard him shout in pain. Then, one of James's wild punches connected with the corner of Eli's jaw, and Eli tumbled off him in a stunned heap. He felt his limbs lock, and he knew he had dropped the knife, though he did not know where. His vision went dark.

John saw Eli topple off James's shade and go limp. James went to stand up, and John charged him, hatchet in hand. He roared, leapt on top of James, and hacked at him. John buried the hatchet in his father's flank then tried to use his burst of adrenaline to knock James's head against the ground. James tucked his legs in front of him and pushed off against John's midsection, causing him to stumble sideways.

He laughed at John as James got to his knees and elbowed his son's unprotected back. John's mind returned to his childhood as James's elbow caught one of the scarred places that never healed properly. His hatred and his self-loathing returned, as well, and he felt himself losing grasp on what was real and what was not.

John struck wildly at James's ribs then pushed his father off balance just enough for him to strike upwards with perfect precision. John heard his father's jaw crack when his knuckles connected, and James flew backwards. John stood up on wavering legs, trying to force oxygen into his lungs. His body already felt bruised and beaten. James got up slowly and looked at John. His jaw hung loosely, broken and unhinged. He tried to speak, to summon a taunt, but his jaw refused to do his bidding. A vicious, throaty yell came from deep inside him then, and James ran at John again.

Eli was floating through the darkness. His head was swimming, and he felt like he would be sick. He had never experienced violence like this before. Never thought he would (or could) attack someone like he did.

No.

Not someone.

Something. For that was not truly their father. It could not be. It was a phantom. James's phantom. Just as how Katherine was a phantom and nothing more. Eli then heard a distant commotion. A loud yell.

"Eli! Wake up!"

John?

"Wake up, Eli!"

Eli struggled to regain himself but soon found that he was looking up at the night sky. The moon was bright tonight.

"Eli!"

Eli blinked several times, looked around, and saw John trying to fend off an animalistic attack from James, who had the hatchet deep in his side. Eli snatched the knife from the ground and stuck it in his belt. Then, he got up and staggered over to the musket. He picked it up, took aim, and recalled the one thing that John had told him to always remember about shooting.

"Aim small, miss small," Eli told himself.

A feral hiss came from his right, and Eli swung the musket around. The witch was charging at him on all fours like a rabid dog. She was *fast*. The sight was unnatural and so horrifying, Eli felt his body seize up with fear. She stopped dead in her tracks just a few feet from him. She stood slowly, very slowly, and her yellow eyes speared him without warning. His mind was suddenly flooded with horrifying images that his human brain could not process. But they left him with a sense of foreboding and dread.

Eli pointed the musket at her, and she reached out and grabbed the end of the barrel, placing it against her bloody chest. Eli's eyes widened when she did this. He cocked it, and though he could not see, he knew that she was grinning from within her tattered hood. Eli pulled the trigged.

Click.

It was not loaded.

It cackled and pulled the younger brother closer to It, hurling him to the ground. It tossed the musket aside and stood over Eli. The fear rolling off of him was intoxicating. It

-261-

looked toward John, who was doing battle with the shade It had summoned. It saw John's attention divert from James and lock eyes with It as It loomed over his brother. It smiled when John yelled his name. It drank in the despair. It would be time soon.

John watched the witch in horror as she began to claw at Eli. His fear paved the way for rage, and he felt the blood boil under his skin. He intentionally allowed James to come closer, and John took two furious blows to the head as he reached and found the handle of the hatchet, still deep in James's side. He ignored his body's desire to fall into unconsciousness and operated on instinct. He yanked the hatchet free and ducked under a wild punch from his father, whose momentum carried him too far forward and made him lose his balance. He collapsed to the ground.

John turned quickly and, with all his might, brought the hatchet down on the back of James's head. A wet, sickening crunch erupted from the skull, and blood and other fluids splashed John in the face as he pulled the hatchet free. James twitched violently from the impact, and John buried the hatchet once more in James's skull. He stopped moving.

"John! Help me!" Eli shouted.

It felt the boy's blood stain Its fingers. It felt stronger as It bathed in his terror. Its talons in his flesh, Eli choked out a call for his brother, but John was too--

It suddenly stopped and felt that something was wrong. A piece of Its power had been broken. The shade of the father had been destroyed. It looked up and saw John charging at It, hatchet raised, and screaming like a wild man.

John swung manically with the hatchet, but the witch seemed to anticipate where his strikes would land. She dodged them effortlessly and laughed faintly as John's swings grew slower and slower from exhaustion. She then lashed out with her claw-like nails and cut deep into his face. Blood ran down his cheek and spilled down his neck. The pain was blinding.

Eli struggled to get up. The pain from his wounds was overwhelming. He rolled onto his side and saw the blood, *his* blood, which drenched his clothes. His torso sent electrifying pain signals to his brain so intense, he could not seem to see straight, but he focused and did his best to overcome. He steadied himself on his knees and stood. He gripped his side and groaned, using all his willpower to remain upright. Eli watched as John tried to take the witch down, but he knew she was just toying with him.

Eli noticed the musket nearby and picked it up. It still was not loaded. Where did John leave the powder and the bullets? The cottage. On the supper table, most likely. Eli rushed off toward the cottage, giving John and the witch a wide birth. He silently begged for John to keep her busy for just a little longer.

It noticed the younger brother enter the cottage and knew he was going to prepare the musket again. Its focus remained on the elder, however. Despite his exhaustion beginning to take its toll, It knew It could not underestimate his strength. It called out and brought forth another shade from the darkness.

Eli entered the cottage and looked around frantically. He searched carefully but quickly and finally found the powder bag on the supper table. Eli poured the powder as quickly he could.

"Hello," Katherine said from behind him.

The powder bag flew through the air as Eli nearly jumped out of his skin at the sound. The powder scattered everywhere, and Eli realized the severity of his error. He turned around and faced her. Her face was bloody and her eyes glowed red. Her nude body was covered in slashes and satanic runes. She grinned broadly.

"Eli," she purred.

Eli's breathing became erratic. His heart raced against the ice-cold fear that washed over him. His eyes were wide and terrified.

"You have been very wicked," she said, taking a step closer, "and ill-behaved children get punished, right?"

Eli's mind became overwhelmed. Her presence forced the memories to the forefront of his mind. He relived each and every moment growing up with her *multiple times* within a matter seconds. The shame. The revulsion. It all came back. She was at his door, in his bed. She was caressing him. She was kissing him. She was coercing him to lay with her. His stomach did somersaults, and he feared he would be sick. But something began to stir in his heart.

Eli forced his breath to stabilize. The cool air entered his nostrils, steady and slow. He felt calmer suddenly. The fear was still present and the sight of Katherine horrified him, but he found something within himself then. His hand gripped the handle of the knife tucked away in his belt.

"What do you think you are doing?" she asked.

He pulled the knife free and pointed it directly at the shade of the woman he detested so fiercely. His eyes narrowed, his heart slowed. The pain from his wounds did little to hinder his courage.

"You dare raise that thing at me?!" she barked, taking a step closer.

"Begone," Eli said in a calm and even tone.

The shade of Katherine hesitated.

Something happened, and It knew. It avoided another swing from the elder's hatchet, and he began to breathe heavily, pausing his assault. It sensed the shade had disobeyed Its command. It pressed her to move. To kill. She resisted the command, and It wondered just how weak Its power had become. The need for a new host was almost unbearable. It ordered the shade to kill the younger brother and put Its fury behind the command. The shade obeyed, and It felt the spirit of the girl growing louder. The rune was wearing off.

Katherine screamed and lunged at Eli. Her hands wrapped around his throat, and Eli desperately stabbed her stomach repeatedly. She shrieked again and threw him out of the window. The pain of the wounds that flecked his torso was renewed as he crashed to the ground, and Eli cried out.

It needed a moment. Just a moment to recuperate. It needed to rest. The girl's screams that rattled through It were unbearable. Her will to break Its control was becoming too much. Her commands frustrated It. John threw himself at It in some desperate attempt, and It dodged the blade of the hatchet but only just. It lashed out quickly and drove Its talons into John's chest. He wailed loudly. Satisfied, It pushed Its claws further into the brother. The talons were ripped out of his chest as he slid off them, falling to the ground, and blood splattered Its face. It fled to the barn and hid.

John saw Katherine throw Eli through the window and saw him hit the ground hard. Eli shouted in agony, and John's expression fell as he noticed the fresh blood that seeped from his brother's torso, his clothing already dark with drying blood. Katherine perched herself on the windowsill like some demonic gargoyle, and she watched in satisfaction as Eli writhed on the ground. She stepped lightly on the ground and prowled toward his brother. John roared. He pushed himself off the ground and used the pain in his chest to fuel his anger and his drive. He sprinted at Katherine, fully understanding he was exposing himself to the witch.

It gathered Its strength to attack the older brother. It needed to weaken him. Hurt him. Then, It would only further his anguish when It flayed young Eli in front of him. But when It tried to sprint after him, to tear flesh from the elder's back, It was restrained. It felt strong, invisible hands grip Its shoulders and hold It in place.

I told you to leave them alone! the girl shouted. *You will not succeed! I will not let them suffer as I have!*

It roared. It cursed. It fought. But she held It in place, and It was forced to watch the one called John save his brother.

John launched himself at Katherine, who screamed at him. Her red eyes and bloodied body were a frightening sight, but his determination outweighed his hesitation: Eli needed him. He rammed his shoulder into her gut, and the momentum sent her sprawling backwards. John helped Eli up from the ground while she was down.

"Keep an eye out for the hag!" John ordered Eli, who nodded.

John went to Katherine and stood over her foul and horrific body.

"You will not touch him!" John shouted. "Never again!"

He swung with finality, and the hatchet struck her throat with a wet thud. He swung again and again and again in a frenzied rage. He imagined everything she had done to Eli. Every disgusting and unsightly act she ever forced on him drowned him, and it fueled his arms to continue to strike her already-rigid and decapitated corpse.

"John!"

Eli was watching in horror. John looked back at him, puzzled. He pointed to where Katherine lay. John looked again and saw that it was no longer Katherine. Her shade had disappeared, and a decomposing pile of organs and other horse parts had taken her place. A disappearing vapor of smoke swirled around them and into the inky night sky.

It fought her off just long enough to rush at the brothers again. The girl's presence and her voice tugged at It, but It would not allow her the satisfaction of stopping It. The young one would die. *Now*.

No! the girl screamed at It.

John turned to look for the witch. He saw her on all fours, barreling directly towards Eli. Time slowed around John. He tried to alert Eli, who was still distracted by the sight of the organs and the hooves. Eli turned in her direction, but he would not comprehend the immediate danger until it was too late.

John could only watch as the witch lunged at Eli, her hands outstretched. The talons protruding from her fingers were poised and aimed with precision. As Eli faced her, his eyes recognized and acknowledged what was coming.

But John was quicker. He leapt in front of Eli to intercept the witch's attack. Her claws sunk into his stomach, and the pain erupted with a violent ferocity. She hissed and slashed wildly at John. His vision went red around the edges as she then turned her attention back to Eli.

Eli dove through the window of the cottage and grabbed the musket, the hag tearing at his heels. She climbed inside and crashed on top of him, and as there was no time to load it, Eli used the firearm to keep her from plunging her claws into him. He knocked her aside, jabbing the butt of the weapon into her temple, and scurried away from her clutches. He was cornered in the back of the cottage with nowhere to go, and Eli's heart skipped a beat as she forced herself to standing position, her head cocked to the side.

John leapt to his feet. The pain slowed him, dulled his ability to process what was going on. All he knew was that Eli was in trouble, and he had a promise to keep to his little brother. He looked through the window and saw Eli backed into the corner of the cottage with only the empty musket to protect himself. John summoned his strength. He ignored the pain that coursed through his body. He focused instead on his promise.

I will protect you and watch out for you always, Eli, he thought to himself.

John shouted and swung the hatchet with as much force as he could. It struck true. The hatchet slammed into the witch's back with tremendous power, and he heard not only the bloody thud, but also a loud crack as her spine snapped. She toppled into a lifeless mound.

John and Eli looked at each other in stunned silence. John looked at the witch's body and gave it a kick, half expecting her to jump up and attack again. But she did not. He removed the hatchet from her back and struck her one more. She did not move or react.

"Just... making sure," John said breathlessly.

Eli nodded, understanding. Eli sunk to the ground, and John sat beside him. They sighed simultaneously. They were both wounded and exhausted. They looked at one another, and, to John's surprise, Eli wearily grinned.

"I am tired," Eli confessed.

"I am, as well," John agreed. "Come on."

John helped his brother to his feet and embraced him tightly.

"It is over," John said "It is done."

"Good," Eli said.

They walked outside, into the cool night air. They both took a cleansing breath. There was a different air surrounding them. A lighter one. Things felt... different. John pointed at the pile of horse intestines.

"So," he said, "I guess she--"

"John," Eli interrupted, "I do not want to dwell on it, *any of it*, anymore. I think it best if we leave."

John nodded.

"Let me grab the musket," John said, "and then, we can be off."

Eli nodded and filled his lungs with the clean air as John went back inside. A sense of freedom electrified him, and a blanket of ease began to settle over him.

It had been cast out. The host had been irreparably destroyed. It looked briefly at John, roared voicelessly in his face, then It flew through the window and into the night. It looked at the sky, and It felt the eyes of a greater enemy boring into It. The enemy knew It had broken the laws, and It knew time was short. But It would not allow them the chance strike, not yet. Not until the law had been shattered completely.

It soared over the trees of the forest and searched. It knew it had to be near. It flew downward, through the trees, and past the river, and soon, It came upon it. The object of Its current needs could not be mistaken, for the thing had been marked. At first, It could sense the fear and hesitation from what It sought. But then, the creature had no choice but to accept the dark force and Its beckoning call.

It consumed the creature and manifested within it. It hated the feeling of such a beast, but there was no choice. It needed a way into John's heart, and It knew that this was Its last chance.

Filthy mongrel, It cursed into the void.

Eli stretched, looking up at the night sky.

"Almost done?" Eli asked loudly.

"Almost," John called from within the cottage. "I just need to load it, and we will be off."

"What will we do now?" Eli asked.

"I am not sure," John said. "I figure the same as we spoke of before. I am well suited to physical labor. I can work with my hands and handle cargo. What do you suppose you might do?"

"I am not sure," Eli said honestly.

"Well, think on it," John said. "We are lucky enough to have a fresh start ahead."

Eli shrugged to himself. He did not know why John insisted on reloading the musket when the witch was dead. He pressed a hand to his wounds. Still bleeding, but not as badly anymore. He kept pressure on the worst of them and cringed at the wound's painful reply. John and he would both need a doctor as soon as possible.

Eli heard it then: the soft thudding of padded paws. The fear he had so happily rid himself of greeted him with a conniving smirk. He stood from his relaxed position and searched the immediate area. His eyes widened when he saw a wolf. Its fur was as white as snow, save for something on the top of its head. As it drew closer, Eli realized it was a rune, drawn in blood, that adorned the crown of its head. Eli was too stunned to cry out, too afraid to react. He stood there, petrified, as the animal charged at him. Its eyes were a milky white color, as if it were blind.

In an instant, Eli felt its claws sink into him. Its jaws snapped at his jugular, and teeth as sharp as daggers punctured his neck. Eli felt emotions surge through him. Anxiety, confusion, and anger poured through him. But when the cottage door opened and he saw the face of his older brother, the shock and the horror displayed on his features, Eli felt overcome with sadness.

John felt his soul shatter into millions of fragments. He had failed. He had sworn to protect him, to always be there to save him. And he *failed*. He watched Eli fall to the ground, writhing in a pool of his own blood. Terror flooded his eyes. Terror, confusion, pain, anger, shock, too many thoughts to count.

He noted the bloody rune on the wolf's head. The creature's gaze leveled with John, its eyes a fiery red. And John heard the thing's voice in his head once more. The perverse sound of unnatural, guttural gurgles trying to formulate words.

Hell cometh.

John fired the musket at the beast and drove the hatchet into its neck until he was sure it was dead. After enough blows, he left the weapon lodged there, John's teeth clenched in a white hot rage, its tainted blood splattered across his face. He looked at Eli, who trembled and choked on his own blood. John dropped to the ground, cradled Eli's head with one arm, and, with his free hand, applied pressure to the fresh claw marks across his little brother's chest.

"Eli?" John whimpered.

Eli coughed and sputtered. Blood spilled from his throat, and his eyes were wild, searching. They pleaded with John to save him. To do... *something*.

"Eli..." John could not stop the tears from falling. "Stay with me."

Eli's eyes welled up. The distress and the anguish in them broke John's heart. With every wet murmur from his brother's throat, he knew that he was that much closer to losing him. John stripped a piece of his shirt and wiped the blood from Eli's lips as best he could, but it did little good as more and more blood came.

"What do I do?" John cried to himself. "What do I do?"

Eli placed a hand over John's and gave it a weak squeeze. John held Eli's in turn and wept.

"Do not go," John whispered. "I failed you. I cannot fail you, Eli. Please."

Eli's brow furrowed. The pain was intense, but nothing pained him more than the tears and the words that flowed out of John. He desperately wanted to tell him that he should not blame himself, that he loved him. He wanted to tell him he was the greatest brother he could ask for. He wanted to set his soul at ease and assure him that this was not his fault. But every time he tried to speak, the taste and smell of iron suffocated him. His own blood was drowning him as his lungs seized against the fluid filling them.

The edges of Eli's vision began to darken. He was afraid. He was no longer hurting. The pain in his throat and chest was no longer there. This terrified him. The darkness at the edges began to creep inward. He was not sure he was ready to find out what was on the other side. He feared that he would be denied entry to Heaven. He wondered if it truly existed. And if it did exist, then that meant there was a Hell. And he knew that if Heaven turned him away, there was only one place his soul could go.

Fear of the unknown gripped Eli's heart as he felt himself slipping away. He tried once more to give John some word of comfort, but he could not. And he focused on his brother, before the darkness overtook him, as John cried and began his descent into despair.

Chapter 30
Of the Interruption

It watched the scene before It. The young one was slowly fading, and the elder brother would soon give in to his despair. It watched his heart darken. His sorrow, his anger, and his disparaging soul fed It. It drank it all in and became intoxicated with anticipation. It laughed and snickered wickedly. It knew It would have John soon. It would know what it feels like to be strong again. To be... human. It began to move toward John, for It desired to whisper in his ear. To intensify his suffering. But It was halted before It could move.

It felt eyes bore into It and soon felt something burning into Its back. It dared to turn and look, and Its eyes were blinded by light. Its enemies had come. It tried to make one last desperate attempt to consume John, but a legion of immoveable forces grabbed It, their grips vice-like. It felt Itself being taken up into the sky, into the light that burned It. Thunderous, echoing voices condemned It, and It shriveled and cowered from the sound. It pleaded for mercy, but none would be offered. It was told Its crimes and sentenced to Its punishment. It felt their hands wrap around Its limbs, and It felt them break. Though in agony, It could not make a sound.

It felt as It was hurled back down to the Earth, and It crashed into the ground; further still, It fell. It could hear the tortured screams and tormented pleas. The light that burned It was gone. Instead, It felt the darkness encompass him. A darkness so deep and abysmal, It felt afraid. It crashed into the Pit, and Its face struck the ground. It whimpered pathetically and breathed in. Sulfur and ash filled Its lungs, and the searing pain on Its back felt like droplets of fire licking at It.

But more than this, It felt a severed connection. A hopelessness. A darkness in Its own heart. A true feeling of nothingness as It realized that It was trapped and could no longer walk among men.

Chapter 31
Of Those Clad in Light

John cradled Eli's head in his arms and gently rocked his brother back and forth as he wept. He silently begged for him to stay. Begged for him to hold on somehow. He gazed into his little brother's eyes and saw the light leave them. They became glassy and lifeless, and John felt his brother's grasp upon his hand relax.

"Do not go," John whimpered. "Eli. No."

Eli's hand became limp and fell to his chest. John looked between Eli's blank stare and his wounds. He then frantically searched in every direction, as if searching for the spirit that just left his brother's body. He screamed and cursed. His grief was too much to bear, and he felt his heart burst. His oath, his promise to always protect his younger brother, had been destroyed, and in turn, he knew his soul, too, was in the same state of carnage.

"God, help me," John whispered again and again, "I do not know what to do..."

His thoughts became as dark as the night sky, and he thought about how quickly and easily he could end his suffering. He thought about loading the musket and taking off his shoe, shoving the barrel into his mouth and using his toe to pull the trigger. It would be instant. For what else was there now? He had lost himself in his boyhood, and as a man, he had broken his vow and lost his brother. The despair he felt was holding his heart down like the weight of a thousand anchors.

John was about to set Eli down. He was about to go fetch the musket and allow his grief to take over. He knew he was going to destroy himself in that moment when something stopped him. A voice. An innocent, gentle voice, like that of a young girl, reached his ears. She seemed far off, but he still heard it clearly enough that he remained in place. He looked around and saw nothing.

"Not another trick," John said. "Please, God, end this torment."

"John," the voice said carefully. "John, can you hear me?"

John wondered if his mind was lost to his sorrow. He wondered if it was all in his head or if this was just some ruse sent from the Devil himself to play upon his already broken mind. John wondered if he should even answer it at all, but when the voice spoke again, he listened.

"I know, John," the voice said. "I see your heart, and I weep with you."

"Who are you?" John asked. "Where are you?"

"I am the one in the cottage," the voice said. "The girl you set free."

"The witch?" John asked, anger beginning to stir inside him.

"Yes," she replied, "but I was not of myself."

"You did this," John said, pain emanating with each word. "You took my brother from me."

"No, John," the girl said. "No, I was a puppet, a tool to bring you and Eli to ruin. I am truly sorry for... everything."

"Your apologies will not bring Eli back," John growled.

"No, but..." she said then trailed off.

The silence around John began to nag at him, and he looked around again, wildly looking for the source of the voice.

"SPEAK!" John shouted.

"Eli is here," the girl said. "He is with me now."

John's eyes grew wide.

"What?"

"We are both here," she said.

"Eli?"

"Let me open your eyes, John," the girl said gently, "to the world beyond this one."

John felt a presence then. He thought he could feel a hesitant hand touch his shoulder. He felt calm then. The storm of emotions that was consuming him seemed to subside, and he regained control of his breathing. Another hand, warm and reassuring, touched his cheek, and the darkness in his soul seemed to melt away.

"Close your eyes, John," the girl said.

John felt doubt creep into him, but he could not deny the lightness he felt in his heart. Whatever force or being that appeared to him had completely taken away the anguish that saturated him just a moment ago. John slowly closed his eyes, and when he reopened them, he gasped.

Eli stood there just a few feet in front of him with a smile on his face. John looked around and saw that the night sky had seemingly been replaced with light. A sun, or something akin to it, shone in the sky and painted it with bright color. He looked toward Eli again, who stood there watching his brother. John looked down at his lap: Eli's lifeless body was no longer in his arms.

"What is this?" John asked.

"I am not sure," Eli replied, "but it is certainly--"

"Beautiful," John finished.

John's eyes produced fresh tears as he saw his brother whole again. The splendor of the land around him made him briefly forget all the ill that had befallen them. The darkness of the forests on the outskirts of the farm had changed, the trees now a brilliant green, their leaves abundant. The grass was bright, and the air around them was pure. The cottage had disappeared as if the land had never been touched.

"Am I dead?" John asked.

"No," the girl's voice answered.

John saw her then. A young, radiant girl with sticklike limbs and a fragile frame came and stood beside Eli. Her raven hair was long, falling past her waist. She gave him a timid smile. He noticed scars in her arms and legs, faded but still there. Runes that had once bled fiercely.

"You are the witch," John said.

"In a way, I was," she replied, "but no longer. You set me free, John."

"I do not understand," John said.

"I was under control," the girl said. "I was a tool used by something from Hell."

John remembered the night he hurt Eli. The night he had fallen under her control. Or so he had previously thought.

"You... you did not make me harm Eli?" John asked.

The girl shook her head.

"I was only Its vessel," she said. "I would never purposefully put anyone through what you both have endured."

John frowned. Eli approached, and John noticed just how... lively he was. A light shone around him, *through* him in some ways. His wounds were healed. Scarred but healed.

"She is not our enemy," Eli said.

"If you are not our enemy," John said, "then who are you?"

"I... I do not remember my name any longer," she replied after careful thought. "I am sorry. I was under Its control and shrouded in darkness for so long, I cannot remember what I was called."

"What do you remember?" John asked. "Do you remember how you fell under Its possession?"

Eli gave him a grave look as if he had asked one too many questions.

"What?" John asked.

"I remember fragments," the girl said sadly. "I remember someone hurting me. I remember feeling alone and scared. I remember..."

She trailed off, and her eyes glistened. John was not sure he wanted to hear the rest when she spoke again.

"I was weak and wanted to hurt them back. I remember running into the wood, crying. I remember asking for someone to help me bring harm to the one who had caused me pain and... It spoke to me. It promised me things. It promised to help. I was too young to understand and too foolish to flee or ignore It. I allowed It to manifest within me, and It fulfilled Its promise. I remember reveling in Its power, and I remember seeing him suffer."

Her eyes stared off in the distance as she quietly relived the details of her fragmented history.

"But when I tried to regain control of myself, It would not relinquish my body. I became Its host. It hurt me. For... so long. I-I cannot remember how long I was in the darkness. And every time I woke up and tried to fight, It..."

She held her arm out and showed the scarring of the runes in her flesh. She traced one gently and shuddered.

"It put me back to sleep where I was visited by those who were damned eons ago."

Eli spoke then, trying to distract her from her tormented thoughts.

"She helped us, John," he said.

"How?" John asked.

"My body had become weak," she explained, "and as my body grew weaker, It grew weaker. I saw the horrors It caused you and wanted to help however I could. I distracted It as best as I could, but..."

She fell silent again, and John nodded in understanding.

"That was not enough," John finished for her.

She nodded, and tears rolled down her cheeks.

"I am so sorry," she said. "Truly, I am. I wish I could rewind time and make it so that I had never accepted that thing's offer. I wish I had done more for you both."

Eli nodded and said, "I do not place blame on you. It was not your doing."

John also nodded after some thought as he came to terms with the idea that the girl before them was no monster or witch. Just a victim in the grand scheme of it all.

"I do not blame you either," John said. "Lord knows that you have probably endured as much Hell as we have."

She wept quietly but found a way to smile at them both.

"Thank you," she whispered. "*Thank you*. I have repented countless times for my mistake. I just hoped you both would forgive me, as well."

John looked around them again and smiled. Such beauty and marvelousness prompted him to ask the question that had formed in his mind.

"Is this Heaven then?" he asked.

The girl shook her head. "No. It is... a bridge, I think."

"A bridge?" Eli asked.

"Yes," she said, "one of two. I have seen the other one, and it leads to... a place where no light can touch. But this place is another bridge, a gateway, maybe."

"To where?" John asked.

As he asked this, a brilliant light erupted beside them, as if a doorway had been opened. The girl turned, saw something inside the light, and she smiled broadly through renewed tears. John looked at Eli, whose eyes widened in amazement and shock. But when John looked toward the light, it was simply that: blinding white light.

"Eli?" he asked. "What is it? What do you see?"

"Oh, John," Eli said, a single tear cascading down his face. "It is... beautiful. Is that? Oh, John..."

"What is it?"

"It is him," Eli cried softly. "It is Father Benjamin, John. He is there with his wife and boy."

John felt himself tear up and his mouth fell open at what Eli had said.

"I cannot see them," John said.

"No," the girl said, walking toward him, "you will not be able to."

"What? Why?"

"You are not yet ready," she said kindly. "It is not yet your time to see."

John tried to see. He squinted at the source of light and thought he saw several silhouettes inside. Their faces were indistinguishable, and their clothing seemed to emit luminescence. But when they stepped away from the doorway, John felt his heart swell. Every feeling besides pure joy had evaporated in their presence. They were tall and seemed to be human silhouettes, but his mind could not fully process what they truly were. The girl turned to Eli, and she smiled.

"We have been invited," she said.

"Invited?" Eli asked.

"Yes," she said, "they want us to go with them."

"Where?" John asked.

She looked up at one of the beings. It held out a hand, and she took it with a nod. She walked with the being to the doorway and stood for a moment at its threshold. She turned once more toward the brothers. She looked at the being of light again and asked it something that John and Eli could not hear. It nodded, and she smiled back at the brothers.

"Where are you going?" John asked, still blinded by the light.

"We will see each other again," she called out. "When your time comes, we will meet again, and you will see. It is lovely beyond any description."

She walked through the doorway, and both brothers could hear her laugh from beyond it as her voice faded away. One of the beings approached Eli then. John tried to look at it, but its light was so intense and pure, he had to close them.

"Can my brother come too?" John heard Eli ask.

There was a silence then, and John strained to listen for the answer. After a moment, Eli spoke as if responding to the being's reply, a reply that John did not hear.

"Please," Eli said, "I do not want to leave him alone."

John understood then. The invitation was for the girl and Eli alone. His mortal ears could not discern the words of the being, and he knew the words were only meant for those it allowed to listen. John then felt a strong hand on his head, firm but gentle. He knew it belonged to the being of light, and he felt warmed by the touch. John was made to understand that he was not meant to see what lay beyond the other side of the door. He was not meant to see the beings in their true form as the minds of men would not be able to comprehend it. And finally, he was made to understand that his time would come, but this was not his time.

You still have a purpose, Johnathan, a fierce yet sympathetic voice washed over his mind. *When you have fulfilled it, then... then you may join us.*

John felt himself crying but not of sadness or grief. Of relief and of joy. The voice filled him with solace, and he nodded. He looked at Eli, who began to shine more brilliantly than before. John smiled at him with tears in his eyes.

"Eli," he said softly, "go. Do you see what is on the other side of that door?"

Eli looked toward the doorway, and he smiled as he wept. He nodded quickly.

"I do," Eli said. "John, it is... it is amazing."

"You have been through enough," John said. "I think you have earned a bit of peace."

Eli looked at his brother and sobbed while still maintaining some semblance of his smile.

"You have not smiled like that since... I cannot rightly recall since when," John said. "But you have been called, Eli. It is time."

One of the beings approached Eli and extended a hand. Eli hesitated and looked to John for approval.

"Go." John smiled. "Go now."

Eli smiled broadly and took the being's hand. He allowed himself to be led to the doorway, where he stopped at the threshold and looked at the being. John saw them converse, and Eli nodded to it. He looked back at John.

"What will you do?" Eli asked.

"I have a purpose still," John said. "Now, go on. I will be along one day soon."

"Promise?" Eli asked.

John closed his eyes and felt the tears he was trying to hold back roll down his cheeks. He opened them and saw that the night had returned. He was holding Eli's body in his arms again. The other world was gone from his sight.

"Yes," John said quietly, "I promise."

John sat there holding his brother in his arms, rocking back and forth. He wept. He wept for no longer being able to see the beauty of that other place. He wept for the girl, happy that her suffering had finally ended. He wept for his parents, who he knew would never see such a place. Finally, he wept for Eli, glad that he no longer felt the pain of his wounds, physical or otherwise. He had been freed of his demons, much like the girl had.

He wiped at his face with a clean part of his shirt. Still seated, he looked up at the sky. The moon seemed brighter than he remembered it. The stars could not be touched by the darkness, and his heart, while heavy, did not despair. John smiled slightly and nodded. The comforting feeling that the being clothed in light left him with still lingered, and he understood what he needed to do.

"Alright," he said softly. "Alright."

Epilogue

It had been five years. Five years since the events that had taken place at the farm. Five years since he buried the body of that young girl. Five years since he buried his little brother.

Sometimes at night, he would have nightmares of that time, and he would wake up in a cold sweat, calling out for his brother. But then, he would calm down and remember everything that had transpired before getting on his knees beside his bed and praying. He would send up his prayers and often request that a message be delivered to Eli, if it was not too much trouble. Today was not much different: he had been awoken by a nightmare. He breathed deeply and reminded himself that it was over as he knelt to pray.

"Oh, Lord," he said softly, "direct my steps to walk Your path. May I not tarry or dwell in darkness. Thank You for Your blessings and for Your light, and may You shine it on those who need it most. And if You are able, will You tell Eli that I love him, that I miss him, and that I cannot wait until we meet again? Thank you. Amen."

He stood then, his knees making popping sounds in his older age, and dressed. He looked out the window and saw the sun creeping into the sky. He absorbed its light and smiled. His heart was full. He ate a modest breakfast and walked down the road. People smiled at him, greeted him, and waved, and he returned all these greetings with a warm expression and a cheerful "Good morning". He entered the building just outside of town and walked inside. It had become a second home to him, and he greeted the man that awaited him.

"Good morning, John," the man said. "Are you ready?"

With a grin, John answered, "I am."

People filed in, and John greeted them with as much liveliness as the townsfolk had come to expect. His smile was inviting, and his eyes sparkled with love and compassion. He went to the pulpit, took his place, and looked over his notes. He then looked out at his flock and saw that it had grown since the last time. He smiled brightly.

"Good morning!" he said.

"Good morning, Father Johnathan," most replied.

He took another look at his notes and said a brief prayer in his heart. His purpose, his calling, had finally been realized. He looked out the window of the church and saw a crow perched on a branch just outside. It unleashed a loud cawing. John paid it no heed, gave the bird a wave of dismissal, and looked at the faces of those sat in the pews.

"Today," he said, "I want to speak to each of you about caring for your fellow man. To be a port in the storm for someone who may need it, for example. Or to try and trust someone with something that may have left scars on your heart. You see, I trusted my brother long ago with a secret that left me hurt and in a state of constant sadness and turmoil. The secret of my past. And today..."

John took a deep breath and reaffirmed his conviction. He reminded himself to lead by example.

"Today, I will share with you all what ailed me for twenty years, as I did with my brother. I do this to offer some comfort to the hearts of those of you in this room that may have your own secrets weighing you down. Some of you may find that bearing such a weight by yourself will drive you to insanity."

The crow cawed once more before flying away, knowing that it was not allowed near a place that dwelled in such a light.

Acknowledgments

I would like to extend a heartfelt thank you to the following people:

To Heidi, for being a fantastic friend, supporter, and editor!

To Anja, for her tremendous love, as well as care for my mental state during the writing process.

To Braden, for his outstanding validation, encouragement, and artwork.

To Cole, Geoff, Nate, Jake, and Bubba, for their unending support.

To Kimmie and Emma, for their encouragement to see this thing through.

To Taylor, for *everything* she did.

To Streeter, for helping me to discover my love for literature.

To my parents, for their love always.

And finally, to those that gave me at least one ounce of support, it is not unnoticed. I thank all of you. One gesture of kindness, no matter how small, can change someone's outlook and mental state for the better.

About the Author

Dalton has always had a way with words since childhood. He has used writing as a way to explore other worlds and communicate his vivid imagination and vision with those around him. His debut novel *Scourge* is a perfect representation of Dalton's pure talent and dedication to his craft. Dalton currently resides in Arizona with his dog, Sandor Clegane.

Instagram: @daltonjameswriter

About the Illustrator

Braden Maxwell is an award-winning illustrator and internationally known educator, whose work has been displayed in multiple galleries in the United States. He works both traditionally and digitally, but pen and ink will always have a special place in his art making.

Website: BradenMaxwellillustration.com
Instagram: @bradenmaxwellillustration

www.ingramcontent.com/pod-product-compliance
Lightning Source LLC
Chambersburg PA
CBHW020558260626
47157CB00003B/767